I0716511

The 24 Hour Bet

Learning to Love Again
Book 2

Rochelle Bradley

Copyright © 2024 by Rochelle Bradley
Cover Design © Alt19 Creative
Edited by Rebecca Adksal
Published by Epic Dreams Publishing

All rights reserved. No part of this book may be reproduced, distributed, or transmitted in any form or by any electronic or mechanical means including information storage and retrieval systems, without permission of the author/publisher. The exception would be in the case of brief quotations embodied in the critical articles or reviews and pages where permission is specifically granted by the publisher or author. For permission requests send a message to the publisher at: epicdreamspublishing.com

This book is a work of fiction. Names, characters, businesses, places, events, and incidents either are products of the author's imagination or are used fictitiously. Any resemblance to actual persons, living or dead, events, or locales is entirely coincidental.

Visit: RochelleBradley.com

ISBN 978-1-947561-33-5

DEDICATION

For my author wife CJ. Sometimes it feels we are
attached for 24 hours or more.
Thanks for being my friend.

ACKNOWLEDGMENTS

Thank you to my prince, Aaron, who put up with my crazy editing schedule, and my mom and dad for aways coming to events and supporting me. Special thanks for Sara and Rebecca—for helping make **The 24 Hour Bet** great. Thank you to my writing buddies CJ W, CJ B, Aliya, Leah, Tony, David, and Chelsea who supported me and kept me company—online, at the coffee shop, and at the bar. Thanks to Alt19 Creative for working with me to perfect the cover. To my amazing ARC readers… you rock!

A NOTE FROM ROCHELLE

Dear Reader,

Thank you for grabbing book two in the Learning to Love Again series. It all started with a dream I had with Vanessa and her evil twin, Veronica.

I wrote ***The 24 Hour Bet*** before ***Destination Escape*** (book 1), but was so compelled with Vanessa's plight and her escape that I had to expand on it. After reading the ***The 24 Hour Bet*** you can see why Vanessa ran away from her inheritance, family, and job in book 1 of the Leaning to Love Again series.

Welcome to the world of the Warsaw and Tanner families.

Thanks again, and happy reading!

~Rochelle

CHAPTER ONE

A LONE. IT'S ALL I WANTED.

Sea spray cascaded over me as the catamaran cut through the waves. I inhaled the salty air and rolled my shoulders to the music from my earbuds, trying to relax.

Soon, very soon, I could sit and ignore the world. Even if my earbuds had to be surgically removed by the end of the trip, I would escape for a week, two, or thirty. Hell, I could disappear forever and that would make me happy.

Once upon a time, I'd dreamed of falling in love, getting married, and starting a family. The American dream with a house, two point five kids, and pets— everything. But the dream began to crumble when my mother died of cancer while I was in high school, and now here I am.

From behind mirrored lenses, I surveyed the other passengers, most of whom I'd also observed while we were on the cruise ship. I'd heard the names Tiffany, Lindsay, and Monique but didn't care who was who—in my mind I just called them all "Barbie." The women took turns consoling a seasick friend.

The sick woman, Karen, I knew from the group's

antics on the cruise ship. She'd been celebrating her newfound singleness after a recent divorce. The group had been a drinking, giggling, tight-clothes-wearing Tasmanian devil consuming and messing up everything around them. At the back of the catamaran, Karen leaned over as she emptied her stomach into the sea. While the ladies were fun to watch, I could only stand them in small doses.

Soon my catamaran confinement would end, and I'd be free.

"She shouldn't have drunk so much last night." A woman in a string bikini with hot pink hibiscus flowers talked over the wind with one of the Barbie clones. Barbie nodded and threw a concerned looked over her shoulder.

Glancing around the catamaran, I noted several couples in addition to Karen's drinking posse. A set of honeymooners, an older Japanese couple, an ancient couple from Wyoming, a gay European couple, and two men, one a tall Jamaican and the other a blond American, who seemed to be friends and not lovers.

Over my music, I heard the Jamaican's laughter ring out. The tall, dark-skinned man was slim in build and dressed impeccably, always in khaki, white, or cream colors. The deep, rich tone of his voice reminded me of church bells, and I couldn't help but smile. His head tipped back as he laughed, most likely at his friend's expense. On the cruise ship, he had commented and teased, then chuckled at the shorter man's discomfort. I hadn't heard most of it but watched as the blond turned bright red. I felt sorry for the American.

The American, whom I'd caught looking in my direction a few times, resembled a surfer with tanned skin and wavy hair. His eyes were blue. He reminded me of my first love, Nicholas Arlington Tanner. His facial expressions and overall looks had had me glancing twice.

I'd met Nick while I was in high school; he'd been a senior and I, a junior. However, Nick had been my height, and while I wouldn't say he'd been chubby, he hadn't been as lean as the blond man. Another difference, my Nick had brown hair.

I thought the blond guy was cute, but only because he resembled Nick. Chancing a glance, I found him studying me again. My face heated, and I turned to gaze at the panoramic view of the resort on the remote island.

The last passenger was a lone man who sat at the bow. His physique was that of a Greek statue. I'd dubbed him Mr. Gorgeous. His damp linen shirt clung, revealing each contour of every muscle. His raven hair, ruffled by the wind, still looked perfect. It was as if he was filming a commercial.

He made a deal with the devil to look that perfect. He probably doesn't get morning breath either. His hot bod is definitely romance book cover material.

My inner voice was right. I snapped my gaze to my lap, where my thumb held the page I'd been reading. Had my fanciful ideas come from a romance book? I closed the paperback and stowed it in my Vera Bradley bag. The bright floral pattern wouldn't reflect my feelings until I was alone.

I turned up my music, trying to drown out the others. I wanted to be alone. Closing my eyes, I faced into the wind. The balmy breeze comforted me, and the rhythmic bob relaxed me. I could almost forget there were others around me.

Almost. Until my earbud fell out. Conversations assaulted me once more. I pushed the earbud back in so I wouldn't hear the nasally voice of Mrs. Wyoming.

The waves became choppier as we neared shore. I turned off my music but left my earbuds in, then gathered my things, so I was ready to disembark the moment the catamaran slid onto shore.

The seasick woman groaned again, prompting her friends to murmur about the trip's near end.

The Wyoming couple tried to guess their room's location, but I didn't look at the resort. I studied a long sandbar that extended out in the opposite direction of the shore, a peninsula. Closer toward the resort, the higher the dunes became. I couldn't see the peninsula's other side. I decided I would walk to the end and sit, then I'd wait until everyone else checked in before going to the reservation desk.

My boat-mates appeared excited about the Dancing Winds resort. Mr. Gorgeous stretched his shoulders and flashed an unnaturally white smile. Three of the seasick woman's friends sighed, watching his muscular form move.

"Karen, we're practically there!" Hibiscus bikini Barbie jumped up. Her breasts, bouncing in unison, caught Mr. Wyoming's attention. I rolled my eyes.

The catamaran slowed and slid onto the sand, and two resort workers helped pull it in. I stood before the others could find their land legs and made my way to the edge. A greeter helped me down. I thanked him and turned toward the end of the peninsula.

"Miss, your accommodations are in the other direction." He motioned toward the resort, staring at me as if I was stupid.

"I know." I nodded and set off in the opposite way he pointed.

Walking from the wet, hard sand at the water's edge into the warm, soft sand of the beach. I kicked off my sandals and wiggled my toes. My white button-down shirt and tan capris were damp from the sea spray but would dry in no time thanks to the sun. I shifted my bag to my right shoulder and walked farther away from the chaos.

Once at the crest of the nearest dune, I settled to watch the show. Over a dozen people still needed off the boat. The resort employee returned to his work and helped the plump Mrs. Wyoming down onto the sand. She giggled hysterically when he said something into her ear. It must have been flattering since her face gleamed as red as a cherry.

"He'll be receiving a big tip," I muttered.

Mr. Wyoming was next. He flipped his comb-over back to the preferred side. His Mrs. laughed when he stumbled. The Japanese couple followed, and both sets of older folks headed toward the resort.

I couldn't help but chuckle as a few of the women made a display of needing help. A petite redhead grabbed Mr. Gorgeous' hand as she tentatively put her foot down. She had a scar on the ankle from a car accident in her youth. She liked to talk about it, and I'd overheard three variations of the story on the cruise. The woman extended the foot, showing off the rose tattoo that covered the scar. She gazed admiringly up into Mr. Gorgeous' face while her mouth moved like an auctioneer. The man glanced at his Rolex. Oh yeah, he was done with her. Once on the shore with her friends she waited—for him, apparently, because when he turned his smile on the gay couple, she pouted and rejoined the others.

I turned my music back on, so I wouldn't have to hear the squeals of Karen's posse as they kicked water at each other and ran through the surf.

The earbuds had worked to dissuade most from talking to me on the cruise ship. Especially on deck. I could sit in the sun with my eyes closed and pretend to listen to music. You can learn interesting things when people don't think you're listening.

The Jamaican man and his friend disembarked and stood not far from me. Their hands waved as they talked. I contemplated whether it would be worthwhile to turn off my music.

The blond man glanced over at me and winked. Even with my sunglasses, knowing he couldn't see my eyes, I knew my face was bright red. Crap. I did not come to this isolated isle resort to pick up guys. The American, probably a Midwesterner by his lack of accent, had been a favorite among the drunken ladies. Although, looking back, he seemed to avoid them as much as he could. On the ship, I'd seen him duck out into the hallway when they approached him to dance.

Mr. Gorgeous had cornered me once. I begged off, pointing to my non-dancing shoes. He was much too pretty to be anything other than a model or actor. Perfect teeth, nose, body, face, and hair. He had to be a dream or a lie. Even his toes were perfectly straight and manicured. It was odd he focused on me.

I mean, it was normal for a guy like the American to

smile at me but not a super-hot sex god. My body shivered at the word "sex" in conjunction with Mr. Gorgeous. I couldn't go there, no matter how tempting. Karen's friend, the busty Barbie, would be a much better specimen for his arm. She had all the right curves and a personality that purred when shown attention.

I don't seek or want any attention. Move along. I am not the droid you're looking for.

The Jamaican elbowed his friend. The other man shrugged.

I'd had a brief conversation with the Jamaican in the cruise ship's elevator. His eyes had twinkled, as if he knew a good joke. He had fingered his short goatee as he looked me over. Once again, I'd had my earbuds in, but didn't listen to music. He pointed to my ear and asked me what I was listening to. I smiled slyly and said, "Nothing."

"You're a tricky one." His laugh rang like church bells. "I'll keep my eyes on you." He smiled, his teeth white and straight.

I hadn't wanted to befriend anyone, but what fun is having a secret if no one knew? I'd told him, "It's been entertaining, that's for sure. I've heard some interesting things."

The elevator had stopped, and an elderly couple entered. They must have bathed in wintergreen muscle rub before leaving their cabin. The stench permeated the small space and behind their backs the Jamaican pinched his nose and made a yuck face. I tried to stymie a giggle and ended up coughing.

Later, that same wintergreen man had hit on me. Shocked and amused, I'd told him he wasn't my type, inferring that the main reason was because he had a penis.

I wasn't looking for a fling, so all men were not my type. He assumed I was a lesbian and spread the rumor. It hadn't held Mr. Gorgeous at bay.

Karen's shriek jerked me back to the present as Barbie and the red head chased her. The others took pictures. I frowned, hoping they were far from my villa.

The Jamaican's laugh rang out, causing me to pause. His head tipped back, and his eyes crinkled in mirth.

Nick's look-a-like wore a sheepish grin. He stuck his hands in the pockets of his khaki pants and waited. I'd witnessed this a time or two on the cruise ship. He'd get teased. He took it good-naturedly and always wore a smile, but it bothered me. I had to force myself to not intervene. I wanted to shout "Leave him alone!" to the Jamaican and "Grow some balls." to his friend. But I kept my mouth shut and observed. I sensed a sibling-like relationship, and it seemed to work for him.

I turned off my music to listen. They were arguing over a stupid bet. "Money, that figures."

"I'm not going to do that." The Nick look-a-like crossed his arms over his chest and frowned.

Oh, he was manning up. I can't explain why it made my heart race, but I became intrigued. I wanted the underdog to stand up for himself.

The Jamaican leaned toward his friend with a confident smile. "It's because you can't."

"It's not that at all. It's just stupid, Mike."

Good grief. Nick's look-a-like was sexy when he put his foot down. I studied his jawline, his brow, and the width of his shoulders. Shit, I shouldn't be studying him if I am anti-men. And I am definitely anti-men.

"It's a thousand dollars." Mike, the Jamaican,

shrugged, then threw me a look.

"Easy money, but a waste of time. No one will agree to such a thing." He dropped his arms and stuffed his hands into his pockets again.

"Let's ask this young woman." Mike pointed at me and smiled sheepishly.

I rolled my eyes, removed my earbuds, and walked over to them.

"Miss, would you please give us your opinion about a bet?"

My gaze raked the Nick look-a-like. His pale gray shirt was pulled taut over his muscled biceps and chest. He could handle himself in an endurance challenge. If it required flirting, the drunk ladies would be more than willing to comply. Karen certainly needed a boost in confidence.

"What's the bet?" I asked.

The blond's face turned a deep crimson, and I couldn't help but smile. He shook his head.

"All he has to do is spend twenty-four hours with a woman." The Jamaican's smile reached from ear to ear, reminding me of a bearded lizard.

I sized up the American in a new light. He was easy on the eyes and, from what I'd observed on the cruise ship, polite and well mannered. I could almost handle him. Almost. If I hadn't come here to be alone.

"He's right, easy money," I agreed.

"Thanks." Nick's look-a-like grinned. I nodded and turned away.

"But that's not all he has to do," Mike baited.

I turned to face them again. "What else?" I asked, hoping I hid my impatience.

"He has to remain physically attached to her the whole time." Mike stood with his hands on his hips in triumph.

Linking a man and woman for twenty-four hours? It was physically impossible. Wasn't it? My mind raced. I didn't know if the American had the stamina for such an activity, but my body liked the thought of trying.

Mr. Gorgeous laughed at something a crewman said. All eyes focused on him. He was sex on a stick, waiting to be licked. I'm sure he could handle a day of making love. Again, my body hummed in agreement. Crap.

I frowned and pointed to Mr. Gorgeous. "You might want to try that guy instead."

Church bells rang again as Mike laughed and tried to control the tears forming in his eyes. Nick's look-a-like didn't appear happy. I shrugged at him.

"No, no, miss. Not that kind of attachment. He has to hold hands with a woman."

"Oh," I squeaked out. My face heated, and I wished I could crawl under a rock. "I'm sure one of those single ladies will take him in a heartbeat. They may even fight over him."

"No, we need to find someone who'll put up with him."

Okay… What an odd statement. I sized up the blond again. Maybe he needed medication or had an annoying habit. Before I could contain my curiosity, I asked, "Why? What's wrong with him?"

"Nothing is wrong with me," he grumbled and half-heartedly kicked sand at Mike.

The Jamaican stared at me and the longer he looked, the bigger he grinned. Finally, I realized, he wanted me to bond with this giant frat boy for the bet.

"Oh, no," I said, taking a step backward. "No way. I came here to be alone, not get attached to some whiny, sex-crazed man."

"I'm not whiny," Blondie announced in a mock whine, then pursed his lips in a pronounced pout. He added a stomp for effect.

I bit my tongue to stifle a laugh. At least he didn't deny the sex-crazed part. Mike wore an "I told you so" expression. He started razzing Blondie. "I told you. She doesn't want you."

Inhaling, I couldn't stand the thought of the American being bullied again. "A thousand dollars?" I asked. A thousand dollars wouldn't cover my mortgage—if I hadn't sold my house before enacting my escape.

The American beamed at his silenced friend. Could he behave for twenty-four hours? Did I want to give up my alone time?

"One thousand dollars, if he makes it the whole time," Mike confirmed.

I eyed the man once more. Again, his similar appearance to Nick hit me. Being constantly reminded of my first love for twenty-four hours would be hard.

"Can you keep your mouth shut?" I asked. He nodded, showing me compliance. "Now here's the hard part, listen closely. Can you keep your free hand to yourself?" He nodded again, and Mike laughed.

"Here's the deal." I pointed at Mike. "If he misbehaves, you forfeit your money to me." I faced the blond. "If you misbehave, you forfeit your life."

He put his hand up to interject, but I stopped him with, "Are you right- or left-handed?"

He wiggled the fingers on his right hand. "Right-handed, why?"

I contemplated which hand I should hold. I'm right-handed as well. We might need his strength, so I probably should take his left with my right. I reached out my right hand but hesitated when he tried to take it.

Vanessa, what the hell are you doing? Are you nuts? You left home to get away from people, especially men. Here you go again, trying to help someone. Why can't you just say no? You never say no. You're ruining your chance at solitude. Your vacation will be over. Please girl, get a grip and just say screw you and move on.

The inner me was right. I jerked my hand back. "Double or nothing." I wore my poker face.

"Pardon?" Mike asked.

"The lady wants her share for putting up with me because of your stupid bet," the American reasoned. He smiled at me. Suddenly, we were business associates. We could broker a great deal.

"That's right. If we do this. One thousand for him and one thousand for me." I stretched my arm and opened my hand, hovering it over the Nick look-a-like's hand.

I liked that Mike hesitated. He was actually thinking things through. Chances were I wouldn't have to babysit an adult man on the real first day of my new life. Hopefully, the pressure I added would make them think twice about their foolish endeavors. I sent a prayer heavenward.

"Well?" I asked, panning both men. "Tick-tock. I'm not getting any younger."

The breeze blew a strand of my long brown hair into

my face, and I tucked it behind my ear. I'm sure my once-decent braid was now unkempt since it had been re-styled by the salty sea air.

"How will I know you fulfill the bet?" Mike's dark eyes narrowed. His features held a sudden sternness. And it pissed me off.

"Do you believe your friend to be honest?" I had to ask. He didn't know me from Adam.

"Come on, Mike, you know me." Nick's look-a-like huffed out a breath.

Mike inhaled deeply. He spoke to both of us like a superior giving orders to subordinates. "Twenty-four hours, no less. You must remain touching, one hand or the other at all times. No hanky-panky. Just pretend the other doesn't exist. We'll meet up at the resort, by the tiki bar. Cole, if she comes back alone, then I know you tried something, and I'll send out the dogs to find your body. No money will exchange hands."

Ah. So Blondie's name is Cole.

"But—" I started, but Mike continued.

"*No* money will exchange hands. If he comes back alone, then I'll know you got sick of his ramblings and no money will be exchanged."

Cole winked at me. "And if we both don't show?"

Mike's brilliant white teeth sparkled in the sunlight as he laughed. "Well, I hope you be making love on the beach, mon," he said, exaggerating his accent.

"Fat chance. I'd need a hell of a lot more money for that." I snorted, then felt myself flushing in mortification as I realized at what had come out of my mouth. Cole gazed at me with wide eyes. Yeah, it sounded like prostitution to him, too. I squeezed my eyes shut and shook my head, all the while Mike continued to laugh.

"Excuse me, wouldn't a more rational explanation be that we're too stubborn to admit that we were annoyed by each other and gave in? Therefore, the longer time extends, the more money we would make?" It sounded feasible.

Cole bit his hand to hide a smile. I hoped he enjoyed my business finesse.

Mike stood quietly, digesting what I'd said. "Well, we will see about that. Let's try the first twenty-four hours and see how it goes." He probably assumed we wouldn't last more than a few hours. He looked at his watch. The local time was close to four in the afternoon. "Are you sure about this?" he asked, suddenly concerned.

"Are you?" I questioned. I wanted to make sure he could financially hold up his end of the bargain. Not that I needed the money. After all, I am Vanessa Warsaw, the CEO of Warsaw Industries.

You quit that job, moron. Brilliant move, Ice Queen.

Shut up! I had quit, but I didn't need to worry about money. I had enough to live comfortably and, hopefully, anonymously, for the rest of my days. At least, until I was forty-five. A sigh escaped.

I wanted to make sure Mike didn't make foolish bets without having the means.

Mike threw his hands up in the air. "I'm good if you are."

"I'll be good once I'm alone," I huffed but glanced at

Cole. "So to speak." Grabbing Cole's left hand, I pulled him away from the resort. The sooner we started, the sooner it'd be over.

"Wait," Mike called after us, "Don't you want to be properly introduced?"

"No," I yelled over my shoulder.

"The resort is the other way."

I mumbled while striding forward. "It's the other way. The other direction. Turn around. Blah, blah, blah. Well, for once I'm going the way I want to go." I turned to my companion and said, "Listen, I know this is a sand bar and it ends somewhere out there. I want to go to that spot. Why? Because no one else is out there. I want solitude. I want to see the water, hear the waves and feel the wind in my hair. Once I get there, I might go comatose and stay there all night."

"But—"

I silenced him with a look.

CHAPTER TWO

Cole walked with me in silence to the end of the
sandbar. He'd kept my pace and let our arms swing with
my gait. Once I'd even forgotten he was there until his
weight hampered me when I lifted my arm to shade my
eyes as I scanned the panoramic view.

At the point, I closed my eyes and put my nose into
the wind, inhaling the warm, salty air. I heard soft,
dueling waves break on either side of the bar. I opened
my eyes and peered over the frothy water as I stepped into
the surf.

I was glad Cole willingly joined me barefoot in the
water, but he'd stepped farther into the water than I had.
The hem of his pants became damp as the waves hit him,
then me. Sometimes the water covered our feet up to our
ankles and sometimes it only kissed our toes. The
unpredictability fascinated me.

A gull's cry turned my gaze skyward. The deep blue
was littered with giant, white, cotton ball clouds. I
shielded my face against the brightness of the sun and
watched the clouds' migration. They drifted across the sky
like ships pushed across the ocean.

The dark, damp sand wouldn't be the best place to rest.

I wanted to sit or maybe have a siesta. I should have paid more attention for a suitable spot on the way to the point. "Should we find a place to sit?" I asked Cole.

He seemed shocked I'd spoken to him. Once he recovered, he examined the bar like I had. "I saw a good place a ways back."

I acknowledged him with a nod, and he led the way to a wider place. The center held a few mini-dunes with grasses growing. The dry sand was lighter tan and hot to step on. It was a perfect place to sit and ponder life. He smiled at me, and I grinned back.

We both sat with our legs stretched out in front of us. After a while, I laid back on the sand with a contented sigh, using my bag as a pillow. I must have fallen asleep because I'd been talking with Nick when a gentle prodding on my shoulder woke me.

"Hi," Cole said. His blue eyes were the color of the sea.

I glanced at the sky. The sun had lowered on the horizon. Now hot and sweaty, I wanted to cool off. I stretched, yanking Cole and making him lose balance. He toppled onto me.

"I'm sorry." He righted himself and wiped sand off my arm.

"Are you all right?" I asked. "That was my fault. I'm sorry." He had sand on his chin, and I brushed it off.

His cheeks flared red, and a small smile graced his lips. "Yeah, I'm okay."

"You seem rattled." I examined his face and dusted off a few more grains of sand.

"I'm fine." He continued to wipe his chin. His eyes shifted to the surf. "I'm sorry I woke you, but the tide will come in soon."

Hello. Doesn't it bother you he knows about tides?

Not really. He looks like a surfer dude. He's probably a marine biologist.

Whatever, Cinderella.

"Oh?" I asked, mildly interested. I had more urgent concerns, such as finding a bathroom. The constant water sounds added to the pressure to relieve myself. Would it be wrong to pee in the ocean? Fish do it, right? I hoped Cole wouldn't notice a sudden warm spot in the water.

"Yes, when it comes in, the peninsula will be underwater."

I shook my shirt to remove the excess sand. "How long?"

"An hour or so." He didn't appear anxious about the tide.

"Good. Still time for a swim."

He chuckled until I stood and managed to unbutton my capris with only one hand "What are you doing?" Cole asked with wide eyes.

I couldn't keep from rolling mine. "I don't want to get my pants wet, so I'm taking them off. Do you have a problem?" My free hand found a home on my hip.

He faced away from me and stammered, "I, uh?"

"Have you ever seen a girl in a swimsuit before? Well, I'll go out on a limb here and say my underwear covers more than the average bikini."

My bladder screamed the entire time I balanced,

pulling one leg of my pants off at a time. I hung the capris on some sea grass.

Being in my underwear in front of a stranger wasn't my idea of fun. It was time to earn that money.

I studied him. He averted his gaze. If I'm going to go waist deep, he needed to get wet too. I didn't want to walk around all night in wet pants, but maybe it wouldn't bother him.

I walked to the water's edge. He had to be hot. His hand was as sweaty as mine. "Are you going to get your pants wet?"

"Well, I—"

"It's okay if you do. Whatever you want is fine. I'm going in. I thought you might want to take them off, so they're not wet all night long. Maybe you could roll them up?"

"You want me to take off my pants?" Cole teased with a smirk. His sparkling blue eyes homed in on my face.

A growl of frustration escaped as I threw my free hand in the air. I couldn't care less about the man. I'd only been trying to be polite. Forget him. I stepped deeper into the warm water. I stretched my arm as far as I could while still holding his hand, but I was only shin deep. My bladder protested.

He contemplated what to do. His eyes met mine and his free hand went to unfasten his pants. I smiled with relief and pushed him back until his feet were on dry sand. "You can use me for support if you need to," I offered, turning away and hoping he wouldn't fall face first into the sand again.

"Thanks, but I," there was a plop, "don't need help. I'm done." He laughed softly at my expression. His pants bunched around his ankles. He kicked them away from the water. "My wallet acted as a weight and gravity did the rest," he stated, as an interesting fact.

He wore blue and white plaid Ralph Lauren boxers—thank God, he wore boxers and not boxer briefs. I think I would have liked that too much.

You know it, girl. Finally, you speak the truth.

He tugged my arm and pulled me into knee deep water, then he pranced through the water like a five-year-old who'd never seen the ocean before. I had a hard time keeping up, especially when the water became deeper. He had long muscular legs, and I had short ones. The guy had to be over six feet, and I'm only five four.

Liar. You are not five four.

Okay, I'm *almost* five four.

When he tired of loping through the water without a focus, his attention turned on me. Let me tell you, you can't outrun someone you're attached to. I shucked and jived trying to be a challenging target. It was difficult to catch my breath between the laughter.

After Cole tired, he stood with his chest heaving and a beautiful smile on his lips. I circled him as best I could, switching hands when necessary. His cerulean eyes traced my path.

I stopped, faced him, and pushed on his hard chest. His pale gray shirt felt damp. He remained immobile. The waves hit around his knee level, and I noticed that his boxers clung to his muscular thighs.

I prodded him again, this time with more energy. This earned me a raised eyebrow. Determined, I swung my leg behind him underwater and pulled it forward while I pushed his chest with my free hand. His eyes widened as he lost his balance. Tripping backward, he jerked me forward as he flailed his arms. He landed on his bum with a splash.

I stumbled to my knees beside him, chuckling. Our joined hands rested against the sandy seabed. His long legs were bent like frog legs, his knees breaking the surface. Now wet, the bottom of his shirt turned dark gray.

Glancing at his face, I noticed his eyes had narrowed and his lips had disappeared into a short, firm line. A single drop of saltwater dripped off his chin and fell onto his chest.

"Oh, shit."

Genius. Did you expect him to like it? Way to incite the hottie.

He tugged on my arm, and I fell across his stomach. Quick as a snake, he plucked me up and threw me an arm's length away. I landed between his legs in the deeper water. I'd deserved it.

We rested, sitting in the surf. I may or may not have peed like a fish.

A wave hit, rolling over me. I came up sputtering and drenched. Salt water stung my eyes. Another wave barreled over me. I glanced at the shore. We were back at the point. No wonder the water pummeled me. It was rough where the two sides met.

Cole's large hand held mine and when the next wave

hit, he tugged and I floated into his arms. He tilted my chin up, so I looked into his concerned eyes. "Are you okay?"

He leaned a whisper away, and words stalled in my throat. I swallowed and held my breath. Was he going to kiss me? My heart hammered. I put my hand on his chest. I can't kiss him. "Fine."

Kiss him, dammit, kiss him. You haven't had a toe-curling kiss since Roger. Man, he could kiss. Too bad Roni had to ruin that relationship. He wasn't a suitable fiancé if he couldn't tell you and your identical sister apart. Made it too easy for her to seduce your man when he thought it was you. Good news. She hasn't had Cole... yet. And you're on vacation.

Cole glanced toward the resort, then gave me a quick hug. He stood and pulled me to my feet. I shook off the disappointment that no kiss had occurred.

"Look how far down shore we are," I pointed out, not knowing what else to say.

CHAPTER THREE

COLE CUPPED HIS HAND OVER his eyes, glancing down the peninsula toward the resort. I followed his gaze along the dunes and saw something bright hover then disappear.

"Did you see that?" Cole asked, keeping his eyes focused on the dunes.

"I saw something white."

"It was Mike."

"Really? How could you tell?"

Cole grinned down at me. "He must have watched and followed us down here. I saw his face, and he wears that stupid white hat everywhere. He thinks it makes him look like Panama Jack." Cole laughed.

"Does he stalk much?" I suspected he wanted to check on his investment. We walked toward our pants and other items.

"Not usually."

"Making sure we're not cheating." I frowned. "I honor my word."

"He doesn't know you. He's probably checking to see if we took his suggestion." As we moved, our threaded hands swung between us like any other couple. It felt comfortable and normal.

"What suggestion?"

"Making love on the beach."

I stopped walking. It was my turn to laugh. "Yeah, you wish."

So do you.

I abruptly stopped laughing and turned to him. "If that's true about Mike, he's one serious pervert."

Cole's mouth dropped open. We started forward again, searching for the spot where we lost our pants.

He tugged on the clinging material of his boxers, pulling the damp cloth away from his legs. Luckily, the constant breeze rapidly dried our clothes. His shirt had returned to its original pale gray.

When I found the grass that had been acting as a hanger, I searched the area, looking for signs of Mike. Cole held my capris, my hands over his, while I stepped into them. Then we did the same for his pants. I sat back down in my nap spot, picked up my bag. The turquoise, lime green and white floral-patterned bag had been a gift from my sister. She'd told me my life was too drab and needed pizazz.

"Come on," he said while gently pulling me to my feet.

"Where are we going?" My voice sounded tiny, like I'd been muted by the universe.

"The tide is coming in, remember?" He picked up my bag and slung it around his free shoulder and led us back toward the resort.

His pace picked up, and I grabbed his bicep for stability in the soft sand. I found it hard to keep pace with his long strides.

After a while, we came to the larger dunes. We climbed up, then lowered again. As we crested, I heard music and sometimes laughter. I occasionally caught a whiff of something scrumptious, reminding me we hadn't had dinner. We'd had a late lunch at a stop while cruising on the catamaran. I'd loved the bread and filled up on it, but I didn't know about Cole. He seemed content to play tour guide and hadn't said a thing about dinner or being hungry.

The imaginary path he took finally leveled out. We settled on the warm sand facing the sun.

I fished inside my bag for the journal I poured my soul into and my favorite pen. He sat beside me, holding my right hand.

"I'm glad you don't wear briefs," I said, uncapping my pen and handing it to him.

He chuckled and held the pen. I stuck my hand back in the bag and pulled out a water bottle, offering it to him. He unscrewed the lid, then lifted it to his lips.

"I like your underwear. Especially the little hole right here." Cole poked his index finger to a point in the center lower back below my waistline.

The soft, accurate touch sent tingles through my body. Goosebumps appeared on my arms. I opened my journal, trying not to watch his body stretch beside me. "That hole is called a keyhole," I murmured, willing my heart to slow.

"Hm. A keyhole belongs to something that needs to be unlocked."

"Not without a key."

He's got a key. Reach out and touch it.

No. I clenched my eyes shut.

Was he always this interested in women's underwear? I didn't care about his grasp of fashion.

"I think the keyhole should be on the front so the panties can be unlocked."

My heart tap danced in my chest, and I took a deep breath. I sat my journal on my lap and tried not to steal a glance at him. I focused instead on the waves. They'd crash and retreat, then repeat. I wanted them to douse the fire in my veins.

What have I gotten myself into? Heaven help me. I desired to turn my underwear around and see what he'd say. I swallowed. Or what he'd do.

"But maybe the treasure that has to be unlocked is in the back." He chuckled when I elbowed him in the ribs.

I picked up the journal again and took the pen but found it impossible to write holding hands. He seemed oblivious to my plight.

He's thinking about unlocking your underwear.

I grabbed his wrist and placed his hand on the back of mine. Now I could hold the pen. So far, this bet hadn't been as horrendous as I thought it would be. He'd been a decent companion. The overall result surprised me, and I was reluctant to admit I liked Cole. He seemed a genuinely nice person.

I'd been chronicling the last year or so of my life.

It's depressing shit.

I sighed and glanced over the page about the elevator experience with Mike and the old man who thought I was a lesbian.

I flipped to a new page, dated it, then titled it "The Bet."

Cole tapped me on the shoulder and pointed to the dying sunlight. The colors changed. Blues swiftly softened to periwinkle to rose. I'd been so engrossed in my writing that I'd lost track of time. I set my pen and my journal aside and straightened up.

This moment—when the sky kissed the earth in a brilliant show, I was grateful I wasn't alone. Words couldn't describe it. You had to witness the beauty to understand.

I glanced over at my companion. He raptly watched the magnificent sunset. My heart softened as I studied the wonder expressed on his face. Again, his features reminded me of Nick and a dull ache filled me.

I took up my pen again. I wrote about what I'd experienced attached to another individual. "I now can relate to conjoined twins."

Reading over my shoulder, Cole laughed. I elbowed him again.

"What? I can't help it. Plus, you spelled conjoined wrong. It's an N, not an M." He tugged the pen out of my hand and reached for the book.

I pressed the book against my chest. "Gee, thanks," I said, rolling my eyes. "And it *is* an N, just a cursive one."

"Oh, sorry." He surrendered my pen.

I wanted to finish expressing the freedom I felt when frolicking in the water like a child, but the dark was settling, and I strained to see. I sighed. Suddenly, the paper gleamed white. His mobile phone lit the pages for me. I smiled at him, and he returned it. Surprised by his kindness, I hurried and finished.

I wrote: *I left home to be alone, to have silence, and what did I do? I sabotaged my chance at solitude by opening my mouth. My good sense was thrown out for a bet. What is wrong with me? The irony is, I came out here to get away from people and then I got myself saddled to one. Not just anyone, a man! Although, I will say he has surprised me so far. He hasn't whined or complained about anything. He hasn't made any crude remarks. This alone almost gives me hope in mankind. Almost.*

Losing my privacy was not a complete loss because it caused me to go through some things I would not have encountered if I'd been alone. I played in the ocean as a child, carefree of all things adult. I would not have done this by myself. Alone, I would've walked in the water or sat in it and enjoyed it, but being with someone is a completely different experience.

The sunset this evening was beautiful. The blue sky faded into pinks, oranges, and violets. Clouds were lined with vibrant pink and gold. Words cannot describe the striking beauty. How can I define my feelings? The peacefulness of the night will haunt me, yet I did not encounter this alone. Only he will understand these words as pictures.

His thumb skimmed the back of my hand before he tugged the pen and wrote "I do" in the margin.

I closed the book, capped the pen, and put both away. The meager light from his phone died as he stowed it in his pocket. Blindness momentarily assaulted me. I blinked and my eyes adjusted. That's when the stars winked into existence. Yet another of nature's shows took my breath away.

"There are so many," I whispered in awe.

Cole glanced around, then up. "There are many more we can't see because of the lights."

I laughed quietly. He's crazy. There were no lights. "What light?"

"The resort." He leaned closer. "Look behind me. Do you see the pale orange glow? That's the resort. You'd see tons more if those lights were off."

"Tons?" I couldn't believe it. "Wow." I wanted to see tons more stars. How did I unplug the resort?

The beach had narrowed. If I had stayed out on the peninsula alone, would I have drowned? Water could have cut me off from the mainland. I could have floated away. Did I owe my life to my companion?

We trudged downhill into a valley. He slowed, and I bumped into him. "Sorry."

"It's all right. Are you ready for a surprise?" His voice, deep, quiet, and excited, had my heart in overdrive.

"A surprise?" I sounded like a small child.

"It's just a little farther," he leaned and whispered in my ear. "Trust me." His thumb rubbed the back of my hand again. Shivers from his touch, his warm breath, and my imagination sliced through my body.

"Lead on, Cole."

The light from the resort started to wane, and the dark became even darker. I don't know how far we walked, but the crunch of sand was always underfoot. The sound of waves crashing came from the right. I assumed we'd hit the main isle. We passed a few palm trees. When the path turned along the ocean, I wondered where we headed.

Now you wonder. Isn't it curious how he knows his way around a private resort? He's been here before and probably not alone.

"It's just up here." He led up a slope. At the pinnacle, we stopped. He took my shoulder and pointed the way we'd come. I could see the lights of the resort and the outlines of several palm trees and some of the private villas.

It looked like a fairyland. A dock jutted out into the water. It also was lined with lights.

He pulled me back into the shadow of the dune. Slowly, my eyes adjusted again. "This is a good place. Don't you think?" he asked, setting down my bag.

I tried to make out his features in the darkness. His voice didn't sound malicious, but I wished I could see his eyes. "A good place for what?" I tentatively asked.

"To sleep under the stars," he answered.

I tilted my head and stared heavenward. The sheer quantity of stars kept me from finding familiar constellations. "I, um."

"Stargazing, no more. I promise." He squeezed my hand. "You'd like to sleep under the stars, wouldn't you? What better blanket can you have?" It sounded as if he smiled.

I gasped at the thought. I'd love to lie in the warm sand and stare at the sky until I fell asleep. The pleasant balmy breeze cooled my skin. I was comfortable, but the temperature might drop through the night. Still, we'd be protected by the dunes.

We had to sleep somewhere. Here or in an air-conditioned cabin.

There are food and drinks back at the resort. And a bathroom. Remember, plumbing? You love it.

Mr. Gorgeous was back at the resort, too. I feared he'd come pay me a nocturnal visit. This way, I wouldn't need to face temptation.

Tsk. Cole's a real man, not a surgical wonder.

I don't want anyone to see me with either man. I'm not here to hook up or find love.

"Aren't you hungry?" I asked Cole.

"Yes but skipping a meal won't kill me. Tonight is perfect. I really don't want to go back."

My heart echoed those words, and I smiled into the darkness.

CHAPTER FOUR

THE WESTERN HORIZON STILL HELD a navy scar left by the setting sun; the rest of the sky was black but littered with pinpoints of light. My vision was limited to black, white, and in between. We stood, absorbing the world around us.

I reached down for my bag and opened it. Searching inside for the pocket, I dug deeper. I had a granola bar stashed. It wasn't a gourmet meal, but it would fill the tummy a bit. Trying to open the bar one handed was deemed impossible until I involved my teeth. I yanked the wrapper, and voilà, sweet success.

I wedged the bar between our braided fingers. "You can have half. Help yourself."

"Thanks," he replied softly, "but ladies first."

Chivalry? Was he trying to impress me, or was he just being polite? I broke off half the bar and took a small bite. I'd been hungrier than I'd thought, and my mind wandered to what I could be dining on if I hadn't taken this bet. Known for their seafood dishes, the resort was, no doubt, pulling out all the stops for the new guests.

Here we go. You don't even like fish. You only picked this place because it's owned by Nick's family, and you knew your father wouldn't look for you here.

Cole's piece of the bar crunched as he devoured it. I hated causing the man's lack of nutritional intake. Besides food, I'd denied him a soft bed, bathroom, and shower. He had to worry about his reputation, too. Neither one of us would be seen at tonight's celebration. We'd disappeared off the boat together and then suddenly we'd reappear in the morning. The rumors would fly.

You don't care what they say, only that they'd notice you.

They'll notice Cole. His marital status remained unknown. I didn't want to ruin anything for him.

"Are you okay with this?" I asked. "You know, sleeping with a stranger?"

"Do you mean, do I have a girlfriend?"

I glanced over at him, trying to decipher his features. My stomach clenched.

"No. I don't have a girlfriend or a wife. I'm not dating." He paused. "It would seem the only girl I'm attached to is you."

Chewing the last of my half of the bar, I exhaled the breath I'd been holding. I passed him the bottle of water and he drank, then handed it to me. I finished it, then put it back into the pack.

"Thanks. Should we lie down and stargaze? Our necks will be sore if we keep standing." He squeezed my hand and lowered himself to the sand.

I followed his lead and sat. Never had I slept outside without a tent. Not only was it a new experience to be able to see the heavens from my bed, it was also new to slumber with a complete stranger. He arranged my bag so I could use it like a pillow. I lay in the sand and shifted my body until I became comfortable. I unlaced our fingers and slid my hand up his arm. Was that cheating?

I took a deep breath and relaxed. Sleeping outside in a tropical paradise was just fine with me.

I stared at the space above and studied the stars for constellations I recognized, but I couldn't find any.

"I can't find the Big Dipper. Or Orion."

"You're viewing the sky further south than you usually do," he reminded me.

"Of course." I bit my lip. What an idiot. I can't believe I hadn't thought of that. "There are so many." Magic hung in the air.

His free hand touched my arm then his fingers circled around it. The warmth from his touch filled me with joy. I wasn't alone in the universe.

A shooting star streaked from left to right, then moments later, another came from the north. Visible for only a moment in time, then lost. A light crossed the sky slow enough that I thought it might be a plane, but Cole pointed it out as a satellite. Due to light pollution, I'd never seen one before.

"You know, there's a place better than this to stargaze." His low voice near my ear made me smile. He had to be lying. How could you improve on the masterpiece of nature's own hand?

Masterpiece…? Do you remember when you met Nick

Tanner? Now, there was a masterpiece. And the historical building with the ceiling frescoes wasn't bad either.

Remembering Nick brought another smile to my lips. My mother and his had been sorority sisters. When they reconnected on some social media and found out they'd both given birth to identical twins, they felt compelled to reconnect. Of course, by then Roni and I were juniors and Nick and Scott had been seniors.

I sighed, thinking of the first day we were all together. My parents, Victor and Vivian, had brought us to an old monastery. It was steeped with ghost stories and tales about miracles. The property had a rectory, several outbuildings, and a stone church. I'm not exactly sure why my parents chose such a place to meet the other family, other than it was close to Halloween. We'd planned to picnic in the garden.

While we waited, my mother had talked about Mrs. Tanner and her college days. I had sat down in the sun on the stone steps of the church and started to read. My mother's voice rose with excitement, and I heard raised shouts of joy.

After a minute, Roni pushed my shoulder. "Check out the eye candy." Following her extended arm and finger, I gazed at a family of five. My mother and Mrs. Tanner held each other at an arm's length and chattered like children with a favorite Christmas toy. Their excitement made me giggle.

That's when I first saw him. Looking over our mothers' arms, Nick and I made eye contact. His face also wore a grin. Slowly, the smile on his face changed from whimsical to welcoming, accompanied with a blush.

His identical brother poked him in the back, and we broke eye contact. I studied the two brothers that bore the same face. If they were anything like my sister and me, their personalities were completely opposite each other. They only had their faces in common. Nick's hair was longer than his brother's, and it curled around his ears and neck, while Scott's was short and spiky. Doug, the oldest, bore a similarity but was taller and had dark eyes like his mother. All three boys had the same light brown hair.

Doug stood next to his dad, and they both talked to my father. Doug was a handsome young man with a sexy unshaven look and long eyelashes. His stance was straight and his clothes clean, his shirt tucked in.

I could tell Roni liked Scott because she grinned and tossed her hair over her shoulder repeatedly. Scott's lips were constantly twisted into a smirk and his brow furrowed. He could have been planning something. He was a cute devil.

Nick's smile was natural, from joy and wonder. His clothes were functional and relaxed—jeans with a hole at one knee and a pair of white Chuck Taylors. The polo shirt was the same color as his blue eyes. Hm. Those dreamy blue eyes.

Same color as the guy next to you.

Cole had said something, and I'd been off daydreaming about Nick. "Sorry. I was lost in thought."

"There's a better place to stargaze. Would you like to see it?"

"Is it near here?" I asked. "Do we need to move?"

"It's on the island. Maybe tomorrow after meeting

Mike, I can show you? Would you mind spending more time under the stars?"

"Not at all. I could live under the stars. Actually, I could live out there on that sandbar and be happy for the rest of my life. Do you think the owners would look down on me if I set up camp out there?" I chuckled, but he remained silent.

After a long pause, I continued, "Too bad I'd have to worry about eating."

Or going to the bathroom.

"Yes, the body does need fuel to function."

More silence. Was he lost in the stars? Or maybe he'd just asked me out, and I hadn't acknowledged him.

"Why did you come here?" he inquired, giving my arm a gentle squeeze.

I gave him the simple answer. "I wanted to be alone."

After a while, he asked, "Why?"

"I needed a break from people." I searched the sky, studying the Milky Way.

"Mike and I ruined the first day of your island visit." Cole sounded sad. "I'm sorry."

"You aren't the people I needed a break from and…" I straightened my arm and, finding his hand, I gave it a little squeeze. My problems were not his.

"And?" he prompted.

I sighed, not wanting to admit I hadn't minded his company. "And I've actually enjoyed this time, you know, for being a bet and all."

"Yeah, you were right. Easy money." We both chuckled. "I've enjoyed it too." His fingers slowly laced with mine. The sensuousness of that small act had me breathing faster.

"Well, if you want to talk, I'm here for you." He tugged my arm, gently pulling it to his chest. I could feel his strong heart beating. His warmth and the rise and fall of his chest fascinated me.

"You'll be here for another eighteen hours or so," I teased.

He chuckled again. "Unless you talk Mike into extending the bet."

"Fat chance. I want a shower."

"We could work with that." A low laugh rumbled out of him, vibrating my hand. A shiver ran down my arm. Suddenly, thoughts of Cole in the shower invaded my brain. Would his hands caress my back as gently as his fingers slid between mine?

To hell with your back. Have him touch your boobs.

"My family," I blurted, drastically hoping to change the subject. "Especially my sister."

"Oh? Is she a brat?"

I wish it were that mundane. "She steals the men I date." This included Nick, although she'd never slept with him.

"Steals?"

"We're identical twins, but our personalities are polar opposites. She likes to pretend to be me, but I'd never do that to her. I tend to think things through, but she rarely thinks. She's provocative and promiscuous. Seriously, she makes Hugh Hefner look like a saint."

"Hm," he replied.

I scoffed at that reaction. "Of course, you'd find her interesting. You're a man."

"Thanks for noticing," he quipped. He rolled on his side and faced me. "I only wondered how many boyfriends she'd stolen from you."

"All my boyfriends and my fiancé too. Veronica AKA Roni is the epitome of an evil twin"

"Fiancé, too? That's rough. She's not a very good sister." The fingers of his free hand trailed down my arm then back up. "How long were you engaged?"

I blew out a loud breath. I hadn't thought of Roger for a while. "My father introduced me to Roger, and three months later, we were engaged."

"That's fast. You must have really loved him." His fingers continued to glide up and down my arm.

"I couldn't say it was love." Sure, I liked the guy and cared for him. I could see myself living with him, but there never was passion. I guess by then, I was skeptical that Roni wouldn't get her talons into him. Roger could tell the difference between us at first, but Roni shifted her tactics. She played dirty and won.

"So, if no love, then what?"

"Mutual respect. Roger's business sense had impressed my father. He was funny and kind. Cute for a nerd. He wanted nothing to do with Roni until she came to the office and seduced him on my desk."

"You're kidding, right?"

I turned onto my side and faced him. "No. I went to a meeting, then she called him to my office. About halfway through the meeting, I excused myself and went to find Roger, since he was the head of one of the departments. I pushed open the door and found them going at it on my desk." I shook my head and laid back on the sand. My fingers dug, clawing deeper until they found cooler, dense sand.

All the desktop items, including my laptop, had been sprawled on the floor to accommodate his body. Roni straddled my fiancé on top of my desk. They hadn't taken the time to undress. Roger's pants remained at his ankles, and Roni's skirt had bunched on her hips. She rode him hard and fast because she knew exactly how long the meeting lasted.

"What did you do?"

"At first, I didn't know what to do. I guess I watched them for a minute. It was surreal. When he cried out my name, 'Oh Vanessa,' I'd had enough. I flipped on the lights and marched into the room."

Cole scooted closer. "I would have paid money to see their faces."

The laugh that escaped sounded evil. "I punched her."

"Awesome."

"She deserved it." I took another deep breath. I hadn't wanted to hurt my sister, but I'd been so angry.

"What did Roger do when he saw you?"

I groaned. "I'll never forget the look on his face when he saw me." I shuddered and closed my eyes, hoping to stem the tears. Before I'd interrupted them, his head had rested on the desk, an expression of ecstasy on his face. His big hands held onto Roni's hips. When I suddenly appeared, heels clicking on the floor, he raised his head and opened his eyes. "His eyes were as wide as his mouth. He did a double take, then started to panic. Roni was so into grinding his dick, she didn't see me until I was next to her. I'm pretty sure that's when the screaming started."

I clenched the sand and ground my teeth.

"Vanessa, I'm sorry."

"Yeah, me too. When I hit her, she flew off Roger. I'll forever have the image of her frog-like legs flying off the desk." I don't think Roni had ever been afraid of me before. But she actually looked like she might pee herself. Roger had started making noises, trying to form words while attempting to pull up his pants. I know I kept screaming for them to get out. I was enraged and shaking.

"And I thought my siblings were assholes," he mumbled. "When did this happen?"

"About a year ago."

"Were you close to getting married?"

"I've had the dress for ages, but I hadn't printed the invitations." I rubbed my sandy hand on the side of my leg, then threw my arm over my chest, hugging myself.

"He was a fool. How could he not tell you apart? What about the other boyfriends?"

I sighed. "None of them could tell us apart. Not when she pretended to be me."

"None?"

I rubbed my face and breathed the salty air. "There was one, but my sister ruined that relationship, too."

"She did?"

I sat up and folded my knees to my chest, wanting to keep Nick to myself. I didn't know how to talk about Nick with a man who looked so much like him.

"How did she do that?"

It's almost as if he knows he wouldn't sleep with Roni. How does he know?

"I don't want to talk about him." I rested my forehead on my knees.

"What did she do?" he asked more firmly. He sat up. He switched hands, then put his free arm around my shoulders. His warmth felt good, comforting, and homey.

I hesitated. "It was a long time ago. I was a senior in high school. I don't really know all the details because Roni won't tell me. Whatever happened made my dad hate Nick. I wasn't allowed to see him after that."

He started kneading my shoulder, working his way to the other side. It was exactly what my body needed, and I began to relax. His fingers moved up and down my spine, giving me shivers.

"He'd come to visit me, and I think Roni tried the old switcheroo. Whatever Roni told my father about Nick was bad. Dad forbade me to see him ever again."

"Why don't you ask him what happened?"

I turned my head in Cole's direction. "I'm sure he's married with a ton of kids by now."

"A ton?" he chuckled. "How do you know?"

"I know. He's too good of a catch." I didn't want to go into Nick's personality or our history. I'd loved him. He was my first true love. We'd lost our virginity together. If mom hadn't gotten sick again, I would have stood up for our relationship and things might have been different. But then Mom died from breast cancer. "He's a good person. I bet he's the perfect husband."

So yeah, you let the wistfulness seep in there, honey.

"Have you ever tried to find him?"

Between the water and the wind, most of my hair had

come out of the single braid. He took a strand that had blown into my face and tucked it behind my ear. He found the end of my braid and with a slight tug, he pulled the band off, setting my hair free. I took the band from him, and he started to finger comb my hair.

Strange sensations ran through my body, starting at my scalp. "You don't have to do that. My hair's a mess."

"I don't mind. Your hair is soft and smells good." He kept working his way up. My hair is long, brown and has a gentle wave.

Before I'd escaped, I'd pretended to get it cut. The stylist pulled it up, giving the illusion of cascading layers.

After several dinners with my father and sister, Roni came to my office with shorter hair. Luckily, I had my hair up with a clip, so she hadn't seen I'd not cut it.

I like my hair long. I've grown it down to my bra strap, and I keep it trimmed.

The salty air and sea water made it feel thick and dirty, but if Cole wanted to touch it, I didn't mind. When he reached my scalp, he started massaging. Good grief, I wanted to keep him.

Make a move, scaredy pants. Say something.

"His family owns this resort." I might have purred the words, so contented I'd become. I bit my lip. That was smooth to mention the one that got away.

"So you have tried to find him."

"I know he worked in Europe for his family's business. I made an effort to find him once after I graduated from college. I called place after place, but no one knew him. It was as if he'd gone undercover for the family." His hands had paused while I'd spoken, but they started again.

"What about you? You said you have siblings." I asked, only to change the focus away from Nick.

He leaned close and I could feel his heat against my back. Pulling the hair away from my ear, he said, "I have two pain-in-the-ass-brothers."

Just like Nick.

"One older brother, who thinks he has all the answers, and one little brother, who thinks he's God's gift to women."

"You're a middle child. Well, that explains a lot." I chuckled when he jabbed me in the back with a finger, then gently tugged a chunk of my hair.

"Are they single?" Curiosity moved me.

"Why? Are you in the market?"

"Not for me. For Roni." I sat up straighter as he started to knead my shoulder again. I think I moaned. What could his hands do to the rest of me, other than drive me crazy? "On second thought…" I gasped when his lips touched my ear—or was it only his breath?

"What thought?" His breath tickled me. Alarm bells sounded in my brain, but my body wanted him to take my lobe between his lips and suck.

"Hmm? Thought? Oh, God." He chuckled, and holy crap, did I just say *oh God* out loud?

Leaning forward, I shook my head to clear it. I came here to be alone and get perspective. I didn't want a romance. "On second thought, I wouldn't wish Roni on your family. Even if they are assholes."

"You want her married off?" His palm rested on my lower back.

"I figure once she has her own man and family, she'll stay away from mine." At least, that was my hope.

"Sounds logical." He unlaced his fingers but continued to hold my hand. "For the record, my oldest brother is married. Happily married, I might add. I don't know what my sister-in-law sees in him."

"Maybe he's got a big ding-dong?"

What the hell is wrong with you? Slap your palm to your forehead, girl.

Cole laughed and patted my back. My face felt like it might ignite into flames.

"I don't know about that." He laughed again. "My baby brother is single, but he's a lazy jerk. I wouldn't wish him on anyone, even Roni."

"I don't know. They sound kinda perfect for each other." I snickered.

"That would make us in-laws," he whispered.

I envisioned my sister holding a chubby baby on her hip and a man, who looked like Cole, leaning in to kiss them both. On the table was a cake with a big number one. Cole grinned with his arms across his chest as he waited for cake. My father would be somewhere with big gifts, waiting for them to be unwrapped. I don't know how I'd behave if Cole became my nephew or niece's uncle.

"I don't think that would be good." With a finger, he turned my chin until we were face to face.

I could see the starlight sparkle in his eyes. My lips parted to utter the word "Why?" and his gaze fell to my lips.

A phone rang.

Cole's right pocket glowed, and he struggled to get the phone out with his left hand. The awkward angle made it hard. Quickly, I plucked it out and glanced at the screen. Michael Higgins. I surmised this to be Jamaican Mike. I tapped the screen and put it to my ear. "Hello."

"Hello," Mike laughed, "Is Cole still living?"

"I haven't harmed him… Yet." I sat straight and strained my eyes looking for the light from Mike's phone somewhere on the horizon. I think Cole was doing the same behind me because he shifted to his knees.

"You missed a fabulous meal tonight. The staff performed a show. Oh, my heavens, dessert was divine." The velvety tone of his voice started to hypnotize me, and I yawned.

Cole stood and our arms pulled taut. It reminded me of something I'd been wondering. "Mike, I have a question for you. It's regarding the stipulations of this bet."

My arm lowered as Cole stepped next to me.

"I thought Cole would behave himself. If you back out now, you'll forfeit…"

"No, no, he's behaving admirably, better than I expected really." I paused. "It's just, well, do we have to hold hands? Can we touch other body parts?"

The laugh that came out of the phone was so loud I pulled it away from my ear and stared at it. I hope he hadn't jumped to conclusions. My face burned, and I was surprised I wasn't glowing.

"I'm glad you're getting on so well," he congratulated. I could imagine his big white smile and his telling eyes, crinkled with mirth.

Would it be a crime if I chanted some voodoo curse into the phone?

"Yes, we are, but you shouldn't be glad. It could cost you more money." I used my even-tempered business voice. The one that got things done at work. "So back to my question. Do we have to hold hands? Can we, oh say, link elbows?

Both men were silent. Listening to the waves, I hummed the theme to jeopardy in my mind, waiting for a reply.

"I suppose," Mike said slowly, like he was thinking out loud. "Why not. As long as you are touching physically, that will be fine."

How else would you touch someone, dumbass?

I thanked him and relinquished the phone to Cole.

Mike's voice rang loud and clear. "I can see why you like her." He laughed, and Cole shuffled his feet next to me.

I touched Cole's pant leg until I reached his ankle, then let go of his hand. I stretched my fingers and curled them. As much as I liked holding hands with a handsome man, they felt cramped after being in the same position for hours.

It seemed he was trying to talk to Mike without saying anything, so I figured I'd give them some privacy. I dug into my bag and found my phone and earbuds. I selected some relaxing music and leaned back once more to take in the heavens. Cole's long legs and rear were clearly silhouetted against my view of the majestic sky.

I yawned and Cole's hand touching my palm startled me. He laced his fingers with mine and sat down again. After a minute he pulled out my earbud.

"I thought you were mad at me," he chuckled as I turned down the music.

"No just letting you talk with your friend without eavesdropping."

He leaned slightly over me. Even in the dark, I could see his face. The shimmering starlight touched his skin with a soft silver light. He studied my face as my gaze devoured him. His fingers skimmed my cheek, and I closed my eyes and sighed.

Sucker.

I yawned again, and when I opened my eyes Cole's lips wore a smirk.

"Let's go to bed."

My eyes widened and his smile grew. If he only knew what my body really wanted when he'd said those words. He rested his hand on my face, cupping my cheek as he laid beside me on his side. He propped his head on his hand and waited for a response. My tongue stuck to the roof of my mouth. What could I say?

How 'bout... Take me, I'm yours! Or what are you waiting for? Or I'd opt for: Let's go.

I pried his fingers away from my face and brought our arms to our sides and grabbed his hand.

I let my eyes flutter shut and breathed deeply. The cool breeze with its salty scent and the monotonous, soothing sound of the breaking waves relaxed me. Peace rolled over me.

"I don't think we'll stay connected through the night if we lay this way." He laid back against the sand with his arm behind his head. "Do you move a lot when you sleep?"

"I guess you're right. We could tie our hands together," I suggested.

"With what, your bra?"

I sucked in a breath and coughed.

"Our circulation would be cut off."

"What do you suggest then?" I asked sitting up again. So much for my peaceful moment.

He placed my hand over his heart then released it. I could feel his heartbeat and warmth. He stretched his arm straight out on the sand. "Here, you can use my arm as a pillow."

"Your arm will fall asleep," I pointed out. The bra strap thing would work better.

"Trust me."

I growled but gave in. "Okay, but you can use my bag for your head."

I tried to flatten it, so nothing poked him. He sat up and I dusted his head, neck, and shoulders to remove as much sand as I could. I placed the bag with the large flap open, giving us both a place to lay our heads. He reclined against it then rested his hand over mine.

"Thanks, that's better. Now your turn."

I pulled at my hand, but he held on. "I'm going to need that," I chuckled when he mumbled something that sounded like "mine." I made sure my arm remained touching him even as I laid my head back against the bag, his arm against my neck. I enjoyed the sensation of his body close to mine. I stretched both arms over my head, arching my back. It felt wonderful to move my arms the way I wanted.

Cole decided to bend his elbow, and I rolled against him, the length of my body against his side. I frowned, but he had his eyes closed. An ornery grin rested on his lips.

Two could play that game. I leaned my forehead against his chest and his arm rested on my shoulders. One of my hands completely covered one of his while the other was sandwiched between us.

I snuggled up to him and threw my leg over his, rubbing his thigh. I felt his breathing hitch. I played with his fingers, tracing their length. He plunged his hand into my hair again. I sighed.

His lips touched my forehead in a whispered kiss. "Good night, Vanessa."

I smiled. "Good night, Cole."

I dreamed of Nick.

CHAPTER FIVE

THE MONASTERY THAT WE EXPLORED the first day we'd met had a bell tower. Nick and I had followed our twins upstairs. Roni and Scott were bold and daring. They leaned over the edge and made outrageous claims. They also tried to ring the bell. Nick pointed down the stairs, and I nodded. We took off.

"Trust me," he'd said and offered his hand, and I'd taken it.

We ran to another level and reached a section under repair. Scaffolding and ladders littered the room; plastic drop cloths hung everywhere and were fluttering, even though there didn't seem to be a breeze.

The area was deserted, creepy, and dim. Hand in hand, he led me through, zigzagging around debris.

Roni called my name, and it echoed. As their voices got closer, Scott shouted for Nick. We stopped near the corner and Nick put his finger to his lips, then smiled. I smiled back and I'm pretty sure my face was red. We heard our siblings talking and the sound of their footsteps. They sounded close.

In what looked at first like a solid wall, a door the same color was cracked ajar. Nick pushed it open enough to look in. His head tipped up, and when I followed him in, I saw a wrought iron spiral staircase.

He threw me a grin, then started to climb. We walked softly up the steps. At the top, a door opened onto a narrow balcony overlooking the sanctuary. We paused to catch our breath and glanced over to glean our siblings' whereabouts. They had ventured into the large room. My sister complained about the smell. Nick watched their progress, but I looked up. The vaulted ceiling held painted frescos that, even in disrepair, were beautiful.

Nick squeezed my hand, recapturing my attention. His eyes crinkled in mirth as we watched an interesting scene unfolding below. My sister stomped away from Scott with her arms crossed and a pinched expression on her face. Following her, Scott caught up and grabbed her elbow. He swung her around and she slammed into his chest.

"You hurt me, you idiot," she yelled, getting a shin kick in before Scott silenced her with a kiss.

I blinked my shocked eyes at Nick as I crouched down. Now he frowned and stuck out his tongue. I'd agreed, seeing our sister and brother kiss was gross. Something crunched under my feet. Looking down, I found pebble-sized pieces of plaster all over. I picked up two and handed one to Nick.

Glancing over the balcony, I spied a floor to ceiling drop cloth. Likewise, Nick searched for a place to chuck his projectile. We nodded at each other, then threw them.

There was a metallic ting as Nick's piece hit something and then ricocheted down to the floor. Mine made a swoosh as it slid down the plastic and shattered on the ground on the side of the large room opposite to Nick's piece. Roni screamed and Scott yelled.

"This place is haunted," Roni said in a reverberating whisper.

"Let's get out of here," Scott exclaimed, taking her by the hand.

I put my hand over my mouth to contain my giggles. Nick was red faced and had tears in his eyes from trying to not make a sound. I sucked in a breath, and he started to laugh. He pointed to a door. We pulled open the door and entered the musty room. Just as I shut the door, we exploded with laughter. Nick's hand landed on my shoulder, and I leaned against his chest as I laughed. After we'd sobered, we glanced around at the grayed walls. The room had a slanted roof with exposed beams, dust-covered piles of boxes, and a couple of trunks. A dormer window had all its panes except one. Fresh air blew in, making the cobwebs move.

"This is creepy," I said.

"I won't let anything happen to you." He hugged me, and I let him. It felt right. After he released me, we looked around. The strange, long, narrow room had a high, angled ceiling. The standing candelabras were tarnished. A pile of old books with pink, probably used-to-be-red covers, were stacked in the back corner. One lay open on the floor where it had fallen and something black crawled over the page.

We talked and talked as we explored. I knew this boy was special. He understood my feelings about being a twin, and we laughed a lot. At one point, one of us looked up and froze. The other followed suit. Above our heads was a huge honeycomb, and as we quieted, a low buzzing filled the air.

"I hate bees," I groaned, grabbing his arm and

edging my way to the door as I started to panic. With his hands on my temples, he turned my head until I stared into his brilliant blue eyes.

"I've got you," he stated. "Now breathe."

I inhaled, then blew out a breath.

Nick dropped his hands and turned toward the door which had automatically shut. He reached for the knob. "It's stuck."

He jiggled it, but it wouldn't turn. He tried again, this time putting his shoulder to the door. The buzzing got louder as our noises disturbed them. Then the doorknob on our side of the door fell off into his hand.

Oh my God. We were trapped, and the hive had started to swarm. Nick attempted putting the handle back and making it fit, but it wouldn't catch. He kneeled and examined the hole. He tried to work the mechanism inside but didn't have any luck.

It seemed the buzzing had gotten even louder. I looked up, and every shadow had things moving. I rubbed my arms. My gaze darted around.

"Nessa, you need to breathe." He spoke in a calm voice.

I was breathing, wasn't I? I took a stuttering breath and blew it out. Nick stood and grasped my trembling hands.

"Wow, you're really freaked out." He tipped my head. "Look at me, Nessa. Look into my eyes." His gaze drank me in, landing on my lips.

I momentarily forgot about the bees. Would he kiss me? He touched my cheek and my hair. His eyes grew wide when his hand pulled a bobby pin out of my long locks. He turned towards the door, then just as quickly pivoted back to me and kissed my cheek.

As he jimmied the lock, the buzzing grew louder, and a black cloud came after me.

I sucked in a deep breath and sat up, and it was a few moments before I realized I'd been dreaming.

A shiver shook me. The temperature had dropped some. When I had shifted, Cole's arm had slipped off my back.

The surf continued to roll up onto the shore. The wind brought an eerie sound, a low grunt, and I quivered and leaned closer to Cole. A sleeping man couldn't offer protection, but the chills that ran down my spine could be warmed by his closeness.

I heard the noise again, and this time it seemed to come from another direction. My mind went into overdrive trying to remember if any predators lived on the remote tropical paradise. A large jungle cat? Maybe a monkey. A wild hog?

With every grunt, my heart hammered harder. Being close to thirty, I shouldn't be this afraid of the night. Since we'd sheltered in a dip between the dunes, it was hard to determine what direction the grunts were coming from and if the animals were getting closer.

One sound would come from the vicinity of the resort, while the next came from the long sandbar. Shifting left to right, I watched with wary eyes, expecting scavengers to sniff us out any minute. The longer I waited, the more nervous I became.

Cole grabbed my wrist, and I nearly jumped out of my skin with fright. "Nessa, what's wrong?" he asked.

"I didn't mean to wake you." I felt bad, but I was

relieved too.

Instantly, a wave of calm rolled over me. I needed to share my angst and alleviate the trepidation. "There's something out there. I keep hearing noises, and it seems to be circling around us."

He straightened and tilted his head, listening to the darkness. My hands were clamped on his arm like a vise. When a loud howl met our ears, I jerked, almost breaking contact.

"I won't let anything happen to you," he promised.

My foggy thoughts remembered Nick and how he'd made the same claim. We'd survived without a single sting. Now Cole wanted to protect me, too. I nodded, believing him. I trusted Cole. That realization would have given me a lot to ponder about if I hadn't been too frightened to think.

Another long but faint guttural noise came over the dune, and Cole covered his mouth with his right hand. He bent over, shaking his head.

"What is it?" I whispered.

He chuckled now. "They won't eat us, that's for sure, although they seem to have an appetite." Patiently, but with relieved anxiety, I waited for him to expound. "It's people."

I shook my head. "It doesn't sound like people."

"They've taken Mike's suggestion." Cole stared at me.

Mike? "Oh. No way." Remembering what Mike had suggested about making love on the beach, I shook my head again. "It sounds like wild animals."

"Doing the wild thing. Listen again and see if you can hear the people this time."

The breeze rustled the tall grass around us. The stars had rotated, making new pictures in the darkness. A new sound met my ears and this time after the moan, I heard the murmurings of lovers.

"Well, I'll be…" I started to giggle. "I thought they might bite."

"They might," he said, joining in the laughter.

"What are we to do?" I asked. We couldn't move for fear of interrupting and embarrassing the couple. Finally, they quieted, and we were able to lie back down. As I snuggled against Cole, his breathing changed. As I followed him into sleep, my mind whispered that he'd called me by Nick's pet name for me: Nessa.

CHAPTER SIX

I AWOKE AND STRETCHED. COLE kept a hand on my arm as I sat up. "Good morning," he said with a smile.

"Morning." My stomach rumbled.

"Come on." He pulled me up and grabbed my bag. We started walking toward the resort. "I hope you're hungry."

"I hope they don't mind us tracking sand everywhere," I mumbled.

"Why would they mind? You know the owner." He strode ahead confidently. I swallowed, hoping Cole wouldn't flaunt that information.

We arrived on the patio café. Several people sat enjoying meals at outside tables. A few looked in our direction but went back to eating. Thank God.

Cole strode into the main lobby and straight to the reception desk.

"Good morning, sir."

"Good morning, this young woman is a friend of Nick Tanner's. Please give her anything she needs."

The woman's eyes widened, and she nodded. She smiled at me, but I was dumbfounded. Had I said Nick's last name? Or maybe Cole had put two and two together. I'd mentioned his family owned the place.

"What can I get for you, miss?" Her dark eyes scanned me.

"Uh."

"She'd like a toothbrush and some toothpaste." He glanced at me. "Anything else?"

When I looked into the mirror behind the desk, I frowned. My hair was a greasy rat's nest. "Shampoo and conditioner, please."

She nodded and signaled to another woman. She passed her a note, then the other woman left.

The lobby had a high ceiling with many windows and potted plants. The floor was tiled. As people walked, their shoes made noises.

The woman returned and handed Cole the bag. Hand in hand, he pulled me deeper into the main resort building. We ambled past rooms, down a long corridor, then into a workout room.

At the far side was a set of bathrooms. My bladder rejoiced. Opening the bathroom, I saw it had a toilet, a sink, and a small shower.

"How do we do this?" I asked, pointing to the toilet.

"Like this." He followed me into the bathroom and locked the door. "This area isn't as busy. That's why I came here." He released my hand to his waist, so he had both hands free. He started fiddling with the zipper on the front of his pants.

"Cole." I couldn't believe he was just going to do his thing with his thing in front of me.

"What?" He glanced down at the toilet. "Oh sorry," he said, then raised the lid.

I stood behind him while he used the bathroom, then it was my turn. By this time, my bladder didn't care. He stood with his back to me as I sat.

We took turns washing our hands. While he washed, I stood behind him with my hands on his hips and then we reversed it for me.

He fished in the bag and retrieved all the items. Shampoo, conditioner, two toothbrushes, but only one paste and a comb. We brushed our teeth. I hadn't shared that experience with a guy for a long time.

I turned the water on, trying to find the right temperature for washing my hair. "I should have got a cup and a towel."

"That's an easy fix." He opened the door and on a small table sat a whole stack of towels. I grabbed two. Next to a water cooler, Cole found cups. They were small, but they'd do.

He helped me wash my hair, giving me a scalp treatment similar to the one he'd given me the night before, only this time he'd used soap and water. After washing up and getting rid of as much grime as I could, I felt human again.

Now we could go eat with the others and not stick out. We ate in companionable silence, taking turns touching hands or feet. My long hair air dried, swaying in the gentle breeze. Cole took care of our food, putting it on his room.

After we'd eaten, he suggested a leisurely walk along the resort's beach. We secured a double lounge chair but when I hesitated leaving my bag, he threw a couple of towels over it. His solution both hid my bag and claimed the chair. Then we kicked off our sandals and left my bag.

I stepped on his foot, then rebraided my hair to keep it from becoming a knotted mess in the wind.

As we walked, hands joined, we passed other couples.

They greeted us. Some wore bathing suits and others, like us, merely strolled. A few I recognized from the cruise ship. Walking, we remained mostly silent, but I was comfortable with Cole. We didn't need to talk.

As we neared the last cabana on the beach, I noticed its deck rails held as many brightly colored towels as the UN has flags.

A burst of giggling, then a petite blond in a bikini ran out chased by another woman—Karen, from the cruise ship.

"Dammit Lindsay, where's my freaking bra?" Karen wore a long white tee-shirt and gray sweats. She sprinted while keeping one arm on her chest.

I giggled at the women. They were crazy, but at least Karen had friends to cheer her up.

I didn't have that anymore. I'd made my work my life. But that dry part of my life was over. Maybe Cole would consider being my friend?

Once the cabana was out of view, it was as though we'd left civilization behind. We came to a grove of palm trees. One had fallen, and we stepped over the trunk. It hadn't died but had curled heavenward at the end.

He paused, and I turned to face him.

Cole glanced into my eyes, and I quickly looked at his feet. He wiggled his toes in the sand. I couldn't help but smile. He took a step closer and tipped my chin, so I gazed into his eyes. With his free hand, he ran his fingers through his wind whipped blond hair. "Vanessa, I want to thank you for accepting this bet. If you wouldn't have done it, I might have gotten stuck with one of those from cabana one."

I hadn't seen any numbers, but I knew immediately

which place he'd meant. "They would have eaten you alive."

He chuckled and nodded.

"You might not have wanted to, but I think you could have handled them. Plus, you probably would've gotten lucky."

His mouth opened, then he pressed it closed in a thin line. His cheeks turned red, and his eyes narrowed. "Is that what you think about me?"

I held my free hand up in surrender. "I'm just saying they're crazy and drunk all the time. They might've jumped your bones." His expression softened. "All of them. You could be dead." His lips twisted up in a smirk. "And where would I be? I'd die not ever seeing the best stargazing place in the world."

"Hm. That's true." He walked to the edge of the water. A wave kissed our toes. "I'm considering not taking you tonight."

"What?" I poked him in the ribs. "You are not reneging."

"You think I'd give in to those women?"

Now my eyes narrowed. I had been teasing him since it hadn't happened. "I've learned one thing about men— it's that they never say no to sex. Never."

Cole looked up at the sky and pinched his nose. He took a deep breath and released it before turning to face me. "I'm not Roger or any of your other boyfriends who didn't say no to your sister."

Tears stung my eyes. I tried to blink them away. He wasn't Roger, but he was a man. "So have sex with me," I blurted.

Oh God, what have you done?

One of his eyebrows rose. He stepped, so we were toe to toe. His right hand cupped my face, then his left. He tilted my head and held it, so I had no alternative other than to look him directly in those cerulean blue eyes. He closed the space between us, and I thought he would kiss me.

I chewed my bottom lip. My chest heaved almost as fast as my heartbeat.

His gaze lingered on my lips and his mouth parted as he breathed. "I would love to get naked with you, Vanessa. I would love the opportunity to pleasure you. I would love to have your hands touch me all over, but not today. Not like this. I want you to want me, too. Something more than sex."

I swallowed, relieved and strangely disappointed at the same time. I let my lids close and felt his lips touch the tip of my nose, and I sighed.

You sighed like a freaking adolescent with her first crush.

He pulled me against his hard chest. My arms snaked around his back. He rested his chin on my head, and we stared at the water for a long time.

He'd rejected my offer, yet with his erection pressed against me, I could feel that he wanted me. That made me feel beautiful.

Beautiful and wanted. Something I hadn't felt in a long time. Maybe since Nick.

I hugged him tighter, and a part of me shattered.

"Thank you," I mumbled. Tears streaked my face, but I kept him from seeing.

"No, thank you. You offered me something precious. I'll never forget it."

By and by, we returned to the resort and our chair. He sat, and I stretched out. I found my sunglasses and reclined with my feet up.

Cole raised his hand, and an employee came over and passed him a menu. He ordered something for both of us, then handed the paper back. The employee rushed off to get the order.

I'd retrieved my journal and located my pen. I looked up as Karen and her posse walked by. A few looked over in my direction, one even pointed at Cole and me.

Look! The lesbian scored a hottie. Ha ha.

I grinned and resumed writing. Cole pulled out his phone. "I can't see the screen." He stuck it back in his pocket.

"Cole," a deep voice called. I kept writing even as a shadow fell over me.

"Mike," Cole greeted. "Come out for a swim?"

His laughter rang, and I put my pen down to listen. "Amoya sent me out of the room, so she could have some peace."

"So, you've come to disturb ours?" Cole asked with a smirk.

Mike crossed his thick arms over his chest. "I came to see if Vanessa has had enough of you yet. I asked Marguerite if she had a shovel in case I needed to dig up your bones."

"So little confidence in me?" Cole placed his hand over his heart.

Mike sat on a lounger next to me with his legs crossed. Today he wore shorts and leather flip-flops. His plaid overshirt waved in the wind while his white tank pulled tight over his chest. His white fedora tilted on his shaved head.

"Cole, I'm a little surprised she didn't gag you or slap you for talking. I know that mouth of yours. You probably asked all about her. Trying to find some new information."

"Funny, Mike." Cole said, but he frowned and watched the drunk ladies kick water and toss a beach ball.

I gave his leg a pat, which Mike noticed.

"Looks like the lady has taken pity on you." Mike laughed again. His deep velvety voice intoned, "I can't believe you lasted this long."

"Why?" I asked a little snottily. Cole had been a gentleman. Of course, we'd teased each other, but he'd always been courteous and never taken advantage of the situation. Especially when I asked him to make love to me.

"Cole's a dreamer, miss. He had set his sights on you from the get-go. He'd hoped you'd remember him."

The get-go, so Cole must have noticed me on the cruise ship.

"Come on, Mike. Give her a break," Cole snipped.

"Not a chance." Mike glanced at his watch. "You have five hours until we meet. Should we have dinner together? Amoya," he glanced at Vanessa and clarified, "my wife would like that." Mike looked at Cole and shook his head. "Still don't think you'll make it. Somehow, you're going to screw this up, man."

I gritted my teeth. Mike had spoken constantly to Cole on the ship like this. I couldn't stand how he treated Cole. And maybe, just maybe, it reminded me of Roni teasing me. The pseudo fun and lilting voice disguising a mean spirit.

I didn't understand why Cole never stood up for himself. So I decided to. I jumped up and would have been in Mike's face if Cole hadn't had a death grip on my hand.

"Leave him alone," I breathed through my teeth.

"Oh," Mike's brows raised. "She likes you."

Not reacting to his prompt, I raised our clasped hands. "We are together and when you put him down, you're doggin' me. I would prefer you don't piss me off. I'm on vacation and I'd really hate it if I had to open my can of whoop-ass."

Cole chuckled behind me.

"I like your guard dog. She's ferocious when she bares her teeth." Mike crossed his arms and frowned at me.

Cole moved so fast I had to keep both hands on his arm to stop him from pouncing on Mike. He leaned over Mike, his full height dwarfing the seated man. "Don't say anything about Vanessa. She's not a dog." The veins in his neck were bulging and his face had turned red.

The smile plastered on Mike's face was priceless. His hands gripped the edge of the lounger's seat on either side of him, and his knee bumped up and down. I was proud that Cole stood up to Mike, and he'd stood up to him for me.

My heart warmed, and I longed to kiss Cole. It was a

strange sensation. One that frightened me. I stroked Cole's arm, trying to soothe the anger.

"Give us a minute, Vanessa." Cole said, nodding to Mike.

"Sure thing," I said, not really knowing where to go that I wouldn't hear. I sat back down on the lounger. Cole held my hand standing next to me and faced Mike. I wanted to watch, but I fished in my bag for my romance novel.

Mike got to his feet and he and Cole spoke in low tones. After a moment, Mike huffed off, and Cole turned back to me. I slid over so he didn't have to climb across to the other side.

The resort employee returned holding a tray with two drinks. One large cup with an icy brown liquid, maybe tea, and another with a white slushy drink with a red umbrella.

I rested my calf on his shin so we could have both hands free. Cole handed me the drink with the umbrella. I sipped. Piña colada. "Mmm. Thanks. Cheers." I clinked his glass.

"To a great vacation," he said with a wink.

I took a drink, then he put his arm around my shoulder. Snuggling against him, I laid my head on his shoulder. We enjoyed our drinks watching other vacationers explore the surf. When Cole set his empty glass on the small side table, he raised his hand, and an employee came over. As he spoke, I appreciated the way his chest vibrated. Moments later, a shadow covered our torsos as the employee adjusted a large shade umbrella. I sighed, relishing the coolness.

I stretched and sat up. I took off my white button-up

shirt. Even though it was lightweight, peeling off the layer helped to keep me cool. The white tank I wore had spaghetti straps. The lacy straps of my bra were wider than the tank's, and Cole noticed them.

With a finger, he traced a line on my bare skin. "Your bra matches your underwear."

It did, but I answered, "Maybe."

How astute of him to notice.

"You know, I'm grateful that I got stuck with you and not Mike. I have a feeling he would not shut his mouth, and I'd have had to pop him."

Laughing, Cole shifted to look at me. "No, not much peace with Mike around. He might have talked your ear off. No, both ears." He leaned back and put his hands behind his head. "I don't mind the silence. Sometimes the silence says more than the noise around us."

Mutely, I contemplated those words. Cole was a unique guy. He could make some deep observations. Perhaps there's hope for the male species, after all.

Then again, perhaps not.

"Why do you let Mike push you around?" It wasn't my business, but I couldn't resist asking.

He waited a while before answering. "He doesn't do anything that I don't let him, but he does like to push me sometimes. You noticed?"

"I notice lots of things," I mumbled, not wanting to admit to watching him on the cruise ship.

"Is that why you accepted the bet?"

I bit my lip. Most of the men's interactions I'd observed were playful, but sometimes Mike had teased a little too much. In my point of view, the conversation became lopsided and derogatory. Cole never seemed mad or hurt and mostly laughed or shrugged things off. It might not have bothered Cole, but the subtle bullying concerned me. I'd felt sorry for Cole and had wanted Mike to stop the so-called teasing.

Never in my wildest imagination could I have conceived this stupid bet. I had wanted to be alone, yet I intervened. Why *did* I get involved?

"Yes, it is one reason, I suppose." I didn't really want to think about why I'd sabotaged my aloneness.

"Thank you." He touched my shoulder again. The heat of his touch sent my blood pressure skyrocketing. "I appreciate you giving up your time for me and standing up for me."

I nodded. "You stood up for me, too. It's been quite a while since anyone has done that."

His fingertip followed a line down my arm until he reached my hand. He circled my palm, then his finger traced each of my fingers. He drew my hand to his lips and kissed the back of it. "We make a good team."

I nodded in agreement but couldn't look into his face for fear of pressing him back against the lounger in a heated kiss that would probably lead to more than just an attachment of hands and lips.

I picked up my book and started to read. The heroine in the story tripped, and the hero caught her. It reminded me of the dream I'd had, remembering the time with Nick and the bees.

Nick had worked the lock, trying to get the door open.

I'd pressed against his back, afraid of the bees. He'd smiled at me and just when I thought he had it, the door jerked open, away from him. Scott gripped the knob as Nick and I plummeted through the opening, but Nick shifted so that I landed on his chest. He had clung to me until I could breathe again.

I grinned at the memory and flipped the page.

CHAPTER SEVEN

NICK'S VOICE CALLED TO ME. "Nessa," he whispered.

Mrs. Tanner and the twins had come to visit with us a month after Nick and Scott had graduated. Mrs. Tanner took mom to the doctor while my father was on a business trip. This was when we'd gotten the doctor's bad news.

I'd hugged my mother, holding it together long enough to flee the room. I didn't want Mom to see me upset, but the news had devastated me.

My mother sent Nick to find me. Even then, Mom knew Nick and I had a bond. He'd found me sitting in a shadow at the edge of the pool. I fluttered my feet back and forth as the tears trickled down my face. Nick sat next to me and put an arm around my shoulders. Then I started sobbing.

Somehow, we began kissing. I was needy, consuming, and he complied. He gave what I needed but never crossed the line. That's why I fell in love with him.

"Nessa."

I felt a gentle prodding. I didn't want to leave Nick, but consciousness was calling. "No, Nick," I mumbled, snuggling down against him.

I opened my eyes to high-pitched screeching. "You bitch!"

Even in the heat, I'd moved toward Cole's side of the lounger and was now cuddled up against him with one arm draped across his belly. I blinked up at him.

"Hello, sleepyhead," he said, smiling at me.

"I didn't order a wake-up call," I grumbled.

He laughed, and the vibrations felt awesome. "You wouldn't want to miss the show."

"You're the bitch, bitch," a slightly deeper voice yelled.

I sat up and frowned. Two of Karen's friends squared off. The scrawny redhead held a deflated beach ball in her hand, taunting Barbie. "It's the only thing you're good at blowing."

Barbie lunged, grabbing a fistful of red hair. They circled, scratching and pulling hair as their friends gathered around them, some cheering one over the other.

I leaned to pick up my book, and Cole winced. "You okay?" I asked.

"I'm fine, it's just..." He pointed to three empty glasses. "This is the perfect time for a potty break." He gingerly put his feet on the ground.

"Where's the closest?" I inquired. He'd obviously been here before and seemed to know where everything was.

"By the pool."

"Lead the way." I slid on my shoes, then picked up my bag.

The building, which looked like a hut, had a thatched roof and stucco walls painted stark white. It was on the far side of the pool.

A few guests floated on rafts in the water, sunning themselves. There was a built-in bar in the center where the gay couple from the catamaran sipped cocktails in the shade while watching TV.

Without hesitation, Cole headed straight into the women's restroom. My eyes squinted to adjust to the dimness. There were three stalls, two regular and one handicapped. I pushed open the door, and we raised our free hands, clasping them over the metal wall. Once beside the toilets, we stopped.

"Here, touch my foot." I looked down, and he'd stuck his foot into my stall. With our toes kissing, our hands remained free to take care of business. He let out a big sigh, which made me chuckle.

As I washed my hands, he held my hips, then we switched places. "We're getting good at this," I admitted.

The door creaked open, and two older women entered. I smiled when they shot a look at each other with raised eyebrows.

"Something wrong with your plumbing, boy?" one asked.

"Nope," I answered. "He couldn't live without me for twenty-four hours."

Cole laughed as we headed for the exit. With a tip of his head, he said, "Have a great afternoon, ladies."

"Clever," he said as we skirted the pool, hand in hand. We had nowhere specific to go or anyplace to be. Stopping at the tiki bar between the pool and the beach, he sat and patted the stool next to him. He motioned to the bartender, who was an older man.

"Excuse me, I wouldn't happen to be able to charge my phone here, would I?" Cole asked, laying his phone on the countertop.

The old man smiled. His weathered face wrinkled, and he grinned at me. I had a déjà vu feeling, like I'd met him before. I tried to recollect. He wasn't overly tall or short and had lost most of the hair on the top of his head.

"Sure thing," he nodded and took the phone, looking at the port. "I can plug it in under here. Please don't forget about it. Can I get you something to drink?"

"Thanks." Cole glanced at the resort's specialty drinks. Once again, he ordered for me. I liked the little display of dominance—probably more than I should.

Cole made a funny face. "Which of our fellow shipmates is most likely to wear a Speedo?"

The pool was behind me. I could cheat and look but decided to try to guess. "The Japanese man and…" I couldn't even think of him mostly naked without heating up. "Mr. Gorgeous."

"Who?" Cole asked with a neutral face.

"You know that guy who looks as if God sculpted the perfect man? He has dark hair and dark eyes with long lashes." I gave an involuntary shiver and sighed. "Did I guess right?"

I swiveled my head to find the fifty-something Japanese man wore a red marble sack. He also had goggles and a swimming cap. "Okay, I can't unsee that." I stuck out my tongue.

Cole chuckled. "I'm glad you didn't see the other guy."

"Oh please, like I want to see a banana hammock. Yuck."

The bartender set our drinks down and waited until we each took a sip. "Very good," I said. "This could be dangerous. I don't taste the alcohol."

"Good for me," Cole teased.

"Hey, baby," a voice as smooth as liquid sex sounded behind me. I froze, holding my breath. I'm sure I paled. Cole's face pinched with concern, then anger, when the man touched my arm.

Nothing came out of my open mouth except a gurgle. The bartender saved me. "What can I get you, sir?"

"I'll have what she's having."

He's after you. Surrender, it will be sweet. Oh, and let him lick you everywhere.

I gurgled again. My gaze strayed over the legs next to me. Tanned and toned, one knee nudged mine. Traveling up his thigh, I found he indeed wore a Speedo.

What the hell did he have stuffed in that thing, another arm?

I swiveled my seat until I faced Cole. He looked as if he sucked a lemon. I swallowed. Finding my mouth dry, I picked up my drink and gulped. I set the empty glass down.

Luckily, Cole's phone rang, saving us. Cole took it from the bartender. "Dinner, in fifteen. Sure, we'll be there."

Cole stood and, taking me by the elbow, led me away from Mr. Gorgeous' tempting banana hammock.

The combined drinks and my lack of food had me feeling warm. I needed something to eat. The last thing I wanted was to give in to that beautiful bastard.

The time was early for dinner, but my stomach agreed it was fine. We waited by the door until Mike and his wife appeared.

Amoya was almost as tall as Mike, at least in her heels. The white, shoulderless dress contrasted with her flawless dark skin. The hem of the dress had red embroidery.

After we were seated and had selected an appetizer, Mike started heckling Cole again, but Amoya nipped it in the bud.

"I swear, Michael Higgins, stop your teasing. Let the man be." She smiled at Cole and me as we held hands on the tabletop.

Cole and I agreed that we needed to continue holding hands until Mike deemed the bet concluded.

"We have a guest, and I wouldn't want to scare her away." Amoya grinned.

"I don't think that one scares easy," Mike said with a wink.

I leaned back and crossed my hands over my chest, inadvertently putting Cole's hand on my boob. I quickly dropped our hands out of sight; my face probably matched the red tablecloth.

"She's tough." Cole agreed, ignoring my boob.

"So, how often do these two make stupid bets and crazy dares?" I asked. Amoya hadn't been on the cruise ship or she might have kept Mike from teasing Cole and thus instigating the bet.

"Oh no, what have they done now?" Amoya shifted her gaze from man to man. Cole wore a sheepish grin, but reached for his water. Her husband shook his head.

"Amoya, darling…"

"Oh ho, this is bad." She pursed her lips and crossed her arms. "No sir, don't you darling me. What did you do and how did you get this young woman to play along?"

The men shared a look but stayed silent.

"They ensnared an innocent victim, me. I have to remain attached to this one," I pointed to Cole and raised our joined hands, "for twenty-four hours. I believe it's been over twenty-four hours now."

"Attached?" She arched her eyebrows.

"Sleeping was interesting. We had to make it, so we remained touching." I rolled my eyes. "Don't get me started on the bathroom issue."

"Why did you agree to this bet?"

I shrugged. "A thousand dollars will buy one hell of a spa treatment."

"A thousand…" Amoya's mouth stopped moving.

"For each of us," I said, pointing to Cole again.

Amoya's eyes widened until I saw no lids, and she slowly turned to her husband and slapped his arm. "I can't believe you," she growled so low it was hard to hear.

The appetizer arrived. Cole looked over at me and winked. "Amoya, don't worry. I'll take care of it."

Her angry glare dissipated. "Cole, this isn't like you. I can't believe you'd do this." She shook her head again, then glanced at me. "Well, you must be a trooper. It looks like you survived their bet. I should make them both pay you."

"I'm just glad I'll be free to take a long, hot shower later." I closed my eyes and smiled. When I opened them, Cole wore a lopsided grin and his half-lidded eyes stared as if he'd like to devour me. I swallowed.

Maybe you should have mentioned how you'd like to poop alone.

"See, Cole, she's done with you. Twenty-four hours and she's through." Mike laughed.

I couldn't help narrowing my gaze, but I jerked it to my plate. I'd seen Cole take care of himself. He needed to man up.

"She could handle another twenty-four hours. Hell, Mike, she could put up with your bullshit for a week."

"Probably not," I mumbled. That's a bet I'd refuse. You couldn't pay me enough. "I'd have to ask Marguerite about that shovel." I gave Mike the sappiest smile I could. Cole started laughing.

"I wouldn't wish you on her either," Amoya said to Mike. She patted his arm. "I'm stuck with you."

I smiled as an idea formed in my head. I squeezed Cole's hand, catching his attention. I gestured so only he could see. I swung my finger back and forth from husband to wife, then I pointed to our joined hands. I raised my brows in question. Did he get it?

At first, his forehead crinkled, but then a smile gradually materialized. He nodded.

"I have an idea." Cole leaned forward slightly. "An idea that may save you some money. Some as in all of it."

Amoya took a piece of bread and started to butter it. "I'm listening."

"You need to spend twenty-four hours attached to one another." Cole grinned.

"She's already attached to my wallet, twenty-four seven," Mike said with a frown.

Amoya sat back and I could tell she was thinking

about what it meant to be connected to someone for a full day.

"You can't poop alone," I blurted. Luckily, nature hadn't called while I was with Cole. Neither one of us had had to face that hurdle.

"If you guys go another twenty-four hours, we'll do it too," she said.

"What?" Mike gasped. He took his wife's hand and said, "It's a long time."

"No way." I shook my head. "I want a shower."

"I'm sure Cole wouldn't mind scrubbing your back," Amoya teased.

I sucked in a breath and refused to look at Cole. I couldn't help envisioning his hands all over me. I knew it'd be heavenly, especially after the way he'd massaged my scalp.

I shifted in my seat, antsy to retreat from the room. I glanced from the wall art to the doorway.

Mr. Gorgeous entered in a linen suit—hair immaculate, smile sensual, and walk dominant. All conversations stalled. I swear, everyone in the room stared.

My hand ached from Cole's tight squeeze. *What the*? I glanced at him, and he grimaced.

Amoya gazed unabashedly at the swaggering man. Every man glared at him while their women ogled. A collective sigh arose from Karen's single-again table as he walked past.

I turned around, ignoring temptation. Cole scooted his chair closer, and I bumped knees with him. Warmth filled me.

Cole, a regular guy, with boy next door looks and a

rocking body, was obtainable. He was within my grasp. I liked him, and he respected me. Cole was almost Nick-good.

I stared into his cerulean eyes and our smiles grew. His thumb rubbed the back of my hand. My heart rate elevated and the world muted.

A hot weight landed on my shoulder, and I gasped. Mr. Gorgeous made a show of dominance. I automatically leaned towards Cole. I desperately glanced around. Amoya fanned herself. Her gaze was below Mr. Gorgeous' belt line. Oh my.

"Hello baby," Mr. Gorgeous said.

Looking at my shoulder, I found perfectly manicured nails on long fingers. I loved a man's well-groomed hand. I swallowed. I lifted Cole and my joined hands to the table.

Get a clue, jerkoff.

He lowered so his mouth was an inch from my ear. His sexy voice, oh my God, if he would have talked long enough I could have orgasmed. This wasn't natural.

He's an alien!

"You're mine," Mr. Gorgeous purred.

The words radiated pleasure. My body sang his praise, it wanted him, but my mind, it thought something else.

"Who do you think you are?" I rose, pushing his hand off. With my free hand, I poked him in the chest. "Get a clue buster. I'm here with someone." I immediately sat back down, scooting in my seat.

"You're mine," he repeated, then he walked away and sat alone but facing our table. He stared at me, and I became a nervous wreck. The longer he leered, the more I hoped the second wave of the bet would work out, so I wouldn't be alone. I feared I couldn't resist him on my own.

"If you guys make it twenty-four hours, then we forfeit the money?" I asked, trying to keep the desperation to a minimum. "What if we make it the second twenty-four hours?"

Our dinner arrived, and we started eating. The wine and food Cole had chosen were phenomenal.

I could get used to him doing this.

"We will buy you dinner if you make it another twenty-four hours with him," Mike offered.

I winced. What the hell did I do to deserve this? God, are you listening? I came here to be alone. What would I have been doing if that had come to pass? I'd order meals in my room and sit and watch people from the sidelines.

How would I handle Mr. Gorgeous? I wouldn't. I'd let him handle me.

I glanced at Cole. He glared at Mr. Gorgeous, but Mr. Gorgeous focused on me. I touched Cole's leg and rested our hands on his thigh. Finally, he looked at me. I winked at him, and he relaxed.

He appeared to dislike the other man. I didn't know his reasoning, whether he was unhappy because I didn't like being touched by the man or maybe he was a little bit jealous. That thought made the butterflies in my stomach take flight.

"Why does he think you're his?" Amoya asked. Her gaze flicked from me to Cole.

"I'm *not* his, but…" I had a ludicrous theory. I toyed with my wine glass and picked it up. Cole gave me a sidelong glance, and I swallowed my trepidation. "I think my father might have hired him."

It was possible Mr. Gorgeous had been following me since I'd escaped.

Both the Higginses gasped as their eyes widened. They glanced at each other before looking at me again.

I didn't blame them. It sounded preposterous—a parent hunting down an adult child using a sexy beast of a man.

Cole stared into his water glass, his features relaxed. But then again, I shouldn't expect him to take up arms. Amoya studied me and then Mr. Gorgeous.

"Why would you think that?" Mike asked.

I shifted in my seat, anger beginning to simmer in my gut. I didn't want to go into the details about my inheritance. Thanks to my bossy grandmother who cursed my pregnant mother, only the oldest Warsaw could take over the family business when they reached the age of thirty.

That's not the worst part! It has to be a married thirty-year-old Warsaw.

My evil twin sabotaged any chance of the business staying in the Warsaw family. My father had been trying hard to find me a suitable husband, one I'd be able to tolerate and work with. Someone he could trust with his precious baby, Warsaw Industries.

I tried to hedge around why my father was desperate to keep the business. I'd left weeks before my thirtieth birthday. I didn't see why I needed to stay and be forced to do something I didn't want to do or see the company I ran be turned over to the shareholders.

"Do you see him? Now look at me." I watched their eyes move and heads nod. "Why would the world's sexiest man want somebody like me?"

I put my hands out. It was a fair case, a logical one. I was short and not model material. My hair was average brown with a slight wave, and today it was styled by the salty wind. I wore no makeup, my clothes hadn't been changed, including my underwear, since I left the cruise ship.

Luckily, Cole had the foresight to commandeer a toothbrush, toothpaste, and deodorant or I wouldn't feel or smell fresh.

Cole frowned, and he scanned my face.

I bit my lip as he inspected me, probably agreeing. Heat crept across my cheeks. I studied my plate but suddenly wasn't hungry.

"Don't think like that, Vanessa," Cole said softly. His thumb skimmed the back of my hand, giving me chills.

"Vanessa?" Amoya looked at her husband. "Vanessa as in *Vanessa* Vanessa?"

I blinked. Mike patted her arm and Amoya's smile grew. "Oh, I see."

That makes one of us.

Mike frowned and pointed to Mr. Gorgeous. "That man wants you because you said no."

"That's ridiculous," I murmured. And stupid.

Amoya nodded. "He could be right. A man like that doesn't get told no very often, if at all. You are now a challenge for him. I dare say, he never sleeps alone. There are plenty of women—and men—who would be willing."

Glancing around the restaurant, I found the long table full of Karen's friends. The women either had their heads together whispering or openly gawked at Mr. Gorgeous.

I jumped when Cole nudged my arm. His brow crinkled with concern. "You don't buy that, do you?"

"That he wants me because I said no? Of course not." Although it was a plausible theory.

Cole shook his head. "No, not that. You're beautiful. Any man would be a fool not to want you."

My mouth flopped open and stayed that way long enough to become dry. I fumbled with the napkin on my lap and my face heated.

I wanted to thank him, but I didn't believe him. How could I? No man had loved me enough to distinguish me from my sister. I found myself shaking my head and fighting to hold back the tears.

I inhaled deeply, then again. "Thank you," I mumbled the polite response. I'd been mumbling a lot lately. "I need to go." I pushed my chair back, clutching my bag.

Cole nodded and dropped his fork. His plate was mostly empty.

"What about dessert?" Amoya asked.

"We'll get some later," Cole answered before I could think. I gave him a timid smile.

The heavy hand landed on my shoulder again. I gasped and threw a pleading look at my table mates. I closed my eyes, my lips trembling.

You're totally going to faint. And that god among men will give you mouth to mouth. You might orgasm thinking about it.

I groaned, but he took it as a moan. He leaned close to my ear and said, "My love, where are you going?"

I abruptly stood, nearly toppling the chair, and raised Cole and my joined hands, which I pointed to. "Wherever he wants to go." I promptly turned and stomped out of the room without looking back.

Cole followed me. He didn't have a choice in the matter, did he? He'd kept his hand on my back, and I welcomed the small token of encouragement.

I stopped outside the door, feeling like a fool. Twisting to face him, I lamented, "I'm sorry. You didn't even get to finish your dinner."

He brought me into a hug and kissed my forehead. "No worries. I was finished."

When I turned my head, the entire dining room stared at Cole and me. "They're watching us."

"They're jealous," he chuckled.

Of me or of Cole? He threaded my fingers, and we walked to the outside bar again. Breathing the balmy air, I relaxed while Cole retrieved his phone from the bartender.

"Vanessa, do you need to charge your phone?" With a shrug, he took it from me, and the bartender plugged it in somewhere below the counter.

"Come on," Cole said, tugging me back to the main building. I groaned, but he tickled me, and I walked faster.

CHAPTER EIGHT

In the lobby, I studied a painting while Cole spoke in a foreign language to the woman behind the desk. In the uniform of a white shirt with the resort logo and a navy skirt, her tanned skin highlighted the bright pink lipstick she wore. She listened intently, then nodded. When she talked, it sounded as if she asked questions. She glanced curiously toward me more than once. I smiled but continued as an amateur art critic.

The woman disappeared into an office, then reappeared and handed him a small key. He held it up to show me.

I tilted my head. "Bank vault?"

Cole laughed, then he led me down a dark hallway. He used the key to open an employee's' only door.

How many times has the blond hottie been here? Maybe he knows the Tanners.

"What are we doing here?" I asked, nodding to one of the staff as I passed.

"Private bathroom."

I pulled him to a stop. "Why?"

He leaned close and spoke softly, "I didn't think you'd

want to check in and go to your room in case that guy followed us. If he knew where you're staying, he might harass you for the rest of your trip."

Dumbfounded at his kindness, I stammered. "Thanks, Cole."

"You're welcome." He led me to an office that reminded me of a typical hotel room. One primary area with a bathroom right inside the entry.

"Now, how are we going to do this?" I stepped onto the white tile. The bathroom was clean and had toilet paper.

"You can go first. I'll sit out here," he said.

The toilet was next to the door. I sat on it clothed, so he could see the impossibility of him being outside the room.

"This will work. Watch." He slid his hand to my knee, continuing to my foot, then toes. He switched his hand for his foot.

"You could have just tapped your foot on mine," I teased.

Blushing, Cole ignored my observation. "I'm going to lie out here and look at my phone with earbuds on. You'll have complete privacy. Do what you need to do and don't worry, I've locked the outer door." He disappeared from view.

I waited a moment, then closed the bathroom door as much as I could. If someone did enter, I'd be hidden. I did my business while he talked on the phone in the foreign language again. French maybe. When I was through, I tapped his foot. He concluded the conversation. I needed him to move closer so I could reach the sink.

"My turn." Cole smiled and rubbed the back of his head. "Uh, I might be awhile."

His cheeks pinked up, and he handed me his phone.

"Why don't you turn on some music and look for that guy you lost track of. I'm connected to the resort's wi-fi."

I nodded and mimicked his earlier movements until I was lying on my belly. "Cole, keep your foot on mine. That way I won't move it."

"Will do." I heard his zipper and hastily put the earbuds in. I didn't want to hear any bodily functions. Finding his music app, I punched in Boston. I played the station, then wondered if I should try to locate Nick.

Nick Tanner. Nicholas Arlington Tanner. Should I roll the Google dice? I typed his name, then deleted it.

Oh, for crying out loud. Just put his name in. He'll never know you're stalking him.

I sighed and entered his family's business. The website came up, and I clicked on it. I'd planned my escape by booking from the registration page and had already scavenged the pages for pictures of the family, finding only one when Nick and his brothers were young.

Entering his name again, this time I tapped enter. There are a ton of Nick A. Tanners on Facebook and other social media. It didn't deter me from trying various forms of his name. All too soon, I felt pressure on my foot as Cole indicated he had finished.

After he washed his hands, we returned the key and went back out to the bar.

Cole patted the stool next to him, and I sat. Our hands hung between us.

I set his phone on the bar top with the screen open. He glanced down at the device.

"Any luck?" He touched the screen, scrolling the list.

"Not really. There are too many people with his name."

"Maybe I could find him." He leaned over, but I tapped the screen and backed out of the Facebook search.

Before I'd escaped my old life, I'd visited my childhood home and removed Nick's senior picture from hiding. I'd brought it with me, pulling it out to stare into his deep blue eyes and remember the one man who could tell me from my twin. I wish I'd kept the photo in my bag so I could show Cole.

On the cruise ship, the dreams of Nick became intense and realistic. I saw Nick in Cole and knew I had to hide the photo away in my luggage. I decided to let go of the past.

Too bad it hasn't let go of you.

I swiped the screen until I found my profile. I had the account set so only my friends and family could view it. Well, everyone except Roni. My twin was blocked. As I clicked on my profile picture, my full account opened for a stranger to see.

My privacy settings had been switched to public, another attempt from my sister to spy.

That scheming Biotch.

But, at least, I could access photo albums belonging to my past. I scrolled through until I found my senior prom picture. Nick and I held hands in formal wear.

"Here he is." I pointed to the handsome nineteen-year-old love of my life. "He's inches shorter than you are. He has brown hair and these cute cheeks you want to pinch."

"Fat, huh?" Cole chuckled, leaning over the picture, squinting his eyes. "Glasses too."

"He didn't wear the glasses all the time. I thought they were sexy. And he's not fat at all. He just had those cheeks… I guess it might have been baby fat, but he's probably leaned out. He wasn't a skinny twig, but he wasn't ripped either." I stared down at Nick, probably wearing the dreamy smile Nick affectionately called my Mrs. Tanner smile. "Do you know what Nick was?"

Cole's expression softened as he scanned my face. "What?"

"He was perfect."

Cole chuckled.

"Don't laugh. I'm serious. He was perfect for me. We fit. I only wish…" I couldn't finish the thought because I felt a knife twist in my heart.

"What can I get for you?" The older gentleman with clear blue eyes asked. Again, I was struck with a sense I'd met him before. "Miss?"

It dawned on me that ever since becoming attached to Cole, he'd ordered for me. A practice that had annoyed me at first, but had become a game of sorts. I turned to Cole. "I don't know. What am I having?"

Cole smiled and leaned against the bar. "She'll have a Greta Garbo."

After our drinks were set before us, I sipped while watching the bartender work as Cole trolled my pictures of Nick.

How did the bartender know Cole wanted a Long Island iced tea? Cole hadn't said a thing.

"You really liked him, didn't you?" Cole asked.

"That whole 'perfect for me' thing gave me away, didn't it?" I sighed and decided to inspect the trail to the beach. Laughing, waves, and music all came from that direction.

"What did you like best about him?" he asked without looking up from the phone.

"Besides the fact that he could tell me and my sister apart? I don't know, his butt? What do you want to know? It was a long time ago, and he was my first love. I'm sure he's changed as much as I have."

"Maybe. Maybe not." Cole focused on the screen, and I studied his profile. So strange how closely he resembled Nick.

I covered the phone with my hand, and he gazed at me with a confused look. "Cole, close your eyes and listen." I waited until he complied. "Hear the wind rustling the palm branches. The waves on the shore. The laughter of friends and lovers. The upbeat music. The splash of the pool. All are sounds of vacation. Open your eyes."

He grinned and his shoulders relaxed.

"Cole, have you noticed the deep blue sky and shades of blue in the water? I think God's favorite color must be blue."

He chuckled and squeezed my hand. Together we enjoyed our drinks while relaxing and watching the surrounding beauty.

After a while, I said, "It's been about ten years since I've communicated with Nick. He's had just as much time to find me as I have had to find him, and neither of us has done it."

"Were you afraid he'd lose the ability to distinguish

you from your twin and your sister would sink her claws into him?"

I bit my lip. He'd hit my biggest fear when it came to Nick. I nodded. He turned me until we were knee to knee, taking both my hands in his. "In the future, you need to have a code word or phrase your boyfriend knows that your sister wouldn't guess."

"Like what? She's my twin. She gets me pretty well."

"Let's think of something." Cole's focus shifted as he stared into space, his brow crinkled in thought. Suddenly, the pensive look was replaced by a grimace. His gaze returned to me. "The sexiest man in the world is coming."

I raised my brows. He'd come up with a sexual phrase, and I covered my mouth as a giggle fit hit.

He let go of one hand and ran his fingers through his hair. With a sheepish smile, he repeated, "The sexiest man in the world is coming." His gaze tracked something behind me.

The weight of a hot hand landed on my shoulder. Cole frowned, and the laughter stalled in my throat.

"That sucks balls," I whimpered.

"Among other things," Cole muttered. His eyes narrowed on the audacious man standing at my back.

I started to giggle again, and Cole's expression softened as he studied me.

"You're probably right," I squeaked out, then covered my mouth to hold in a snort.

The bartender returned. He surveyed the situation. "Can I help you, sir?"

Mr. Gorgeous sat on the other side of me. His heavy hand lifted as he gestured to my nearly empty cocktail. "I'll have whatever she's having, and I'd like to buy her another."

I fingered my glass. Lifting it to my lips, I downed the remnants. I wanted to question Mr. Gorgeous but didn't want to face him for fear I'd fall under his spell. It wouldn't look good if I was seduced by one man while holding hands with another.

In my peripheral vision, I glanced at the newcomer. However, he noticed my inspection and moved in my direction—presumably so I might grasp a better view. I inwardly gasped and trained my gaze on the bartender.

Mr. Gorgeous' hand touched my knee and slowly slid up my thigh. I squeezed my eyes shut and wanted to click my heels three times. "How about you and I go—"

"No," Cole didn't let him finish. His one word set my heart to fluttering, and my body was suddenly attuned to his.

My gaze volleyed between the two. From Mr. Gorgeous' flawlessly tanned and toned, unblemished skin to Cole's lightly freckled nose. From perfectly styled, shiny, raven hair to Cole's finger-combed, blond, just-as-sexy hair. Mr. Gorgeous' clothes were starched and clean while my companion's were rumpled and wrinkled and full of memories of our enforced togetherness.

"I think it's for the lady to decide." Thankfully Mr. Gorgeous' hand stopped mid-thigh.

Even his voice makes you need to change your panties.

"Not going to happen. Especially when my father is footing the bill," I stated firmly, adopting my Ice Queen tone.

Mr. Gorgeous stiffened only a nano-second then

pressed into my personal space. "Who's your daddy?" His sensual baritone and warm breath tickled my ear, sending a wave of pleasure to my sweet spot.

My heart rate skyrocketed as his fingers slowly moved toward my crotch.

I turned a pleading look to Cole. "Cole, please," I uttered in desperation.

Cole cupped my cheek in his free hand. I pressed against it and sucked in a ragged breath. He rotated my swiveling seat until I once again faced him, then he pulled me to a standing position. With his palms gently holding my face, I was sheltered between his legs, facing him. Those mesmerizing blue eyes held me transfixed. His voice became a mere whisper as he said, "Trust me."

I gave a hasty nod and rested my hands on his knees. His pants might not be as wrinkle free as Mr. Gorgeous', but they were soft. My fingers curled as he leaned down and kissed my lips.

The gentle kiss did nothing to calm my racing heart. Cole hovered before me with a little smirk, which I matched. My lips tingled and my body warmed. I wanted to taste him, to explore. I glanced down at his lips, then back to his eyes, lifting my brows in question. He wiggled his eyebrows twice before descending again.

This time, the tentative gentleness turned into firm decisiveness. He tilted my head, then his hands plunged into my hair. The sensations that rippled through my body started where his fingers caressed my scalp. I stepped up onto the rung of the barstool and clutched his shirt to pull us closer, needing to feel his body against mine. His tongue touched my lips, and I opened for him. He swept in and our tongues dueled.

He tasted of alcohol, sunshine, and passion. I wanted more. His hands slid down my back, molding to my curves.

I became putty; my body was hot, yet I shivered.

Cole pulled away, and I reluctantly relented. Our chests heaved, but neither of us moved, not even to blink. Oh boy, I was in trouble. I'd climbed onto his lap and straddled him. I contemplated whether to devour his lips again or burrow my face against his chest.

Fate dictated neither as the bartender cleared his throat. He pushed my new drink toward me. Cole had a fresh glass as well. The older gentleman winked at Cole.

Oh God, he'd watched the whole thing.

I should climb off Cole's lap. I'd just participated in the most obnoxious public display of affection and, though I wanted to hide under a rock, I couldn't move. I felt safe in Cole's arms. Protected and cherished.

I couldn't check and see if Mr. Gorgeous was still back there. It was too dangerous. What would happen if he kissed me, too?

Gross. How can you think about that fake thing after kissing an organic man?

I reached for my drink and chugged half. The cold liquid burned, and I laid my head on Cole's shoulder and closed my eyes. He held me like a parent holds a sleepy kid.

I heard muted clapping and my eyes fluttered open to see Mike and Amoya standing only a few feet away.

"That was quite the show," Mike teased.

"Pretty hot show," Amoya said. Her gaze flitted behind

me. I knew Mr. Gorgeous remained. I wondered if we'd pissed him off or if he was adjusting his… strategy.

"We're going to go change. Then we're going to go down to the beach and dance." Mike smiled and glanced at his wife.

"You want to join us dancing, or are you worn out?" Amoya giggled.

"Just their tongues are worn out, Amoya, their feet are fine." Mike's church bell laugh rang, and Cole chuckled.

"My tongue is fine," I murmured, earning another chuckle.

"Maybe I could have a go then," Mr. Gorgeous said, butting into the conversation.

Cole's grip tightened, and I sighed. I'd been sighing a lot lately. I could stay all night like this. Not dodging that handsome, clueless jerk, but wrapped in Cole's arms.

I sucked in a quick breath at the realization that I would be with Cole for another full night. Under the stars, too, which probably meant alone. That prospect thrilled and terrified me.

"We can join you at the dance," Cole poked my side playfully. "Isn't that right, Nessa?"

I pushed back and examined him, astonished he'd used Nick's pet name for me again. He smiled at his friends, his blue eyes crinkled in mirth. So much about him reminded me of my first love.

"Sure," I shrugged. "I'm not a huge dancer, though."

I slipped off Cole's lap but didn't return to my chair. Instead, I circled to Cole's back. I kept one arm wrapped around his belly but reached for my drink with the other. I finished it. Liquid courage. Geesh.

CHAPTER NINE

A GAGGLE OF TIPSY WOMEN lurched past Cole and me on the way to the beach where the tiki torches burned. They laughed, holding drinks. A few other guests sauntered toward the music.

"We will wait for you here…unless we aren't here, then we'll be down there already," Cole said, waving them off.

Mike and Amoya walked away, hand in hand. Mike tripped and almost broke the connection.

"They're going to lose. You know that? There's no way he'll be able to remember," I giggled.

"You're right." Cole chuckled and turned to face the bar once more. "We need to talk."

I lifted my gaze to his, and my heart sank.

He's going to set boundaries, which is a good thing, right?

Cole picked up his drink, indicating he'd like to walk. I accompanied him, holding his hand loosely.

The kiss must have bothered him, but I'd enjoyed it. I wouldn't mind repeating the act. A fact that surprised me.

"This guy, the world's sexiest—"

"That sucks balls?"

"Yes, among other things."

We laughed again. I relaxed and blew out a long breath.

"Why do you think your father sent him?" He stopped walking and faced me. His features in the dark seemed almost grim.

"It's complicated, but the short of it is that my father is desperate."

Cole's eyebrows rose, and I sucked in a deep breath. Owing him an explanation, I started forward again.

"It began with my grandmother. My mother learned she was pregnant at the same time my grandmother learned she was dying. Before she passed, Grandma Warsaw stipulated that the oldest Warsaw child, and that ended up being me, would inherit the family business when he or she reached the age of thirty. Grandma didn't know Mom carried twins. Part of the stipulation is that I marry before the age of thirty in order to inherit the business. My father has been parading eligible bachelors in front of me for years. If I find a decent fellow, my sister pretends to be me and, usually, sleeps with him.

"So here I am, the great disappointment. The family business will be lost, reverting to the shareholders, and I'll be disinherited. There you have it."

"And Mr. Suck-it?" Cole thumbed over his shoulder toward the bar.

"I left. I quit my job and escaped. Dad wants me to get married, but I don't want to marry someone just to get married. I want to marry for love. I think he sent the perfect man after me, so I'd be tempted and fall for him."

We'd circled the pool and could see the bar. Mr. Gorgeous watched us like a wolf stalking prey.

"He's perfect. And I don't mean for me. I mean, he's physically the perfect man. Too perfect. He's flawless. Hair, teeth, cheeks, ears, his lips, eyebrows, neck, fingers—everything has been tinkered with. That's not normal. He might have had a great foundation, but his body has been manipulated. There's no way he was born like that."

I turned back to Cole, slyly motioning to the people stealing covert glances at Mr. Gorgeous. "Everyone is attracted to him. He's a work of art and built to seduce."

We started walking again.

"Are you attracted to him?" he asked, shoving his free hand in his pocket.

"Oh, hell yeah, and it scares me. I don't want to desire a guy like that. I want someone real. Someone organic."

"Someone like Nick?"

We followed the trail toward the beach and continued out onto the sand but headed away from the party. I sighed, deciding it was time to bury the past.

"No, someone like you." I blurted. Thank God for the darkening sky. I kept walking straight ahead.

"Me?" Cole put his hand on my arm and stopped me. We faced each other.

"Yes." I tilted my head. "You're real. You haven't botoxed your face or plumped your lips. Do you have any silicone inside of you?"

"Well, no."

"The only thing that you might have changed is your teeth. Braces, or maybe you wear contacts."

"I've had lasik surgery on my eyes, and you're right,

I've had braces," he admitted.

I nodded. "That's what I mean by real, organic."

He smiled, and we turned back toward the dancers. "So, I'm like ninety-nine-point five percent organic."

I couldn't help but laugh.

Mike and Amoya hovered on the edge of the crowd. Amoya waved when she found us. She'd put on a short, gauzy, pink skirt with a coordinating floral shirt. Cute outfit.

Which reminded me. I needed to change my underwear. All of my clothes really. "Where are we staying tonight?"

Cole's brow pinched. "I thought we were sleeping under the stars again."

"Can I get some clean clothes first? I want fresh undies."

"I like those lacy ones. I'll be sorry to see them go," Cole grinned down at me.

I knew I'd turned red by the sudden heat. Of course, he'd seen them yesterday when we'd gone wading. I elbowed him in the ribs. "If they're not changed soon, you'll see them go on their own two legs."

"Don't worry. I've taken care of it."

How could he have rectified my underwear issue without lifting a hand or me checking in? "What—?"

With a grin, Cole tugged me forward to greet his friends.

While he talked to Mike and chided him on his inability to win the twenty-four hour bet, I watched others sway to the beat. I searched their faces.

Karen's posse was the most fun to watch. One woman staggered around, pinching her friends' butts, causing giggling.

"We are going to make it the twenty-four hours. Mon, why are you doubting me?" Mike asked, placing a hand over his heart.

Cole raised his nose haughtily and pointed to Amoya. "*If* you win, it will be because of her diligence."

I lifted my hand and nodded. "Cole's right."

Amoya smiled, but she said nothing. Her hips swayed, making her skirt flare.

Mike frowned and scratched his chin with his attached hand, jerking her a step nearer. Her angelic appearance disappeared, replaced by something evil.

"Crap, I'm sorry, Love." With his free hand, Mike stroked her cheek, and the irritated sneer faded as she closed her eyes and relaxed at his touch. It was an intimate gesture, and I had to look away. My heart whispered that they might be able to pull it off after all.

"Good thing we didn't make it more competitive," Cole murmured in my ear.

I rolled my eyes. "The night is still young. Let's not give them any more ideas."

"Are you sick of me, Nessa?"

Nick's pet name for me again. It warmed my soul and stole my words. Cole pursed his lips, and when I didn't answer immediately, his brow crinkled.

"Nessa?"

"No."

My clipped answer must not have satisfied Cole. He caressed me like Mike had Amoya. Not fair.

Shut up and go with it. Tell the man the truth.

I took a deep breath and relaxed against him. "Actually," I paused and locked eyes with him, "It's been better than I thought it would be. I've enjoyed our time."

"Better than being alone?" The familiar smirk found a home on his lips. Lips I had kissed. Lips I wouldn't mind kissing again.

I glanced over at the other side of the crowd where the path from the resort met the beach. Mr. Gorgeous stood scanning the throng.

Good Lord. If I had been left alone, he would have hounded me—or maybe pounded me—mercilessly. I didn't know if I should kiss Cole or cry. No, if my father had sent the sinfully beautiful man after me, then I wanted no part of him. But if my father did not play a part, then… how would I know?

Girl, he's too pretty to belong to any one person. Look, three of Karen's posse are jiggling their cleavage at him. Stick with organic men.

"Yes, better than being alone. I guess I needed companionship. I like you, Cole. This odd situation could have been horrid, but you've been fun."

He nodded but glared at Mr. Gorgeous. I nudged him, making him glance at me. When I had his attention, I squeezed his hand and smiled. "Thank you for helping me with you-know-who."

"Lord Voldemort?"

I laughed until my side cramped and tears rolled. I might have snorted.

You totally did.

"Yeah, him. I don't know what I would have done if I would have been alone. Probably hated myself in the morning." I shivered and grimaced like I'd tasted something bad.

"You would have given in?"

"I hope not, but you've seen how persistently charming he is. He practically propositioned me, and I was hanging on another man. What would he have done if I had no one to help me?" I swallowed the bile that rose.

"You wouldn't have left your sandbar," Cole said.

"Ha. Maybe so. You're right. I would have wanted to be left alone." I gave a stiff nod, trying to convince myself. "I should hire you as my bodyguard for the rest of my stay."

"I don't think bodyguard will do it. I'd just be viewed as only a speed bump."

"Hell, Cole, you could be my husband, and I think he'd view you as a speed bump."

"Husband, huh?" He grinned and pulled me to him, taking my other hand in his. He started swaying to the music, and I followed his steps. "We could pretend. Maybe he'd back off."

"Oh, do you think so?"

He wouldn't retreat if he'd been hired by my father, but it could be worth a shot. "I wonder what my father would do if Mr. Gorgeous reported I'd been married. I'd love to see Dad's reaction." I giggled, and he spun me around.

He pulled me closer, and I snuggled against his chest, and we swayed to our own rhythm. I closed my eyes, trusting Cole to keep me safe, and I relaxed, moving with him.

The music, with its steel drums, was tropical and hypnotic. The woman singing crooned a love song in another language. Cole occasionally translated: "nothing will separate our love," "love you forever," and "together we are one."

The words made me wish I had a lover—no, a love. Someone special to care for at all times, someone my sister would never touch.

I sighed.

"Nessa, are you okay?"

"Just wishing I could find my person."

"Maybe you have," he whispered in my ear. His warm breath made me shiver.

"Maybe," I replied, not wanting to think about it, but enjoying being held and protected.

I don't know how many songs we danced to, but it was a long time. I'd enjoyed every minute. Finally, I popped my eyes open when Cole spoke. He ordered us drinks.

After the drinks came, we sat with Mike and his wife and chatted. It seemed like a normal double date—a strange-homey feeling. Cole kept his arm around me most of the time, but our knees brushed together.

I was growing accustomed to his touch. His touch. I thought I wouldn't be able to last twenty-four hours with the man, and now look at me.

Now you want to touch other parts of him, and you want him to touch other parts of you.

I smiled as I listened to the other vacationers. Joyful

murmurs met my ears.

A shout brought attention to the water. A yacht with white Christmas lights floated closer. Someone in Karen's party yelled for them to join us; and the party ship headed in our direction. The yacht moored on the dock and unloaded.

More male fodder for the drunk ladies since Cole was claimed and Mr. Gorgeous was skulking by the bar.

"It looks like the Las Palmas is sharing the live music tonight," Amoya said. Some of the guests headed straight to the band and started dancing while others visited the bar.

"Las Palmas is the closest neighboring resort," Mike informed me.

"Resort, ha. More like a rundown hotel way past its prime," Amoya said with her hands on her hips.

Cole chuckled. The breeze blew a strand of my hair across my face, and he tucked it behind my ear.

"Now Amoya, just because you think the Menari Angin," Cole looked at me and whispered, "That's the locals' name for our resort," before continuing to tease Amoya. "Just because you think the Menari Angin is better, doesn't mean Las Palmas is bad. Their hospitality is renowned. My parents stayed there while—"

Mike started coughing, gave a strange smile, then took a drink of his drink. "I'm sorry, go on."

"I was saying my parents stayed there before this one was built. Just because it is older doesn't mean it's not a great place to stay. It's established. There are people who've returned for years. It's a regular destination," Cole said with a shrug.

"Yeah," Mike said, nudging his wife. "A destination

for generations. My parents, cousins, and my sister all have been there."

Mike downed the last of his drink. He stood and offered his free hand to his wife. She grinned up at him and took it. They disappeared into the throng of dancers. The island music became edgier, faster. I tapped my foot to the rhythm.

"Would you like to dance?" Cole asked.

I squeezed his hand. "Why, thank you, kind sir, I'd love to dance with you."

We walked between the bodies and found a space. Taking my other hand, he pulled me close. An odd sensation of being alone with Cole swept over me. How could we be alone in a sea of people?

He spun me in circles, and I laughed. We weaved through the crowd of dancers, moving to Cole's version of a song. At one point, he twirled me out, then yanked me back. I giggled, and he whirled me once more.

I nearly knocked a drink out of Karen's hand. After I'd circled around again, she was watching Cole and me, wide eyed and talking with two of her posse.

I felt free. My steps were light, as if a weight had been lifted. In Cole's arms, I could dance all night long.

CHAPTER TEN

COLE AND I STROLLED ALONG a path lined with pink flowers leading to the front of the resort. A small car had pulled up under the portico and a man stood with the door open. Amoya and Mike waited by the car. The valet dropped the keys into Mike's hand.

"There you are. You took forever. Mike thought you might have decided to make love on the beach after all." Amoya winked at me.

I chuckled nervously. "Too many people for that kind of thing," I mumbled, feeling my face heat.

"We have plans but lost track of time," Cole said, rubbing my arm.

What plans? "Stargazing?" I asked him.

His eyes narrowed slightly, and he leaned so he was a breath from my ear. "Among other things."

I blinked and inhaled deeply. Oh man, I was in trouble.

Yay!

"Come on, slowpokes, into the car." Mike pointed at himself. "I'm driving."

Cole and I walked beside the car, and I climbed into the back seat. I started to scoot over so Cole could follow me inside when Mike's voice rose. "I am not crawling through over the console. You can do that. You're smaller."

"I have a skirt on." Amoya's hand on her waist and her pursed lips told me we were in for a long argument. I nudged Cole and pointed for him to get out.

"Amoya, sit back next to me." I patted the seat. "Cole can sit in the front."

She frowned and looked into the backseat. "How's that any better?"

"Watch." I glanced at Cole and smiled. "Let's show them how to do it."

Cole pulled open the door and reached his free hand inside and, from the back door, I took it with my other free hand. Voilà. The old switcheroo. Cole sat, and we got comfortable.

"Hm," Amoya said, "that was pretty easy. You guys are getting good at this."

Once Mike and Amoya settled in, he started the car. Amoya touched Mike's neck. This way, Mike had two hands on the wheel.

We drove past a few buildings. Some were houses but most looked to be condos. There was one bar, the windows filled with neon signs, and a nice-looking restaurant.

The road entered a heavily wooded area with twists and turns. We emerged from the rainforest on a hill that overlooked part of the coastline. The road dropped back to sea level and smoothed out. Mike pulled over in a secluded spot ringed by tall trees.

"What are we doing?" I asked.

"We're here," Cole countered.

"Here where?"

"The place for stargazing." He opened the door, and we switched hands again, then he helped me out. "There's a trail here. We are going to follow it."

I squinted my eyes and saw a dark crevice. "We're going in there?" I swallowed. I hoped there wasn't a man-eating spider in the cave, like *Lord of the Rings*.

"It leads to the beach. There aren't resorts or homes near here, so no light pollution. It makes it ideal to stargaze here."

Mike handed Cole a bag from the trunk, and we said our goodbyes to the Higginses. They waited until we disappeared into the hedge before I heard Amoya say she wasn't crawling over the console. Cole and I laughed.

I stayed close to him, only tripping once over a root. After what seemed like hours, the hard ground became soft sand. The earthy smell of the forest turned salty. A dim light lit the trail.

When we broke through to the beach, several tiki torches illuminated a pavilion. Or platform. I didn't know what to call the structure. As we neared, I could make out a wooden deck floor but only one wall. The three other sides had white curtains, I suppose to keep the bugs at bay, but they were drawn aside. The back wall appeared solid and had a door. Hopefully, to a bathroom.

Cole extinguished the torches as we went until there was only one remaining. He untied the mesh curtains and tugged them into place.

A hammock hung on the right side. It was large enough for two people.

"Are we sleeping on that thing?" I asked, hearing the trepidation in my voice.

"Yes, ma'am." He pulled me against him into a hug. "Look up."

"Oh," I moaned. The sloped ceiling was glass. "I'm glad we aren't on the sand tonight."

"Me too. It gets everywhere."

I sat on the hammock and played with his hair as he searched in the bag. The sound of the waves and wind relaxed me. The starlight danced on the water. This place was exotic at night, and I wondered what the daylight would bring.

Suddenly, I had an urge to swim. Earlier, I'd played but not swam.

This idea posed a new set of problems. The number one being we hadn't any bathing suits. We could take a dip in our clothes and sleep wet. Or naked. Or we could skinny dip and sleep in dry clothes.

"Would you like to go swimming?" I asked him. His gaze lifted and held mine, then his head tilted. "Is it safe to wade out there?" I hadn't considered the possibility of deep or rocky water.

"It's a great place to swim but," his voice trailed off. "We don't have swimsuits."

"I know. We could swim in our clothes, like yesterday," I suggested.

"Then they'd be wet. That would be uncomfortable," he said.

"So, we'd sleep naked." Even in the dark, I saw his eyebrows raise. I continued, "Or we could skinny dip, then our clothes will be dry."

I pulled my shirt away from my body and smelled it.

I needed fresh clothes. If I wore them another day, I might have to burn them.

"Let's walk over to the water and check the temperature." He stood and tugged me up from the hammock. I kicked off my sandals before leaving the structure.

The sand was soft and warm but lumpy. Nearer the water, it flattened. He touched his foot to the retreating wave. A blast of hot wind rippled our hair. "This will feel good."

I nodded, and we went back to the structure. He blew out the torch, and we took turns taking off our clothes. I touched his back while he pulled off his shirt and let his pants fall. He waited on the hammock holding the edge of my hair while I removed my capris and panties.

"Are you sure about this?" he asked before we left the building.

"I really want to go swimming."

He chuckled. "Swimming naked with me?"

"Come on," I said, pushing him. He stopped at the edge of the structure in front of me. I could see the shape of his hind quarters outlined perfectly. I trailed my fingers down his back, stopping at the curve of his cheek. "Get moving, or I'll pinch your bottom." I gave him a small push, and he stepped into the sand. I wished it was daylight, as I watched his body move.

When he reached the water's edge, he stopped again.

"No, keep going. I want to swim." I pulled him. This time I led, knowing full well he could see my backside. We waded in deeper and deeper until the water was past our waists. I sunk in the water to my chin. Cole stood firmly, still holding my hand. His head tilted up.

I looked up too and the Milky Way appeared.

"It's beautiful," I said with awe. The indigo sky was a perfect backdrop for the twinkling lights of the stars. They were subtly tinted orange, pink and purple. The only thing that would make this place better is if we were lovers.

I could see falling in love with Cole.

Gasp! The L word.

I can't afford to fall in love. Not with Cole, not with anyone. Roni would wreck it. First, she needed someone to snag her heart and reel it in. I couldn't go there now.

I pushed Roni from my thoughts. It was too beautiful a night to let my twin get to me.

"Thank you for sharing this place with me," I told Cole as I maneuvered in the water to face him. In the starlight, I could see the smooth skin of his abdomen divided by a thin line of hair. A large wave rolled in and I floated with it, but Cole stood bulwark. The water had hit him neck high and his chest glistened.

Light reflected off his teeth when he smiled. "Thank you for being a willing participant. I've never stayed here before, just saw it from the shore."

Another huge wave came in and this time Cole moved with it, otherwise it would have been over his head. We let the current float us toward the shore. The water pushed me into his side. He reached out. I giggled, tickled by the light touch. His fingers found my other arm underwater and soon both our hands were joined.

We gazed into each other's eyes, the stars forgotten. He pulled me closer. "I'm glad you agreed to join me. I don't think it would be as much fun alone."

Alone. I had planned this escape seeking solitude. Now I couldn't fathom his absence. I didn't want to be alone any longer.

"How are you going to top this tomorrow night?" I teased. Good Lord. Tomorrow I'd be free of him and my heart ached thinking about it.

A wicked grin flashed, and he moved so his cheek touched my cheek. His breath fanned my ear. "I can think of something."

Aw, yeah, baby!

"Good." I let go of his left hand and touched his chest, finding the hair I'd seen earlier. He made a humming sound when I skimmed his skin. It made me long to run my fingers all the way down his happy trail, but I stopped at his belly button.

Another wave pushed us closer toward the shore and my knees scraped, and we hovered there—waves pushing us in, undertow pulling us out.

"What do you do for a living, Cole?" I asked, realizing I didn't know much other than he had a married friend and that he'd been to the island before. "What brings you to Dancing Winds resort?"

Cole held my hand against his chest, caressing the back of it. I closed my eyes, enjoying his company, listening to the water and relaxing. I couldn't care if he answered or what he answered at this point.

"I'm in management. The company I work for sends me to oversee their directives are interpreted and implemented correctly. I do more traveling than I'd like. When I first started, I worked in the European branch, but now, I go wherever I'm needed."

The water grew shallow. We laid on our bellies floating and facing each other. I anchored the elbow of my free hand into the sand.

"I came here to reconnect with an old friend." He drew in a deep breath. I felt bad for him. I was taking time away from that friend. "What about you?" Cole asked.

"I came here to be alone," I said with a wry grin.

He laughed. "What do you do for a living?"

"Oh." I thought about Warsaw Industries. The image of my personal assistant, Darlene, popped into my head. "I just retired."

"You quit and ran away." His tone was questioning rather than accusing.

"True, but it was time for a change." I held up our joined hands. "This wasn't exactly the change I was looking for. To answer your question, I ran my family's manufacturing company. We have factories and distribution facilities across the globe."

"You managed the whole shebang?" He whistled.

"Yes. I enjoyed the challenge. We employ people worldwide. They're inventive and clever. I loved seeing their ideas come to fruition." I sighed. I really would miss my company.

"It's a shame that you decided your only option was to quit."

I didn't like the way that sounded. "It wasn't my only option. I could have married one of those men my father paraded in front of me at any time."

"Did you like any of them?" he asked, his voice sounded far away.

I shook my head. "Occasionally there would be one

that I liked enough for a few dates. We could relate when it came to business holdings and dividends, but most were more interested in getting to know my father or taking my job. Besides Roger, there were none that I cared for, and I didn't love him."

"So, you had only a few options. Get married to someone you don't love that your father picked or quit. What about finding someone on your own?" He rolled over on his back, his head now in the damp sand.

I flipped onto my back, too. My head next to his, my feet pointed away from him. I was completely naked and yet content and comfortable. "I tried that too. Remember my sister?"

"You've got time."

"About a month." Oh, why were we rehashing my miserable life? I needed to end the conversation. "Look, I'm not going to find a single man, fall in love, and get married in that time period."

"Sometimes love works fast," he said in that faraway voice, as if he spoke from experience.

I wanted to change the subject but wasn't sure I'd like the new topic. "Who was she?"

He didn't answer right away, and I turned my head. He was relaxed, with his eyes closed and a small smile on his lips. Finally, he drew in a deep breath. "She was my first love."

If he hadn't said another word, I would have understood. Nick had been my first love, too.

"It was love at first sight, really. I saw her before she saw me. She was sweet and cute. Her bright green eyes observed everything. She watched and waited before acting. I guess you could say she was shy."

"What happened?"

"We were young." He took a couple of breaths. "Circumstances, time, differing college paths. We grew apart."

"I understand. It's similar to what happened to Nick and me." Several beats of my heart later, I asked, "How did you know it was love?"

"When I looked into her eyes, I saw my soul reflected there. She accepted me completely. I knew we were soulmates."

Wow. That was pretty deep for kids, but Nick and I had respected each other, too. Actually, Cole's words sounded like something Nick would say. "I'm sorry it didn't work out."

"Me too."

"Maybe you should try to find her."

"I already have." He turned his head and glanced at me, searching my face. "Last time I tried to find her online, I saw an engagement announcement."

"I'm sorry." It had to be upsetting. It's the exact reason why I hadn't tried hard to find Nick. I knew somebody wonderful had to have snatched him up.

A larger wave hit me, moving all my hair in Cole's direction. "Watch out for the seaweed monster."

"All I see is mermaid hair," he teased. "What a lucky guy I am to get tangled in it."

"I am not going to start singing, so don't even think about it."

He chuckled and touched my head, following my hair down its length. "I think it's the crab that sings *Kiss the Girl*."

I gasped and sat up, bringing my knees to my chest.

Did Cole want to kiss me again? My heart pounded, trying to escape.

My hair dripped down my back. With my free hand, I squeezed the excess water. It would take a while for it to dry.

"Are you okay?" He sat up and touched my shoulder. The tender touch sent a wave of desire coursing through my veins. I leaned until our shoulders bumped. He let go of my hand and reached for my hair once more. He gently worked his way down a bunch of hair, milking it.

"I'm fine. It will take a while for my hair to dry. I didn't want to subject you to it wet all night."

"Thanks, but I'm more worried about the sand."

"Yeah, that too." Thankfully, the sand would rub off easier when our skin dried. The saltwater left a briny film that made me feel grimy. "I'm looking forward to a nice, soapy shower. That should help."

"We can do that before we climb on the hammock. There's a shower where we can rinse the beach off. I brought our bag of goodies, so there are supplies we can use."

"Clever boy," I teased. I wondered how this would work. Would he lay on the ground and touch my foot while I washed my hair?

"Are you ready?" Keeping a hand on my shoulder, he got to his knees. I turned my head to look out to sea or else I'd have had a great shot of the getting-to-know-Cole show. He reached under my knees, slid his hand around my back, and pulled me to him. He cradled me against his chest and then stood.

It didn't matter if I was ready. Cole had been. I threw my arms around his neck and held on as he reached the deep sand. He did well to keep his balance, holding me as if I weighed nothing.

CHAPTER ELEVEN

WE NEARED THE STRUCTURE, AND Cole paused before shifting me as his hand reached out. He twisted a handle and water rained down from a shower head I hadn't noticed. The clean water would wash all the grime away. I tipped my head back and let my hair gather. Cole wiped my back, getting rid of any sand.

"Where's the shampoo?" I asked. He leaned, picked up something and tapped my backside with it. I let go of his neck to grab what he had. I recognized the small bottle of shampoo. He needed to put me down if I was to be able to wash my hair. I couldn't do it in his arms. "Cole, you're going to have to set me down."

"I can't guarantee I won't touch you if I put you down," he replied in a husky voice.

"Would you like to wash my hair?" I asked because he liked to touch it. But also to keep his mind and my hormones in check.

He buried his nose in my damp hair, nuzzling me, and whispered. "I'd like that very much." I wiggled my legs, and he leaned over without removing his face from my hair.

The water still rained on us. My feet touched the

ground, and he slowly removed his arm. The sensual feeling of his skin gliding over mine gave me a shiver. When I was stable, he placed his hands on my shoulders. I tipped my head forward, relishing his massaging thumbs. After a few moments, his hand slid down my arm to my hand and took the shampoo. I moved all my hair over to one side and his lips found the crook of my neck.

I sucked in a breath and stepped back into his hard body. His teeth grazed my skin and I moaned. He uncapped the shampoo and squeezed some onto his palm. I inched forward out of the spray, and he stepped into it while he worked the soap into a lather.

"God, I could get used to this," I said, as he massaged my scalp.

"So could I," he chuckled. "I wouldn't mind being your official bathing attendant."

There's an idea: bathing attendant. Roni would be so jealous.

He methodically continued to the tips of the strands, then I tipped my head to rinse the soap away. Cole uncapped the conditioner and started the whole process over.

I must have moaned because he laughed. "If you like it so much, I can arrange my showers to coordinate with yours." He lifted my hair and kissed my neck again. "Although I'd like to wash more than your hair."

"Perhaps you should judge my hair washing skills before firming up your plans," I teased.

"Something is already firm and up."

I couldn't help stepping back against him and his

erection.

He growled against my skin and slid his hand over my belly. I tilted my head to give him better access. His tongue darted out and trailed the length of my neck. Even with water running over my body, I was hot enough to spontaneously ignite. My core throbbed. It had been a long time since I'd wanted a man like I wanted Cole.

I twisted in his arms until I hugged him. Pressing my ear against his chest, I listened to the rapid rhythm of his heart. My breasts rubbed him with each breath.

He finished squeezing the excess water out of my hair and he shifted us so I was out of the main stream. He started rubbing me on the shoulder but slowly worked his way down my back. I relaxed against him and began my own exploration.

Every muscle on his back seemed defined. I couldn't reach his shoulders, so I decided to go lower—to his butt cheeks. I massaged like he had kneaded my scalp, and he moaned.

"You're hired," he mumbled. "I think all the sand is gone."

"Oh, should I be searching for sand?" I nuzzled my face into his chest and bit his nipple. He gasped and tipped my chin up. I longed for another kiss, but I'd probably end up straddling him again.

With hands on his chest, I pushed my body away. "Turn around and get on your knees."

He raised his eyebrows and gave me an amused look but did as I ordered. I picked up the shampoo and dripped a dab into his wet hair. I lathered, starting at the front and progressing towards his neck. As the soap rinsed, I trailed the white foam down his arms and back. I did want to wash the sand away. I worked on his shoulders and then his pecs.

Long after the shampoo had gone down the drain, I pressed against his back, and I leaned forward, working my way down as far as I could reach. My fingers played with the hair that ringed his nipples. He threw his head back onto my shoulder, and I sucked his earlobe.

"Christ, Nessa, you're making me want to break that promise I made to you this morning."

Promise? What promise? I hope his promise involved his tongue. "And you're a man of your word." I muttered the words on his neck and felt him shiver.

"Yes, dammit, I am." He inhaled through his teeth. "I told you I wouldn't have sex with you tonight."

Oh crap, that's right. And that's exactly where all this touching and caressing was headed. I started to withdraw my arms, but he clasped them. "Do you remember what else I said? I wanted your hands all over me."

I nibbled his neck again. "I can handle that."

"I also said I wanted to pleasure you."

I swallowed and my heart rate skyrocketed. So many awesome versions of Cole pleasuring me simultaneously flowed through my mind, cutting off all ability to speak.

He stood up and reached, twisting the knobs and turning off the water. My hands remained on his back as he reached down to a cubby I hadn't noticed. He unfolded a towel and began drying my body, starting with my face, then my chest. He wiped each arm and leg, then indicated I should turn, allowing him access to my rear.

"Are you going to massage an orgasm out of me?"

You did not just say that.

He chuckled and kissed my neck again. I rushed on. "Your hands are talented. I bet you could."

"It's not exactly what I was thinking, but it is something to keep in mind for tomorrow night, though." He toweled my back and underarms.

Tomorrow? I shivered. Would we get naked again?

The bet ended tomorrow afternoon—maybe he wanted to have dinner. My contemplation came to an abrupt halt when he kissed my lower back. The towel wiped one leg, then the other. He stopped and hovered his hand over my thigh.

"I was thinking more along the lines of massaging someplace else." His hand slid upward to my apex, only coming close enough to make me glad I hadn't worn any underwear to swim.

"It could work," I breathed. One of his feet rested next to mine, touching as he toweled off my hair. He took care to dry it. "That area has been out of order for a while. The hinges might be rusty."

He chuckled and handed me the towel. He turned, and I started to wipe his shoulders.

"I can perform some maintenance. I'll make sure that area is well lubed."

My legs trembled with anticipation, but I continued to dry his shins. I flipped the towel to the dryer side and stepped in front of him. I worked my way up his thighs. When I reached his manhood, I covered it and rubbed his belly.

I glanced up at him. "What's the point if it's out of order?" I asked with a grin as I dried the length of his shaft. He closed his eyes and gripped my arm. I fondled him lower, trying to be thorough so he wouldn't have chafing. I patted his chest, then I touched his face, but it was dry.

I threw the towel over my shoulder, and I ran my fingers through his hair. I loved the soft length.

Cole's arms encircled my waist, pulling me against him. He looked down into my eyes. "The maintenance I intend to perform will get it in working order and it will be functioning for the test run tomorrow evening."

"So that's what you have in store for me tomorrow. Giving my nether regions a good lubing." Resting my chin on his chest, I smiled at him while I played with the hair on the back of his neck.

"No, you've misunderstood me." He gave a little squeeze and continued. "The lubing will happen right now."

He picked me up for the second time tonight. He walked to the hammock and laid me on it. The moment my back hit the hammock's material, I was grateful that it wasn't a net. This hammock was wide and solid, and though it moved with our weight, it didn't sway as a normal hammock would.

He climbed next to me on his belly with his one leg between mine and an arm across my stomach. Cole's whispered kiss on my shoulder gave me goose bumps. As he moved his arm, the hair grazed my nipple, making me shiver.

He stroked my face, then tilted my head, so our lips met. I sighed and opened for him. His tongue plundered my mouth, claiming it as his own.

Desire simmered in my veins and, even though he was next to me, I wanted closer. My fingernails dug into his flesh on his hip and my leg rubbed his, hooking it.

He moaned, a deep feral sound. Cole caressed my breast while our tongues dueled. I arched into his amorous touch. His lips trailed down my neck, nipping and sucking his way to my breasts. He took his time, first working one then switching to the other. His tongue swirled around my nipple making me writhe.

My fingers curled into his hair and held him there. When he tried to move away, I muttered, "No."

He playfully nibbled the tip sending waves of fire through my body. He acquiesced, keeping his mouth there, but his hand dipped lower. His warm palm slid down over my hip to my thigh. He rubbed my muscles, which felt heavenly, but anticipation grew as he worked higher. His fingers brushed my sweet spot, shooting a shiver up my spine.

"Cole," I whispered, locking eyes with him. "Kiss me."

With a final lick, he let go and claimed my lips once more. I wanted to wrap my arms around him to pull him closer, but one arm was trapped by my side. I was drowning with desire, and only Cole could rescue me.

The kiss, fast and hungry at first, became slow and methodical. Lingering and tantalizing. His lips felt amazing. I hadn't enjoyed a man's kiss this much in ages. Since Nick.

His fingers grazed my inner thigh, and I sucked in a breath. He smiled at my reaction, and he nudged my legs apart with his knee. His finger traced my seam, and I opened my eyes. His eyes glittered with mischievous delight when he slipped a finger into my wet folds. I moaned under his administrations.

Pressed against my hip, his erection pulsed, alerting me I wasn't the only one turned on.

"Don't stop," I ordered.

Chuckling, he kissed my jawline near my ear. "I told you, I'd pleasure you."

"Hell no," I said, my voice a raspy whisper, "This isn't pleasure, this is ecstasy." My eyes rolled back in my head, my body responding to Cole's touch.

He reacted to my moans with sounds of his own, and so close to my ear they turned me on even more. His warm breath breezing my skin, his tongue on my neck, his fingers gliding over me had me spiraling towards orgasmic rapture.

His manhood throbbed next to my hand, and I stretched my fingers and skimmed its length. It was Cole's turn to gasp. He shifted to allow me access. I continued down his shaft until I cupped his balls. Yes, I'm a ball girl.

Cole's lips consumed mine once more. His kiss became frenzied, and he stroked me faster. Our breathing labored as we worked each other up. I pistoned his erection, relishing the hard length. We moaned our pleasure. I was close to reaching the heights, and he knew it.

"Come with me," he mumbled against my lips before kissing me again. It was only a matter of seconds for me, three, two, one, blastoff.

He ejaculated onto my side while my body spasmed next to his. Our kiss became gentle and his touch tender. He pressed his forehead to mine. Our breaths were ragged, our bodies sated.

I wanted to stretch like a contented cat and roll over

and sleep. He cleaned my side with a towel then reached under the hammock. He handed me a chilled bottle of water. The place must have had a refrigerator somewhere. I took a long drink, and then passed him the bottle. He finished it.

Cole then reached again and pulled a sheet over us. The color was light and appeared white in the darkness.

He laid on his back, and I put my head on his shoulder. I played with the hair on his chest tracing its path and circling his nipples. I touched the points, and he grabbed my hands.

"That turns me on," he said with a growl.

"It turns me on, too." I flicked the closest with my tongue.

"Christ." When I did it again, he laughed. "It tickles."

When he stopped laughing, I asked, "Is this how we're going to sleep? Like last night."

"Like last night—minus clothes." His fingers slid over my forehead and tucked a wayward strand of my hair behind my ear. I turned my body more and put my arm over his chest like I did the night before.

While staring up at the stars, Cole's breathing deepened. I wondered what he dreamed about.

CHAPTER TWELVE

Nick laughed and chased me around our room. I kicked a high-heeled shoe at him. It didn't deter him. I followed with the other.

"At this rate, you'll be naked soon."

I turned, giggling, and tossed my wrist corsage. He caught it and set it on the night table. I jumped up on the king size bed. Turning in a complete circle, I shook my bottom at him, and over my shoulder said, "If you want me naked, you'll have to unzip me."

He joined me on the bed and kissed my shoulder. He started to kiss and nip. I heard the zipper, and the sleeveless dress fell to my ankles.

"Christ, Nessa, a thong?" Nick caressed my cheeks, then traced the edge to the front. "You're so damn sexy."

"Only for you," I murmured before I turned around and kissed him. We made short work of our clothes. It was our first time, both of us being virgins. My father had already declared Nick off limits, but tell that to my heart. Soon we were making love.

The next morning, he took me home, but the long kiss in the car had been too long, and Roni spotted Nick's car. She ran into the four-car garage screaming.

I held onto Nick. I knew this would be the memory of one of the last times I saw him.

Suddenly, it turned dark and stormy. My father and a handful of his friends, each carrying guns and dressed in fatigues, came out. They pulled him out of the car, dragged him into the yard and ordered him to his knees. They aimed the guns, firing squad style.

"No Daddy, I love him." I dove in front of Nick as the guns blasted.

My eyes flew open. The sun was rising, but it was still dark. I drew in a deep breath. I'd turned in my sleep and Cole now spooned me. Our legs tangled, his arm over my breasts and his nose in my hair.

Luckily, when you sleep in a hammock, you naturally roll to the center. It kept us together.

Grateful for Cole's steady breathing and the fact that Nick's death had been a dream and not real, I closed my eyes and basked in the peacefulness of the predawn until I fell back asleep.

I wore a white dress. The one I clipped out of my mother's magazine.

"This way, Nessa." Nick was all grown up and looked like Cole, except with brown hair. He stood in a tux next to a minister. We stood on the beach, holding hands. We recited vows, and the minister pronounced us husband and wife. Afterward, we went to a party. People swirled around us as we danced. I looked forward to him unzipping my dress again.

"Good morning, Mr. Tanner, where would you like

me to set up?" a man's deep voice interrupted my dream dance.

"Over there, Gustavo. Leave the covers on." Nick's voice replied in a whisper.

"Oh, I'm sorry, sir, I didn't know the Mrs. was with you." He lowered his voice. "I'll just be going. Enjoy your food. Call if you need anything."

"I will."

I opened my eyes again, and the morning had arrived. Not just dawn. The sun had risen.

Cole shifted next to me, and the sheet moved. Had I overheard something he'd spoken with the staff? I clutched the sheet and abruptly sat upright.

"It's all right, Nessa," Cole said. He relaxed back with his right arm cradling his head on the hammock. The sheet covered his groin and most of his legs.

"Did I hear voices or was I dreaming?" I glanced over the platform. The sheer curtains had been drawn, revealing the beautiful beach and breaking waves. I sighed and snuggled back onto Cole's chest.

"I had breakfast delivered. Whenever you're hungry, we can eat."

As soon as he said it, my stomach grumbled. "Are they gone?"

"Yes, they've gone back to the kitchen." He touched my face, then smoothed my hair. "It's just us. Here, put this on." He handed me a t-shirt with the resort's logo. It was dark blue. He grinned and said, "I don't want to be tempted."

"What about you?" I teased. He lifted the sheet and showed me white boxer briefs. I liked them but said, "That's not fair."

He kissed the top of my head, then I sat up and put on the shirt. We went into the small room and took turns brushing our teeth and using the restroom. We were getting good at functioning while attached.

He pulled out the wooden chair for me, and I sat. He scooted close, then lifted the metal lids. An assortment of fruits under one and omelets and home fries under the other. Somehow, the omelets had stayed warm.

Cole cut while I gripped the fork. I lifted the piece to his mouth. His gaze held mine while he took a bite, but then his eyes closed in ecstasy. "That's awesome. Try it."

I sampled a tiny morsel and the flavor burst onto my tastebuds.

"Good, huh?" he grinned when I stole his next bite. I nodded and hummed. "Dang, it must be good if you're sounding like that. That's the noise you made when I touched you last night."

I swallowed and started coughing. Heat flared, and I downed a glass of orange juice.

After we ate, we sat at the table and watched the morning. The blue sky, clouds, branches swaying in the gentle breeze, and an almost naked man made it perfect. I tugged my bag to me and found my journal. I flipped to a new page and wrote about what had transpired yesterday: the Higginses taking the bet, Mr. Gorgeous, and the kiss.

Cole didn't watch everything I wrote, but he was close enough to read it. When I got to our private villa, I jotted only a few words after a brief description. Oceanic skinny dipping, shower, and wow.

I showed him what I'd written, earning an ornery grin. He stuck out his hand, wanting the book and pen. I handed them over, trusting him completely and wanting his writing in my book. I could remember him then years later. He penned something, then returned it to me.

He'd circled the word kiss and written above it: Best kisser ever. I smiled when I spotted the 'double wow' next to my single wow.

I gazed up into his blue eyes, keenly aware of the fact that I didn't have any underwear on. My body knew it, too. I was half tempted to climb on his lap.

"You called out in your sleep," he said, putting the kibosh on my musings. "What were you dreaming?"

I looked away with a frown. I'd dreamed of Nick, like I had ever since escaping from my family. The recollections started on the cruise ship after seeing Cole.

He placed a hand on my shoulder. "It was him, wasn't it? I heard you call his name."

I nodded, not wanting to go into detail, but he asked, "What happened? You sounded desperate and frightened."

I inhaled deeply. "It started out as a memory. We were dressed up and then he drove me home. My father and some of his friends grabbed Nick and were going to shoot him." I turned a horrified face to Cole. "That never happened, but it felt real."

"Dreams sometimes manifest our worst fears. You didn't want to lose him."

I bit my lip. I took a drink and twisted to face Cole. "I've already lost him." I closed my eyes, wincing at the pain that admittance brought. A tear trickled down my cheek; Cole wiped the renegade tear away.

When I opened my eyes again, I said, "I had another dream after that, Cole. It was a better dream. We stood on the beach and got married."

"We did, huh? What color was my tux?"

I stared at him. Clearly, my confusion was plain on my face, and he smiled, touching my cheek. "You said *we* exchanged vows on the beach?"

"Oh." I looked away.

"It was him, wasn't it?"

I wasn't certain and shrugged my shoulders. "I'm not sure who it was. I assumed it was Nick, but…"

He took my chin and turned my face to meet his gaze. "But…"

My mouth hung open, but no words formed. I had to swallow and try again. "But he looked an awful lot like you."

He rested his hand on my arm and leaned back in his chair. Rubbing his scruff with his free hand, he turned introspective. "Hm. I guess we'll need to go shopping."

His comment stumped me, so instead, I studied his sculpted abs. The tanned hue of his skin, his sexy mess of blond hair, along with the smirk when he caught me staring, had me breathing rapidly. Good grief, I didn't want to leave this magical place.

"Shopping? This place is beautiful and relaxing." I stretched out my legs to make a point. "I don't want to go anywhere."

"We can't stay here. This space is rented for a week. Honeymooners." He shrugged. "We need to get out within an hour." He picked up his cup and took a drink of juice.

I slumped in my seat. Bummed. I wanted to be alone with Cole. Now it seemed we would head to town.

I suspected the village would be quaint, with postcard worthy residences and historical buildings. Cruise ships liked to dump tourists on places like that. The tourists would usually pick from a few guided tours, including treks into the jungle to the oldest plantation on the island. The shops close to the docks tended to be touristy, with apparel and trinkets. I had no desire to visit tourist traps or move with a throng of people.

"Do we need to shop?" I asked. I supposed I could have been pouting. "What do you want to buy?"

"Guess."

"Souvenirs?"

"I know a jewelry store. It's not in the heart of town." His blue eyes twinkled like sunlight on the water. His lips formed a faint smile.

"Jewelry? You want to buy a toe ring or something?" I teased.

"A ring, yes, but not for toes."

I narrowed my eyes at him, and he laughed. Maybe a pair of diamond stud earrings would make me feel better. I scratched my thigh. "Fine, but I'll need something other than a t-shirt to wear."

"I kind of like this look." He placed a hand on my thigh and moved it up my leg.

"Well, look who stole some smooth moves from Mr. Gorgeous." I tugged the hem of the shirt down.

Cole blinked and his mouth formed a perfect O. He removed his hand as if I'd slapped him. He recovered and grinned. "That sucks balls."

"Among other things." I waved my hand as if to shoo him away. I tilted my head and looked down my nose at him. After a breath, we started laughing. Poor Mr. Gorgeous, the butt of our inside joke.

"Come on," he stood and stretched. Lord have mercy,

but I yearned to touch his skin. I wanted to run my fingers down around his navel, following the trail south. He squeezed my arm. "Let's get dressed." He must have seen the desire on my features, because he stepped as far from me as he could.

Slowly, I pushed the chair back. One bare footstep, then another in his direction. I felt like a predator stalking my prey. He gave me a wink and turned around. I had a perfect view of the boxer briefs clinging to his muscular bottom.

In the small bathroom, there were shelves on the wall near the shower stall. Folded on the shelves were clothes—including a bra and underwear set that I recognized as mine.

Pinching the bra strap, I picked it up. "This is mine and not the one I was wearing before."

Cole sat on the toilet with the lid closed. He placed my hand on his shoulder. "Hope you don't mind, but I asked them to bring you some clean clothes." He threaded his legs into a pair of khakis, then looked up at me. "You did say you wanted clean underwear. Is everything all right?"

I swallowed my angst and tried to smile at his courteous gesture before turning away from him.

Someone had rifled through my suitcase, my belongings. Some stranger had touched my underwear.

"I had Marguerite make sure a woman picked your outfit. Does it look okay?" I heard concern.

I plucked up the ecru panties and sat on his lap, threading my own legs through the holes. I could feel his dick harden. Serves him right. I frowned. With his hand on my leg, I quickly stood and pulled them up. The white skirt was next. It was shorter than knee length but comfortable. Feeling a smidgen more clothed and less vulnerable, I inspected the blouse that had been picked for me.

Buttery yellow with lime green and white pinstripes, it looked like something that fit the tropical island vibe. With a sweetheart neckline and capped sleeves, both edged with soft lace, I would be cool. The bra she had chosen was a demi style and, with the sweetheart neckline, would accentuate my cleavage.

Not that Cole couldn't see down the front of my shirt from his six-foot vantage point, anyway. But these garments might enhance his view.

"Close your eyes," I told him. Grabbing both his hands, I placed them on my hips. I pulled off the t-shirt and draped it over his head.

"Hey," he said with a chuckle. "Don't you trust me?"

"I know what I would do," I answered. I put on my bra.

"Fair enough."

I poked my arm and head through the holes of the blouse and tugged it down. I took the shirt off his head and he blinked those beautiful blue eyes.

I'd messed up his hair, so I tried to straighten it. That's when I noticed his blond hair had dark roots. His hair was brown? Holy crap. With brown hair, this guy could be Nick's identical twin, if Nick didn't already have a twin, that is.

My heart raced. Could Cole be related to the Tanners? I touched his scruff with my knuckles and hoped my voice didn't give away emotion. "So how long have you been a blond?" Darn it, my voice quavered.

He arched a brow, then glanced at my neckline. "Not terribly long."

"Let me guess, you and Mike?" Under my shirt, he rubbed my belly. I placed my hands over his and tilted my head.

A sheepish grin and a shrug, followed by a "maybe," confirmed my suspicions.

"What happened?"

He sighed and looked over at the doorway. "Let's just say he completed the task. I thought he'd never get it right and my punishment is this." He pulled strands of his hair. "You should have heard him laugh."

"I can imagine." I had to bite my lip not to laugh myself. These men and their stupid bets.

We gathered our items and walked to the road. A limo awaited us. I stopped, squinting at the white car and expecting the newlyweds to pop out. Instead, a tanned man with a slender figure opened the door for Cole and me. The gentleman took our bags and put them in the car, then closed the door after Cole had followed me in.

Cole didn't say a word, but the man drove to town. We exited with a few stares from the locals. Some waved like we were celebrities.

The first shop we entered had expensive odds and ends, like a brass ship's wheel and ships in a bottle. Local artists had painted seascapes in oils or acrylics. In the jewelry cases were handmade earrings, necklaces, and all kinds of small jewelry. It didn't really interest me, but I looked around. The air conditioning felt good.

We walked the streets arm and arm. Talking, laughing, and observing. I had that sensation of freedom again, and when I wasn't actively doing anything, I wore a smile.

"Cole, are we still going to the jewelry store?" I asked, seeing a small shop at the end of the street.

"Do you have anyone you'd like to buy for?" He grinned as he held open the door for me.

"Yes." I stopped just inside the entry and stared. Talk about sensory overload. Lights and shiny, sparkly things. "Oh."

"Something for your sister?" He teased, stepping next to me.

A short, balding man rose from a chair at the desk in the back. "Hello Mr—"

Cole raised his hand. "It's okay, Oliver. This is Vanessa Warsaw, and we're going to look at rings today."

I frowned at the use of my surname. When had I mentioned my last name? Or did I drop Warsaw Industries' name? I must have.

Oliver's eyes widened, and he clapped his hands together. But before the little man could speak, I replied. "He might be searching for a ring, but I'll be looking at everything else."

Oliver laughed and gestured to the case in front of him. "Watches are here. Men's on that side, women's here." He walked to the left and started naming gemstones and settings.

I smiled and nodded but didn't pay much attention. Cole carried on a conversation with him while I searched the cases. I loved the pale purple tanzanite. I studied the jewelry with rubies, my birthstone. Finally, Cole sat down in front of the rings, stretching our linked arms.

"What are you looking for?" Oliver glanced at me quickly before settling his sights on Cole.

"Well, she had a dream we were married." Cole thumbed in my direction. I rolled my eyes.

"He's looking for something for his mother," I said, walking behind Cole and placing my hand on his shoulder. "What are you doing?" I hissed in his ear.

"Humor me. I'm curious." He turned and caught my lips with his. It was quick, but my body quivered at the touch and ached when he pulled back.

I huffed out a sigh and plopped unceremoniously into the chair next to him.

Placing my hand on his thigh, I thought I'd let his body react for a while. While he and Oliver pulled out ring after ring, discussing cuts and the quality of diamonds, I studied the tennis bracelets in the case next to them. I hadn't realized how many styles there were.

My mother had had one with square looking diamonds set in gold; it had been linked. Some of the ones in the case were called channel cut. I preferred the gray metals.

"What do you think about this, Ms. Warsaw?"

I glanced from man to man, then down at the ring Oliver had taken out of the case. The diamond was huge. Maybe four carats. I glanced back at Cole and found him intrigued. I sighed and scooted closer.

"Look," I started. "An engagement ring is personal. Inspiration should come from here," I poked Cole in the heart. "That being said, there are a few other things to consider. Take, for example, this ring." I picked it up and slid it on my ring finger. It was way too big. "The stone is no doubt beautiful but look at my hand." I glanced into Cole's eyes.

"This ring looks out of proportion for my hand. My

fingers are small." All of me is small. "But if the woman you were buying a ring for had long fingers—"

"Like a piano player," Oliver chimed in.

I nodded. "Then the ring would be better proportioned for her hand."

"What about a solitaire versus a ring with multiple stones?" Cole asked.

I kept from rolling my eyes because I could tell he was truly curious. "Depends. A solitaire is simple, and you always can add a jacket or a wrap with it for style and color or an anniversary. One with stones, well, again you have the proportion thing, but…" I scanned the case and found what I was looking for. I tapped on the glass top. "Oliver, may I see that ring there? No, the one with three stones."

Oliver took the small display out of the case, slid the ring off the velvet faux finger, and he handed it to Cole.

Cole examined the ring. The central diamond was larger than the two on either side of it. The band was a silver color metal, but I didn't care if it was platinum or white gold.

I offered my hand palm up and expected him to place the ring in it, but that's not what he did. He flipped my hand over and slid the ring down my finger, and continued holding my hand. Strange sensations had me staring at the piece of jewelry. The intimacy of that small act had my heart in my throat. Finding my nerve, I lifted my hand to examine the ring.

I cleared my throat. "This looks better proportionately on my hand. And the three stones can signify something."

"Like what?" Cole asked.

"Your past, present, and future relationship, of

course." I stood up and glanced around. "Where are the men's wedding bands?"

Oliver grinned and pointed two cases over. We moved down, and I looked in the case. I pointed, and Oliver retrieved the ring.

"Look, Cole, the cool thing is the man can get one, too. Larger diamonds across the width of the band or a smaller one the other way. You both can remember the past, live in the present, and look forward to the future."

Oliver handed me the ring with a sappy grin. He must think Cole and I are picking rings for each other.

I fingered the ring and glanced at Cole. He wore a smirk. Fine. I extended my hand to him and he gave me his left hand. I slid the ring onto his finger. It was too big around, but the style looked good. It was strange seeing both our hands with rings.

Quickly, I tugged the engagement ring off my finger and handed it to Oliver. "May I see a bracelet?"

Cole gave the men's ring back, too.

With Cole's hands on my hips, I tried on several and settled on a bangle style with princess cut stones. The whole time I studied the different bracelets, Cole and Oliver conversed in a language I didn't understand except once or twice when they mentioned my name or the resort.

"I need to get my bag," I told Cole. It was in the limo.

"It's okay."

"No, it's not. I need to pay for the bracelet."

He smiled and patted my arm. "I got this."

"No. You can't get this. I want to buy it for myself."

Cole turned to Oliver and spoke to him in the language I didn't understand. Oliver nodded. "Yes, Ms.

Warsaw. Jewelry can be charged to your room."

"Oh," I nodded. I supposed that would work if I had checked into the resort.

Pulling Cole near, I whispered, "We have a problem. I haven't checked in yet."

Cole's brow crinkled, and he frowned. He'd been with me since I stepped off the catamaran. He fished out his cell and pushed a button.

"Thank you for calling the Dancing Winds today. My name is Marguerite. How can I assist you?"

"Ah, Marguerite," He met my gaze and smiled, then continued in the foreign language. "Thank you." Cole patted my arm. "Everything is good. Your villa is ready for occupancy when we get there."

I breathed out a long breath. "Thank you." He squeezed my hand.

After we left the jewelry store, we walked the streets of town. The temperature rose, but with the sea breeze, it was bearable. I didn't care. I was on vacation.

CHAPTER THIRTEEN

IN THE RESORT LOBBY, COLE smiled at the woman behind the desk. Marguerite glanced from me to our linked hands, then back at Cole.

"Ms. Warsaw is here to get the key to her villa."

"Yes, sir." Marguerite nodded, then tapped on her computer keyboard. "Here we are."

I reached into my bag and pulled out my wallet so I could show her my ID. She glanced again at Cole, then took my license and scanned it.

"Everything is in order," Marguerite said, handing it back to me. "Welcome to the Dancing Winds. I hope you enjoy your stay. If you have any problems or questions, please call the front desk and I'll be happy to assist you."

She smiled as she passed me a folder with the keycards in it. I thanked her and took out one of the cards, noting the six and one on it. Sixty-one. Now, where could that villa be?

I stuck the keys in my bag and took a deep breath. We strolled toward the back of the resort, the seaside. Stepping into the sunlight, I blinked and saw Amoya waving. She sat where I had yesterday at the bar.

Cole raised a hand, and we walked toward the

Higginses. I looked around, hoping that Mr. Gorgeous had found someone else to bother. We moved to a small circular table and ordered a drink. Cole and Mike spoke in low tones on one side, while Amoya informed me in a whisper how miserable Mike was.

She leaned in and said, "He has to go, but won't go with me there." She glanced over at her husband and with a crinkled brow. "He's really in pain."

Cole held my hand against his thigh. I curled my fingers slightly, and he glanced at me. I raised a brow, but now everyone looked at me.

"Do you like my bling?" I placed my wrist with my new bobble on the table. I shifted, and the diamonds caught the light and sparkled.

Amoya's eyes widened. Touching my knee to Cole's, I freed my hand, removed the bracelet, and handed it over for inspection.

Amoya brought it close and Mike leaned in. "Why don't you get me things like this? You could learn a thing or two." She gave her husband the stink eye, then focused back on me. "It's beautiful. You're lucky."

"You did nicely, my friend," Mike said to Cole.

"Thanks. Sometimes a girl has to pamper herself," I declared.

Amoya's brows rose and she and Mike glanced at each other, then Cole. Cole shrugged, and the Higginses resumed admiring it.

I tugged Cole's shirt to pull him closer and turned to whisper what Amoya admitted about Mike. "What do you think we should do? I don't want him to suffer."

"He does look in a bad way, doesn't he?"

We glanced over at Mike, and he shifted

uncomfortably in his chair, moving his legs from one side to the other.

"Although he did do this to himself." I prodded Cole with my elbow, earning a grin.

"What are you two whispering about over there?" Mike asked with narrowed eyes.

"The bet. Vanessa really wants a private shower, but I thought we could go another day. How about you?" Cole was quick to answer.

I sucked in a breath and started laughing. Both Amoya and Mike frowned, then looked at each other. Amoya patted Mike's arm.

"How are you getting along?" Cole prodded.

Amoya pursed her lips together, then sighed. She handed my bracelet back, and I slipped it on.

I know it's stupid, but the bracelet helped me feel pretty. I hadn't styled my hair or worn makeup for two days, so I had a little bling pick me up.

"Well, I don't think we're in for another day," Mike said. "Not that I don't want to spend time with my lovely wife."

"Yes, you guys are the clear winners," Amoya said with a smile.

I grinned and leaned back. Cole threaded his fingers with mine. The bet hadn't been concluded. It hadn't quite been twenty-four hours for them.

"Does that mean we're done?" I asked. I had gotten used to Cole. Now the thought of losing him was hard. I tightened my grasp.

"That sounds good to me. Mike?" Amoya twisted and poked her husband in the side.

"I don't know." He stroked his goatee. Amoya pouted

her lips at him. "Okay, fine dear. This concludes the bet. I suppose we owe you dinner."

"Actually, you owe us a few dinners," Cole said, pointing at Mike. "But not tonight. I am taking Vanessa on a date."

"Really?" I asked. "Dinner and a movie?"

Cole raised an eyebrow, then his eyes narrowed in on me. I swallowed. He looked like he planned to devour me. My body reacted with a quiver. "I don't know about a movie, but there will be quite a show."

"Hm." It was my turn to raise a brow.

"I'm going to take you somewhere cool."

"Not another honeymooning villa?"

"You didn't mind." He chuckled. "No, this place has been used as part of a movie set."

"Hm." I wanted to question him some more, but Mike stood up, scraping his chair's feet on the concrete. Mike excused himself, and Amoya followed after him.

"Vanessa, I would like to take you someplace special for dinner, if you're not sick of me?" He placed his hand over mine. We had yet to quit touching.

"I'm not sick of you. And dinner sounds great." I looked down at my clothes. "Do I need to dress up?"

He stood and pulled me to my feet. "Actually, the only thing you need is a bathing suit and towel."

"No skinny dipping, huh?"

"Not at this place. There are tours that come through." He continued, "Besides, I don't want to share you with anyone."

We started walking, and I saw a sign that pointed to the group of numbered villas that included mine, but he walked me past that path and forward. We wound our way up a hill passing several larger villas until we were near the end. He paused, and we faced each other.

He touched my cheek tenderly. I pressed my face against his hand, not wanting him to leave. How quickly things had changed in my life.

"I'll leave you to have a few peaceful moments to yourself." He stooped to brush his lips against mine. All too quickly, he pulled back, leaving me wanting more.

Glancing around, I found the villas numbered in the teens. "Where are you staying?"

"Over there," he pointed. "Come on and check it out." We walked past three more buildings, and he paused at the last one, which had the largest deck. "This is me."

No wonder he hadn't blinked at a thousand-dollar bet. That was chump change. A villa this size probably cost over ten grand a night and that was being generous. He hadn't even stayed there yet and had food catered to us at the honeymooner's cabin. He couldn't be hurting for money.

"It's okay." I said, pulling away from him. "I'll go get ready. When should I expect you?"

"How about at five?"

I nodded and started walking toward my villa. I turned back once and found him watching me from the steps. We waved, then he disappeared inside.

CHAPTER FOURTEEN

IT TOOK ME A WHILE to find building number sixty-one. It was small, but it had a nice shore-side patio with a cute grouping of chairs.

The sliding glass door was open, so I stepped in. Housekeeping must have wanted to freshen up the place. Clothes were hung in the closet and a makeup kit was open on the dresser. I studied the opened case. I didn't have anything like that.

The door to the bathroom swung open and a tall African man walked out. He froze, looking me up and down. "You're not housekeeping."

"No. You're not housekeeping either. What are you doing in my room?" I inspected him as well. He wore a polo shirt, khaki shorts, and boating shoes. His hair grayed at the temple.

"Your room? You're mistaken. This is my room, and I'll ask you to kindly leave." He put his hands on his hips.

"I'm not going anywhere. This is my villa." I walked over to the closet, and he shadowed me. I was intimidated by his size. What looked like my silver suitcase was on the floor of the closet, but I'd have to flip it over to find the palm tree sticker to prove it.

"Get out, miss, or I'll call security."

I heard footsteps at the door and pivoted to see an older woman with long hair. Her face turned fuchsia when she saw me.

"Oh my God, Reginald! You brought a bimbo in here while I was at the spa." She dove at me across the bed, and I dodged her spindly arms.

"No way, baby. I caught her casing out your jewelry. I asked her to leave but she wouldn't," he said with hands open.

"You're both in my room," I shouted, getting angry. I used my Ice Queen voice. "Leave now."

I pointed to the sliding door, wearing my corporate takeover face. Okay, so business dominatrix doesn't trump crazy, psycho jealous girlfriend.

She jumped at me again with her long red nails like daggers going for my throat. I dodged to the right, and she tripped over the boyfriend's foot. She staggered but picked up her bag and chucked it at me. It hit the glass and stuff went flying. When I heard her mumble something about a knife, I left. It would be easier for someone else, hopefully the resort bouncers, to handle those party crashers.

I rubbed my arm and felt something sticky. I'd been cut. That crazy lady had cut me. My eye pricked with tears.

All I wanted was to take a shower. Shave my parts. Get pretty for a date with Cole, but now I didn't have time. I had to deal with crazies. I started running and when I stopped, my breath heaving, I was at Cole's villa.

Timidly, I walked up the steps.

"Leave your brother alone," a woman's voice

scolded.

"Mom! He did it again," a squeaky child whined.

"Oh, for heaven's sake, Joshua. Go to your room." The woman's voice grew louder.

I stepped up to the door and peered in, shocked there was a woman with children in Cole's residence.

The woman walked through a living room with a large sectional sofa. Toy cars and airplanes littered the floor. On the console, I saw some family photographs. A man entered the room and saw me at the door. His face bore a resemblance to Cole's. Maybe one of his jerk brothers.

"Hello," I said. "I'm looking for Cole?"

"Cole?" the lady asked, glancing at the man.

"Cole is Mike's *nick*name for him," the man thumbed over his shoulder. He wore a Disneyland shirt and basketball shorts. "This is Vanessa."

"Vanessa? *The* Vanessa." The woman's eyes glowed as she scanned me. Her smile a million watts.

I gasped, bewildered. Had they never heard the name Vanessa before? Of course they had, because I am *the* Vanessa. But which Vanessa was I?

The woman reached for my hand and pumped it. "It's so nice to meet you. I've heard a lot about you."

"Cole's in the bathroom shaving and showering. He'll be out in a few minutes."

One of the children started crying. The man glanced at the woman before hurrying down a hallway, out of sight.

"I'm glad you're here. He really likes you. So does Doug."

"Doug?" My mouth went dry.

"My husband. Oh, how silly of me. I haven't

introduced myself, I'm Grace Tanner."

"Tanner?"

Oh shit. I tried to tell you, but no…

I couldn't breathe. Studying the photos, I found—Nick, Scott, and Doug—the grown up versions. Holy cow.

My Nick had been here the whole time. I should feel angry, betrayed, but I felt numb.

What should I do now? Oh, yeah, my room.

"I should probably go. I need to get ready. Nice to meet you, Grace." I grabbed the door handle.

"What's wrong, honey?" She put a hand on my arm, and I sucked in a breath.

"I think someone is in my villa. I have to go back to the main desk and get things worked out." I lied, but it wasn't a complete lie.

"Let me see your key, and I'll call for you. We'll get everything straightened out."

I pulled the folder with the keys out of my bag and handed it to her. Her dainty hands opened it and picked one up. "Oh, nineteen. That's just a few doors down."

"Nineteen?" I started laughing. "I thought it was sixty-one."

"Oh." She turned it upside down. "You can tell because the resort logo is on the bottom here." She pointed and then returned it to me.

"There's no problem then. Nothing a hot shower can't fix." I nodded and waved. "Thanks." With each step, I found it harder to breathe.

CHAPTER FIFTEEN

NUMBER NINETEEN WAS THREE DOORS away from the Tanner's private villa. I swiped the keycard and stomped through the living space directly into the master bedroom. I balled my trembling hands.

Glancing around the room, a flat screen TV was mounted on the wall over a wide dresser, and my clothing hung in the closet. I opened the dresser and found my underwear and bras in one and socks and other accessories in another.

Stepping into the luxurious bathroom, I stared into the large mirror. I had a slight pinkness to my cheeks from being in the sun.

"Cole, I can't believe you didn't tell me who you were," I lamented with a sob. Gripping the countertop, I inhaled a stuttering breath.

Starting the water, I let it warm while shucking off my clothes. My soul wept while I went through the motions of washing. I missed Cole's touch when I lathered my hair. With my arms wrapped around my legs, I sat in the stream of hot water and let the tears flow.

Anger, relief, excitement, trepidation… Love? All these emotions tugged at my heart and strained my sanity.

I didn't know what to do. Pretend I hadn't found out and carry on with the charade or confront him? Why hadn't he been honest?

I hadn't given him a chance at the beginning. But now… I pressed my palms against my eyelids. I'd talked about him like a lovesick fool.

I turned the water off and dried my body before wrapping my hair in a towel.

But he talked about you, too. Remember? What if he loves you the way you love him?

I shook the thoughts from my head and brushed my hair. I could take my time and style it tonight. Despite the deception, I still loved him.

Listen, from the first time you saw Cole on the cruise ship, you were reminded of Nick. That's because you recognized him. He tried several times to approach you. Mike tried to introduce him. You flat out told him no.

I walked into my bedroom and opened the drawer to get my bathing suit. I had two. I picked up the one piece, then dropped it back. It was aqua and blue. The pattern looked like waves. I lifted the other suit. A string bikini with a red bottom and a white top.

"I like that one better," a velvety baritone voice crooned.

I sucked in a breath and turned around. In the middle of my king-size bed lay Mr. Gorgeous. His hands were behind his head, and he smiled when my gaze raked his completely nude body. His tanned ankles were crossed and his dick flopped to the right.

Oh, my God! I scurried into the bathroom and locked the door.

Chicken.

In my hand, I still held the bikini. I put it on and waited, wringing the towel. Taking deep breaths, I counted the seconds until Cole would rescue me.

"Vanessa, darling. Come out and play with my cock." Mr. Gorgeous' voice was sinfully sweet.

"Nick," I huffed, "Cole, where the hell are you?" I paced the bathroom.

"Nessa," I heard Cole call.

"In the bathroom," I hollered. Desperation made my voice warble. I cracked the door open, spotting Mr. Gorgeous pumping his dick slowly. He focused totally on me. I swung the door wide open.

Cole stood at the entry to my bedroom. His face was red, and he looked like he could kill the man on the bed.

"Cole?"

"Come on." He motioned with his arm. "Let's go."

I took a tentative step forward, pressing my back against the wall, then worked my way around the dresser.

Mr. Gorgeous rolled to his side, letting go of his erection; it flopped down. His head rested in his hand.

With a beautiful smile, he taunted Cole, "You can't compete with me. Don't you understand she wants me? She wants this." He took hold of his dick again.

Ignoring Cole, he stared at me and started pumping his dick, slowly hypnotizing me. I couldn't take my eyes off the erotic scene.

I squeaked when Cole touched my shoulder. I threw my hands around his neck, and he picked me up and carried me out of the room. He lowered my feet to the ground and, hand in hand, we ran out the door.

I didn't have shoes, but I didn't care. I needed to get out of there.

When we reached his family's villa, we stopped and caught our breath. I leaned over, my hands on my knees, sucking in air. Cole kept a hand on my shoulder. I peeked up at him. His eyes were closed. I wondered what he thought about Mr. Gorgeous' attempt to seduce me.

"He didn't want me," I stammered through breaths. "Not really."

Cole's brows knit together. "What do you mean?"

"I didn't excite him. Not even in a bikini."

Cole shook his head.

"I'm serious. He had to, you know," I mimicked a man masturbating, "jerk himself to get hard."

"What a dick."

"I know, right? Did you see the size of that thing? It's a monster. His ding-dong is probably bionic."

Cole took my hand, and we started walking again. This time, we took a path that went behind his villa. "I think you may be right about him." His forehead creased in thought.

"About what? Bionic?"

He snorted and shot me a strange look. "Not about his pecker. About being hired to seduce you. You're a beautiful woman, Vanessa. A man's body will react to a sexy woman, especially if she's checking out his junk. It has a mind of its own. He shouldn't have needed to jerk his gherkin."

I pulled on his arm to stop him. My heart raced and my thoughts stalled. "You think I'm beautiful?"

Cole's features softened, and he touched my face. "You are beautiful, Nessa. Don't let anyone tell you otherwise."

I rose to my tiptoes and threw my arms around his neck. My lips met his with anticipation and longing. I was kissing my first love, Nicholas, again. I melted against him, molding my form to his. He opened his mouth, then moaned when I ravaged it. His hands plunged into my damp hair, holding my head in place.

When we broke apart, we smiled. My face echoed my heart. I needed to gulp air, or I'd pass out from delight.

He still held my hand, even though the bet was over. I didn't mind. It felt right to stay in touch with his body.

As my legs grew stable and my heart slowed, I glanced at his attire, realizing for the first time that he wore navy swim trunks. They were a thin material and showed that he had reacted without needing self-priming. A gray short-sleeve shirt clung to his muscled chest, making me want to touch him all over again.

The blacktopped path wound through the resort gardens, between rows of large blooming bushes with either yellow or pink flowers. Palm shadows shaded our journey.

"You don't think he'll follow us, do you?" I asked.

Yeah. Thinking about the beautiful naked man again.

"I don't want to be stalked." I chewed my lip.

"If he did follow, he'd be running around naked," Cole said, trying to lighten my mood. "You'll be staying with me from now on."

I nodded. I liked that. He took his phone and pushed a button. "Marguerite? I have a request. Can you pack Ms. Warsaw's things and bring them to my personal villa? Yes. No. She was pleased with the size and cleanliness of the rooms. Thank you."

I stared open-mouthed at him. No wonder the staff jumped into action when he spoke—his family owned the resort. He was the boss. I supposed he didn't need to speak another language now that I knew his true identity. I wanted to ask him a million questions about his life, but mostly I longed to kiss him.

Between two bushes, a gravel footpath turned inland. We followed the twisting trail as it started to climb uphill. The vegetation became denser, but the ground became softer and easier to walk on. The temperature rose and bugs buzzed around. I was beginning to think we were trekking to the other side of the island.

I wanted to pause and rest, but Cole seemed a man on a mission. He kept checking his watch, then looking into the distance as if calculating something.

"Are we almost there?" I asked, hoping it hadn't come out as a whine.

He grinned and answered, "Not much further now."

He slowed as the path ended abruptly at a grassy oasis surrounded by trees. We stepped into the open area. The trees thinned, exposing a cascading waterfall. I froze, staring in wonder. What magnificent thing would he show me tomorrow?

The water bounced down a high cliff face into a pond about the size of a backyard swimming pool. A pink sand beach offered tempting access to take a dip.

"Come on," Cole said, tugging me gently. "Over here."

We walked to the edge of the beach, the side hidden by heavy leafed bushes. The current flowed rapidly into the pool. Cole moved a large branch, and I gaped.

"No way." I stepped past a bush and pointed. A water slide hit the pool. It was a dark, almost black substrate. "How in the world is that here?"

"The slide?" He shrugged. "Dad had it built when we were younger. Come on." He led the way up the steep slope to the top. From the top, we couldn't see the pool. He kicked off his slides and tugged off his shirt. I touched his belly, combing his hair with my fingers.

"Would you like to go first?" He caught my hand and leaned to give me a quick kiss.

"Sure." He held onto my hand as I stepped into the water at the top of the slide, then sat. The water felt refreshing. I scooted to the edge where he indicated, then without warning, he placed his hand in the middle of my back and pushed. I screamed as I jetted down the side of the cliff. I went under when I hit the deep pool.

Ugh, salt water. It stung my eyes as it dripped.

Cole's laughter echoed as he slid down the slide. He hit the water like a pro and didn't even get his hair wet.

His eyes squinted as he looked at me. "You're all wet."

I chopped the water, sending a giant splash in his direction. He started laughing.

For the next half hour, we used the water slide and swam in the pool, all to the ambient sound of the falls.

Questions churned in my mind like the current at the bottom of the fall, but I was loathe to ruin our time together.

"We need to go soon," Cole said when we were once again on top of the cliff.

"Oh?" I turned to face him and closed the distance, putting my arms around him. "Are you going to show me something else?"

He touched his lips to mine, and my tongue darted out, earning a moan. "I've got plans, remember?"

"Dinner and a movie."

"Dinner and a show," he grinned, and his hands slid over my hips. "Would you like to go down the slide on your stomach? It's fun."

"Like Superman?" Sure, why not? The surface was slippery. I laid down in the water on my stomach. Cole knelt next to me, touching my back. His face became serious. "What's wrong?" I asked.

"Your bikini bow is coming untied."

"Fix it, please."

After he retied it, he massaged my shoulders. I slowly moved out of the pool area. "That feels great. You're hired. Let's skip dinner and just go with a massage."

"I need dinner for energy because I plan to massage you everywhere all night long." Cole pushed my butt, sending me down the slide.

I stretched out my arms in front of me, trying to keep the water out of my face, but it didn't work. The water sprayed in my eyes, nose, and mouth. I felt my bikini top shift but couldn't stop the momentum. When I hit the pool, I went under but skimmed the surface. I coughed and stood up when Cole entered the water.

"I like your bathing suit," he said, looking at my chest. Glancing down, I wore nothing on top. I crossed my arms to cover my breasts, but he'd seen everything.

When I heard voices over the sound of the waterfall, I glanced over my shoulder, then back at Cole.

The tease left his face when the smile fell off it. He pointed to the beach near the path. "Go."

"What about my top?"

"I'll find it in a minute."

I sat on the pink sand with my knees pressed to my chest and my arms wrapped around my legs. He moved my hair, so it covered my back. He winked and dashed into the water. He swam to the far side of the pool and dove under.

A man in a white polo and black shorts came into view, walking backward. A group of people followed him. They all had their phone or cameras out taking pictures.

"This waterfall was used in the movie Bikini Breach. They took three weeks to film it. The crew all got sunburnt." He laughed and turned. If he was shocked to see me, he didn't show it.

"Bikini Breach? Never heard of it," someone mumbled.

"It's an adult movie," the guide said. A collective wave of ahs rose from the group. After they took a few pictures, the group moved on. "Down this way, we have the beach house they used as a prop."

Cole walked through the water over to me, then knelt in the sand. His pockets leaked water. Less than an inch of a string from my suit hung out of his pocket, but he made no effort to give it back. He stroked my head, moving my hair.

I smiled at him. "Did you find my top?"

He shook his head but sported a sheepish grin. "I couldn't find it. I think it got sucked down the filter."

"Well, I guess the tourists can get a few pictures of me topless." I stretched my legs out and leaned back on my arms, pressing my chest out.

His gazed dropped, then his hand reached out, grazing my tight nipple. The sensation went straight through to my core.

His mouth fell to mine, consuming. His hand cupped my breast, thumbing my nipple. His other hand snaked behind me and pulled me closer.

Deciding he wouldn't be the only one fondling the goods, my fingers teased under his trunks' leg until I rubbed the mesh of his suit. He moaned into my mouth.

He pushed me back against the sand, his weight on top of me, grinding. Our kiss became fevered.

People's voices, laughing and talking, floated over the sound of our passion. Cole rested his forehead on mine, catching his breath. "Okay. Let's head to the path and grab our stuff at the slide."

"Your stuff. All I have is my bikini bottom unless you want to shove that in your other pocket."

He winked at me, then rose and offered me a hand up. I covered my breasts with one arm and used the other for balance.

Once again, my hair was ruined by salt water and my feet were dirty. Cole followed me up the trail, playfully tugging on the string of my bottoms.

At the crest, Cole stepped into his slides. I ogled his junk straining his swim trunks, wishing we had more time. He picked up his shirt and tossed it to me. I put it on.

He placed a sweet kiss on my lips and tugged me forward once more. "I see that look in your eye. We'll do something about it later." His lips lifted in a smirk.

"Tease." I couldn't help sticking out my tongue.

CHAPTER SIXTEEN

"Back to the villa?" I asked Cole, anxious to learn more about the show he'd promised me.

His hair was dark and damp, and I touched it. "Your blond looks natural, but I like your hair brown. I've always liked it."

"I know." He hugged me. "You might kill me, but we need to walk awhile again. We aren't going back to the resort."

"Another beachside shack?"

He laughed. "You considered that a shack?"

I put my hands on my hips. "It didn't have any walls."

The breeze blew my hair, and he tucked a wayward strand behind my ear.

"This one has walls—well, some are windows, and an indoor bathroom, including a fancy shower where I can wash your hair." He picked up a strand and brought it to his nose. Closing his eyes, he sniffed.

"Somebody has a hair fetish," I mumbled through a smile.

We started down a path that followed the ridge of the cliff. The gravel was lava rocks and hurt my feet. I had to walk slowly.

Cole lowered and said, "Get on my back. I don't want you to cut your feet." I climbed on and he carried me piggyback.

"Don't you remember why I like your hair?"

As he walked, my head next to his ear, my arms around his neck and my ankles hooked in front, I shifted through the memories. His earlobe became too tempting to resist, and I took it between my teeth gently, then licked it.

"Nessa," he groaned as he stumbled. "Better not distract me. I wouldn't want to fall down the hill." He paused. "Have you remembered about your hair yet?"

I rested my head against his and sighed. "Prom?"

He nodded and his hands squeezed my thighs. Warmth spread through my body. I closed my eyes. "That was a magical night," I whispered in his ear.

"Because you got to see me naked?" He chuckled.

"That was a bonus." I giggled.

Because of my father's disdain for Nick, I had to pretend to not have a date to prom. My best friend picked me up, and we met our dates at a restaurant. We went to the dance from there.

Roni had had a date and flaunted it. I knew she'd show up eventually, but she'd be late because I'd called the restaurant where Roni's posse had reservations and made them an hour later.

It wasn't my best moment, but it bought Nick and me some time. We danced and had our pictures taken. I took separate pictures with my best friend in case dad wanted some kind of proof we stayed together.

Roni sent me a picture of her food and her friends in the limo they had rented. Nick and I made our exit before my sister arrived. I told her I had a headache from the loud thumping music, and I was heading to my friend's house for a slumber party, hoping she'd buy the story. She did, and luckily Roni's partying fun distracted her from focusing on torturing me.

My friend and I, and our boyfriends, headed to a hotel where each couple had a room. Nick and I went to our room. Our secret aloneness and physical desires made me nervous and excited. We started making out. He unzipped my dress, then made quick work of his shirt and pants.

We'd rolled around in our underwear before, but this time it was different. Even though Nick was a freshman in college, I knew I was his first. When he unhooked my strapless bra, I couldn't believe the look of wonder on his face. I felt beautiful. He touched me with reverence. We gave everything to each other.

Our second time, later that night, I let my hair trail over his skin. I started at his feet and worked my way over his legs, tickling him. He squirmed under the sweet torture. I took my time on his groin, swiping my hair back and forth over his erection. He was ticklish on his sides and, as I finally covered his face with my long locks, he gripped my hips. I claimed his lips.

I sighed at the memory, rubbing my hands on his chest. "Would you like a repeat performance?"

He laughed low. "You know it, sweetheart."

Cole continued to trek along the narrow path. The branches hung over the trail, and occasionally, I had to duck. In the humid tropical heat, I started to sweat, and I know Cole had to ache from carrying me.

"Do you want to stop and rest?" I asked, concerned when he tripped on a root.

"I'm good." He turned his head and kissed my cheek. I used my legs to give him a body hug.

I tried another tactic. "Would you like to stop and make out?" I wiggled my eyebrows.

"That sounds good." He glanced around. "Just around that next curve, we'll stop, okay?" He trotted, and the ground crunched.

He set me down, and I stretched my legs. I raised my arms over my head.

He arched his back, then moved side to side, stretching. I rested against the trunk of a palm tree; the bark was coarse but stringy in some places. It was wider than my body and it felt good to lean on it and watch my beautiful man stretch.

Cole caught my eye and sauntered over to me, placing one arm on either side of my shoulder. He tilted his head and kissed me. A sweet, tender kiss.

He pulled back and our eyes locked. I stroked the hair on his chest, feeling the dips of his muscles. His hungry gaze canvassed my body. Finally, his lips closed in on mine again.

I hooked my leg around his and yanked him roughly against me. He groaned and his hands cupped my face. After a few breaths, one dropped away. The roaming hand ventured under my shirt, rubbing first my belly before finding my breast. He gently squeezed it, making me hot all over.

My hands explored his back and my leg held him tight to me.

Cole whispered against my lips, "I want to taste you here." His hand dropped to the apex between my legs, and I shivered. "But I have plans." He kept rubbing me there, and my eyes rolled back in my head.

"Holy hijinks." I dropped my leg, giving him better access. He nudged my thighs further apart. "Right now?" I glanced in both directions down the path.

"Right here, right now." He slid a finger under the material and stroked me. "I'm going to make you feel good. Later, I will taste you everywhere."

His finger glided between my folds and circled my clit. He pushed away and his other hand slipped under the material of my bottoms, and both his hands ravaged me. I flopped my head back and hummed my pleasure.

"Open your eyes, Nessa." Cole kissed my lips. "Open your eyes." When I complied; he smiled and said, "Watch."

My red bikini bottoms were getting plundered. One finger entered me. He started moving it in and out. I gasped and held his shoulder.

Groping the front of his bathing suit for the package that strained against the material there, I rubbed, mimicking the timing of him in me. It wouldn't take me long.

"Kiss me, please?" I whimpered.

His lips covered mine and our tongues dueled, hard and wet.

Fire consumed me. My tenderest area throbbed with longing. "Two fingers, now. Faster."

He acquiesced with a grunt and moved, grinding his dick against my hand.

Heat pooled at my core, and I threw my head back as I climaxed. My fingernails dug into his shoulder flesh as I cried out his name. He kept moving, slowing and eventually pulling out all together.

He held me until my legs felt strong enough to stand without support. I took a staggering step onto the trail. I turned to face Cole, and he wore that smartass smirk.

Something in me snapped, and I reacted by pushing him against the trunk, kissing him while fondling his junk. His hands plunged into my hair and held my face close.

I kept rubbing while my other hand worked on loosening his trunks' tie. Finally, it loosened, and I pulled the front down enough to free his package. One hand caressed his sack while the other jerked him off. He moaned into my mouth, but I wouldn't stop kissing him. I couldn't.

I wanted to inspect and taste his manly bits, but I had to settle with touching his long hardness and the velvety smoothness of his boner. His sack pulled tight against his body. I knew he was going to explode. A moment later, his body was racked with seizure-like tremors as he orgasmed. I pulled back and gazed into his eyes.

Christ, I loved his cerulean eyes. It felt like I could see into the future.

He kissed my nose. And tucked his junk away. He pulled my bikini top out of his pocket and offered it to me to clean my hand.

"Aw, playtime is over, but I want to play some more." I teased, wiping my hands.

"Nessa, if you don't stop touching me. I will take you right here. And I hadn't planned on making love to you on a trail." He caressed my cheek. His face was tinged pink and his breath still rapid. He turned and said, "Hop on."

"I get to ride you again?" I laughed when he inhaled. I climbed on his back and locked my ankles again. He practically ran down a small hill and around a curve. The main route turned, but we continued straight.

"Hey, I think you missed the trail." I pointed back the way we came.

"Nope. Look up."

I tilted my head and glanced through the treetops, seeing a steep cliff face. Something glinted in the sunlight. "Is that a building?"

"Yep."

As we neared, I noticed a zigzag path that connected the ground to the building. "Oh no, are those stairs?"

"Yep."

When we reached the sand, he set me down, and we walked to a beach directly in front of the small building up on the hillside. I could see the mouth of the stairwell. He threaded our fingers, and we approached the base of the stairs.

"At the top of these stairs is your home for as long as you stay." He gestured upwards. "I guarantee Mr. Suck-It will not find you here. And I will not let you out of my sight, either."

I leaned against him. "Promise?"

He kissed my nose. "I promise."

We started climbing the wood stairs; but at the second landing, Cole stopped and pointed toward the ocean. I gasped at the view. Three yachts with rainbow sails headed in the direction of the resort. "Beautiful."

After catching our breath and enjoying the landscape, we began ascending again. It appeared only half of the building was built on solid ground, with the rest cantilevered over the edge. I studied the supports, holding it up.

As we closed in on the private villa, the last set of stairs was concrete. We crested the top, finally arriving at a large square patio. The floor was tiled and the half walls stucco. A metal table and chairs plus two loungers were arranged across the space.

I walked to the edge, and gripping it, I inhaled the salty tang of the sea breeze. I soaked in the panoramic view—tan beach, rolling surf, and the blue horizon where sky met water.

Cole's arms encircled me, and I leaned back onto him, relaxing in the perfection of the moment. He kissed the top of my head, and we stood in comfortable silence.

A buzzer rang, startling us.

Cole pulled away but took my hand and led me through a sliding door built into a glass wall. He let go and walked to the main entry, but I stayed at the threshold, hovering and inspecting the space.

The bedroom was simply decorated with one king sized bed covered by a solid white blanket and pillows. Each side of the bed had a small espresso wood table and a decorative lamp with a white shade. Behind the bed was a wall without windows but with a painting and two doors, one beside each of the nightstands. Hopefully, one of the doors led to a bathroom.

The wall with the entry door where Cole stood also had no windows, but against it was a dresser, a full-length mirror, and metal art. The wall opposite Cole was floor to ceiling glass like the patio wall. I walked over to the glass wall. It was a grand view.

Cole stepped outside, exchanging words with a man in a foreign language. I knew he had something planned.

With only one bed, I started anticipating how soon we

would make love. I hugged myself and tried to calm my rapid breathing.

We'd trailed sand inside. I frowned and looked down at my legs. Yuck. Grimy and soiled. I needed another shower. Or, at least, a foot bath.

I turned the handle on the door nearest me and pushed it open. The wall continued on as glass. A white commode sat directly in front of me. The floor was dark stone square tiles. Daylight lit the space.

A floor to ceiling see-through wall in the bathroom? Anyone could spy you doing your business. But there wasn't anyone on the beach.

There was a pocket door separating the toilet from the rest of the bathroom. I opened the door and stood in amazement. The room was long with double basin sinks, each with a waterfall faucet set into a dark wood vanity. Small bamboo floor mats had been placed by each sink and the shower entry.

The shower—oh wow.

Dark brown stone tiles lined the floor and walls. The walls had a few niches for shampoos and soaps.

I shouldn't have been surprised to see my shampoo and conditioner brand was in the bathroom already. In the far corner of the shower, there was a seat wide enough for two people to sit side by side. There wasn't a curtain or frosted glass door, it was a long, clear glass wall with an opening. You could watch whoever was showering while you brushed your teeth. There were many water jets, but the feature that excited me most was the rain showerhead.

I pulled open a vanity drawer and found cream colored towels and washcloths. Extra soap, too. On the other side of the vanity and shower were two doors—one was open to the bedroom. The other I opened.

"What the…?" I gasped at the size of the closet. It ran the width of the building. The tan, ten-foot walls had wood fixtures. Rows of glass blocks edged the outer wall ceiling, keeping the room light and airy.

One part had men's shirts hanging and the bar below had pressed trousers on hangers. Floating shelves divided the hanging clothes sections. Men's shoes lined the three lower shelves while women's shoes filled the rest.

My heart lurched. How many women had Cole brought here? Not that I had any right to know.

I stepped closer and inspected a pair of platinum gray heels. They looked like a pair I owned, so did the sandals next to them. Actually, all the shoes were replicas of ones I owned. *Wait. Those are my shoes.*

On the next bar hung my dresses, shirts, and pants. My under garments were arranged in two drawers, one for undies and the other for bras. I shook my head in awe. I know Cole orchestrated it, but still, I couldn't believe the preciseness and professionalism displayed.

"What do you think? Cole asked, waving his arm and making me jump.

"The closet is awesome." I spied the full-length mirror by the door for the first time. "Thanks for having my clothes brought here."

"Oh, no problem." He scratched the back of his head, and a sly grin formed. "But I don't think you'll be needing them."

I crossed my arms. "Oh, really." I tried to keep a straight face.

"Mr. Tanner?" A man called.

"Be right there." Sighing, Cole turned to leave the

room. "I'll be back in a minute."

He exited, and I leaned to watch him. He stalked through the bathroom toward the entry door, where the man waited for him.

"Here's tonight's special menu, sir," the man said.

Cole took the sheet and studied it. After a moment, he glanced over his shoulder and met my eyes. I nodded, and he grinned.

I turned back to gawking at the closet while listening to Cole order for us.

My stomach growled. At this point, I'd eat anything. Like Cole had stated, I needed to keep my strength up.

CHAPTER SEVENTEEN

IN THE MIRROR, I STUDIED my greasy hair with a crooked part. *Ugh. Not sexy.*

Also reflected was the tempting shower. I opened the drawer and picked up a fuzzy towel. I hung it on the bar and stepped out of my bottoms, then pulled off Cole's shirt. I stepped onto the cool tile. The faucet handle moved only one way. Water gently rained down, and I adjusted the temperature.

I longed to wash away the briny grime and feel clean. I shifted into the stream and raised my face.

I squeezed some shampoo into my palm and started to lather it in my hair.

"Not without me," Cole said.

I wiped water from my face and whipped my head around as he stripped off his shorts. He smiled, not at all shy, and stepped behind me. Hair circled his belly button, then dipped lower, and as my gaze raked his body, his dick reacted. His arms encircled me, his erection firm against my backside.

Even though water rained over me, heat threatened to consume me. I needed his hands to roam everywhere— claim everything.

Cole worked the shampoo into a lather. I froze. The tingles started at my scalp and traveled to my toes. "You are *so* hired," I moaned.

He chuckled and began massaging my neck. "You've already hired me. Three times, I think."

We moved into the stream and the suds ran down my back and arms. Cole continued to knead my back.

"You're going to spoil me." I mewled.

"That's the idea." He lifted my hair off my neck and nipped me.

"How the hell am I ever going to take a shower alone ever again?"

Stop your bellyaching.

Right. This is an awesome problem to have.

"If I have a choice, you won't." Next, he massaged my buttocks. I hummed my pleasure while he reached around my hips and started working his way up my stomach. His erection rubbed my butt, igniting my core. His hands caressed my breasts in circular motions, and I pushed back against him, earning a nipple tweak.

He stretched past me and uncapped the conditioner. He dove into my hair with a gentle ferocity that amazed me. God, I loved his touch.

When I couldn't stand it any longer, I spun in his arms, my nipples grazing his chest hair. I molded myself to him. He tilted my head back, and we entered the cascading water once more. His fingers combed my hair several times to remove the product.

Relaxed under the water, eyes closed, his lips touched mine. My arms eased over his shoulders, and I played with his damp hair. He licked the seam of my lips, and I opened for him. His tongue teased mine.

Staying forever in his arms wasn't a logical choice—the hot water would run out eventually, but my heart was so full, it prevented me from moving. We stayed locked in the erotic embrace for an unknown time.

I finally broke the kiss. My arms dropped, and I groped his firm rear in an attempt at a massage. "My turn."

I uncapped the bottle, and as I shampooed his head, he bent and took my nipple in his mouth. Waves of desire coursed through me, but I had a task to complete even as I held his head in place.

I stepped backward into the water. Once in the stream, Cole straightened and tilted his head back, rinsing.

I skimmed my fingers down his chest, not stopping until I had a firm grasp of his erection. He was big but not porn star ginormous like Mr. Gorgeous had been. I knew for a fact, his dick was Vanessa sized. "Mine," I claimed.

Cole moaned and squeezed my shoulders, and I released my hold.

He adjusted nozzles I hadn't noticed before. The seat warmed and steam rose from small holes.

"Sit here." He motioned to the tiled seat. He knelt before me, and pulled me to the edge and parted my legs.

"I'm going to taste you now." His gaze locked on mine and his fingers touched my seam, coaxing it open. His head dipped, and he kissed my inner thigh.

"Oh yes, I could get used to this."

His tongue explored my slit, and I gripped his shoulders, trying not to squirm. My blood boiled.

"Oh my God," I uttered, need seeping into my voice,

"I want you."

Truth bomb!

"How about this?" He slid two fingers in deep, and I was floating. A river of desire had me flying high. He played my body like a Vanessa master. I climaxed as his tongue lapped my clit.

I leaned forward, and he caught me in his arms. We sat on the tiled floor, steam swirling around us like a comforting blanket. The man had rendered my legs totally useless with the flick of his tongue.

"Are you ready for dinner?" he asked, as his finger trailed down my cheek, neck, and over the swell of my breast.

"How about dessert?" I countered, touching his balls. "I want to taste you, too."

"Soon."

I wouldn't relinquish my hold.

"Nessa, you'll undo me, and I want to take my time loving you tonight."

"Fine," I pouted.

We toweled each other off, like we had in the dark, but this time we could see all our bits. He handed me a fluffy robe from a drawer, then took one out for himself. We put them on. The Dancing Winds logo was embroidered on each robe and we looked like a commercial for the resort.

He picked up the brush, and we exited the bathroom. I followed him to the patio. It was a strangely private oasis. He sat on the lounge and tapped the seat between his legs, beckoning me. I complied.

As he brushed my hair, I confessed, "You make me feel like a princess."

"You're my princess."

"But Prince Charming doesn't do servant stuff." I tilted my head.

"Prince Charming?" He pulled the brush through my hair. I loved his hair fetish. "I'm more like a frog."

"You were never a frog. You were always a prince." I turned around to look him in the eye. "You were always a prince inside and out, but your brother might have been a toad."

"And your sister's a witch."

I chuckled and spun back around. He continued brushing long after it all had been untangled.

"Oh." I'd noticed the table had candles and covered trays. "When did this happen?"

He shifted my hair off my neck and kissed where it met my shoulder. "When I was sampling you." I shivered at his warm breath breezing across my skin.

We moved to the table and uncovered the platters. There were several seafood dishes, vegetables and rice. We sampled all the plates, even fed each other. We laughed and held hands. As the sky darkened, stars started to appear. It was going to be another beautiful night. I sighed happily.

Cole stared up at the stars with a little boy look of wonder on his face.

"Why the hell didn't I go find you?" I asked.

He closed his eyes and his brow crinkled. In a soft voice, he said, "We both had some growing up to do."

That's a sucky answer. Why didn't he come find you?

Ask him.

He stared into the unfathomable depths of the night sky and, as if reading my mind, he said, "Once, I came for you."

I put both feet on the ground and positioned my chair, so I was directly in front of him. My heart galloped as I waited, letting him pick his words.

"I came to Warsaw Industries' executive offices and spoke with the receptionist. Your sister passed me on her way in but didn't say anything. Minutes later, your father took me to an office and told me you were seeing someone, and it was serious."

Cole swallowed and turned to face me. He reached out his arm and his fingers touched my cheek. "I should have talked to you. Found out the truth from you, but your father seemed," he paused, "reasonable. He even thanked me for coming and kind of apologized for being an asshole. He didn't use that term, mind you. He told me he'd been under a lot of stress from your mom's illness and reacted stronger than he should have."

"Wow. If you got that much, that's good." I sighed and took his hand. I brought it to my lips. "You should have talked with me. I might have kissed you."

"You can do that now."

"Maybe," I teased. He leaned toward me. "Isn't dessert being delivered?" I asked innocently blinking.

"I can call for something if you'd like or," he parted his robe, "you can have this." He pointed to his dick, which rose for the occasion.

Girl, you don't even have a choice.

I jumped to my feet, shucking the robe. It landed next to him. In two breaths, I kneeled, sucking his dick like I was the thirstiest woman alive.

"Nessa," Cole moaned with longing. He leaned back as I rubbed his balls. I glanced at him, catching his hooded gaze.

I worked harder to please him, swirling my tongue around his head.

Then I decided to play. I released him. Offering an impish grin, I swiped his groin with my hair before going back to work.

In one long stroke, I licked his cock from base to tip. He shuddered and my heart filled with a yearning to pleasure him.

I stroked his shaft while eyeing his balls. One at a time, I sucked the delectable morsels. He moaned and gripped the chair's arms as if I tortured him.

More!

"Enough!" he rasped.

Glancing at him through my lashes, I smiled wickedly then took his length in my mouth again, nearly swallowing it whole.

Cole launched upward, pulling his dick out of my mouth and nearly knocking me to the ground. Before I could scramble to my feet, he lifted me and carried me to the bed. He tossed me, and I landed on my back.

He crawled over me, kissing as he went, although he didn't pause anywhere long. His dick had other ideas. He rested his weight on me and kissed my lips. Hard. I moaned and hooked my leg around his waist, rubbing his erection against my swollen clit.

He rolled to the left and reached out of my line of sight. In seconds, although it seemed like minutes, he slipped a condom on. His finger lingered near my wet spot, stroking me.

"If you don't make love to me right now, I'm going to roll you over and ride you until you're blind."

His lips parted in a smile, and he chuckled. "Yes, ma'am. I aim to please."

"Please me faster."

He nudged my legs wide apart then, and, with his eyes fixed on mine, plunged in. My body tightened and flexed, and we both moaned.

"God, you feel good." I uttered as he started to move.

"So do you." He breathed against my flesh, giving me goosebumps.

He pressed up and gazed down at me, his expression tender. My heart thumped; I thought it might swell so full it'd explode.

Making love to him was more than physical—it was spiritual. Our fingers became entwined, and we stared into one another's eyes. He found a rhythm, and I surged up to meet his thrusts. Our bodies were joined, our hearts united.

A light sweat broke out. The tempo changed, becoming charged and hurried. I gasped as my orgasm hit. My body clenched his, and he jerked as his apogee hit.

Spent, he lowered himself and gently caressed my face. He kissed me, then got up to visit the bathroom.

The rest of the night we cuddled, made love twice more and stayed awake long enough to watch the sunrise. When exhaustion found me, I rested safe in Cole's arms.

CHAPTER EIGHTEEN

"BE QUIET. SHE'S ASLEEP," COLE whispered.

My eyes fluttered open and I yawned. My arm hung off the bed as I gazed out the window at the powder blue sky and the foaming surf.

I sighed happily and was about to roll over when I heard a woman's soft voice reply, "Yes, sir. We'll be fast and quiet."

Cole pulled the sheet over my back, and I didn't move. The door creaked open and shuffling footsteps crossed the floor. I tipped my head, so my hair fell away enough to see three pairs of legs in the patio area.

Someone clanged something and the feminine voice hushed them.

They shuffled out. I turned my head to see if everyone had gone.

I spied Cole in the white fluffy robe sitting at the table, pouring two cups of coffee. He fixed one with just a hint of cream and one spoonful of sugar. It was for me. He put half a cow in the next cup.

"You remember how I take my coffee? That's impressive," I teased, rising from the edge of the bed. He handed me my robe and then the cup of coffee.

I sipped the steaming liquid and settled into a chair in the late morning sunlight. Inhaling the bold dark roast aroma, I lifted my face to the sky.

"I remember many things about you," he said, clinking his mug to mine.

"You sure know how to make me moan."

He almost snorted out coffee.

"That's something I aim to perfect." He arched a brow, daring me to disagree.

"I'm all for that." I sipped my coffee. Heat flushed my face, and I glanced at the domed metal serving dishes.

"Hungry?"

"Other than for you? Maybe a little. Bacon. Everything is better with bacon."

He lifted a lid. A plethora of breads, muffins, jams and butter had been artfully arranged on the charger. The next container held scrambled eggs, country ham, and bacon. The third container boasted fruit salad.

"Wow. Quite the spread." The scents tempted my tastebuds, and I licked my lips.

Cole handed me a plate, then picked up a scoop and tongs. "What would you like?"

I pointed to the items, and he placed them on my plate. "Thank you."

He poured us each an orange juice and then sat down with his plate.

As we ate, we reminisced about the past.

"Did you know your mother and mine had planned our wedding?" he asked, staring out at the sea.

"I know," I said wistfully. Before she died, my mother and I picked out a dress. Tears stung my eyes, and I took great care cutting my ham.

"I'm sorry, Nessa." He frowned and reached out and patted my hand. "I didn't mean for you to relive the pain."

"It's not that." I closed my eyes and dabbed the corners. "Mom wanted Roni and I to be happy. Thinking I would be married to you one day made me happy, and my mother, too. She encouraged me to get to know you and your family, despite how my father behaved. Mom knew I believed you were the one. She saw how much we loved each other. She was happy for me—for us."

Cole sat back, stunned. I'd just dumped a whole heaping of past pressure on him. I'd mentioned the L word and the M word.

Might as well go for the gold.

I sighed and met Cole's eyes. "We bought the dress."

"What do you mean?" he leaned forward, rubbing his chin.

"Mom ordered my wedding dress before she died." I swallowed, holding his gaze.

To his credit, he didn't appear frightened or freaked.

"We ordered it, but it didn't arrive before she died. She had it delivered to your mother instead of our home because of my father." I inhaled.

"Mom never told me."

My mother's funeral had been the hardest time for my family. Hard on my father because he'd lost the love of his life. Hard on my sister and me because we'd lost our advocate and best friend.

I couldn't talk to Dad. He'd withdrawn from the world, and Roni had turned into a royal bitch. My father had banned me from the one person who I wanted to hold me.

"Thank you for sneaking into town for the funeral." My voice was rough. I glanced at him through tears.

"God himself couldn't have kept me away. I loved you too much to not be there. You needed me."

I had. Like a body needs water and air, I'd needed him. "You gave me hope." I nodded.

The day of the funeral, I'd gone through the motions. They told me to stand there, sit here. On automatic pilot, I complied. Many faces filtered through the line, complimenting my mother and offering empty condolences.

Other people's tears flowed, but I had yet to weep.

Then I saw Mrs. Tanner. She motioned to me with a subtle shoulder movement. I excused myself, claiming a bathroom break. Outside, she handed me a card to a local hotel with a room number on the back. She embraced me, holding me until Veronica had been sent to find me.

The rest of the day, I'd touched that tangible hope in my pocket. The Tanners, minus Nick, stayed and even went to the graveside with us. Afterward, at our home, my aunts, uncles, cousins, and other family friends reminisced and fed us. They'd told stories, and I'd feigned interest. I couldn't believe my mother was gone.

"She was too young to die," I told Cole. "It's not fair."

I sniffed, sounding like a child. It'd been ten years, and the wounded little girl still lived. "She was such a sweet woman. Why couldn't it have been Dad instead of Mom?"

"Hey."

Wincing, I said, "I know, but he was horrible to you.

I became caged after the incident, not that I wanted to go anywhere. Roni went out and partied while I stayed home and moped."

"Thank you for meeting me that night." I gazed into those deep blue eyes and smiled. My heart soared, remembering.

"It was my pleasure."

"It was both of our pleasures." I chuckled and closed my eyes. The sunshine caressed my body, and I stretched like a contented cat as I continued the memory.

I'd left my depressing house without a word, hoping no one saw me. I knocked on room 315. Nick opened the door. He'd lit candles and had my favorite foods, but I wasn't hungry. The room had a jacuzzi, and the air was damp and warm.

I fell into Nick's arms and wept for the first time. He'd held me as I grieved, letting me vent and handing me tissues.

Soon I'd kissed him. Then we were naked. He loved me slowly.

We soaked in the hot tub and relaxed, and I cried some more. I stayed in seclusion with him for three days. I looked like shit, with purple bags under my puffy, red eyes. I hardly ate and, if it hadn't been for Nick prodding me into the shower to bathe, I don't think I would have.

"Do you still have it?" Cole asked, cocking his head like a lizard.

"Have what?" I asked, drawn from the past.

"The dress."

I blinked, then looked away. Of course, I'd kept it. It

would be the dress I got married in, no matter who or when I married. My mom bought it for me. It was her one contribution to my wedding, and I'd never give it up. "Yes."

"Good. Is it at your place?" He stood and refilled his coffee.

"No." I paused when he lifted his brow, giving me a curious look. "I couldn't keep it there. I didn't want Roni to have access to it. She'd either ruin it or wear it. I couldn't let that happen."

Cole nodded and sat back down. Putting his coffee to his lips, he stretched his legs out on the lounger. His robe parted, and the slit exposed the tip of his relaxed penis. I refilled my cup, pulling my gaze away from his body.

"Good thinking. Hiding it away." When I didn't offer any more, he asked, "Where is it, Nessa?"

I took my coffee, walked to the glass banister, and leaned against the railing. Gazing at the ocean view, the breeze blew my hair from my face.

"Do you really want to know?" I twisted towards him, studying his curious features. "You might not believe me."

His lips tilted into a lopsided grin. "Well, it's not hanging in my closet." He crossed his arms.

I bit my lip and sighed, hoping he'd accept the revelation. "Close. Your mother's."

Cole's grin dropped and his eyes widened. "No shit."

He stood and started pacing the small patio, his brow furrowed in thought. "All this time, Mom has been in on it."

Worry gnawed at my gut. He didn't appear angry, but I wouldn't want him to hold anything against his mother.

"Your mother has been a godsend to me." Picking up my coffee, I took a large gulp, enjoying the robust flavor. "I've kept in touch with her. She's the one who recommended coming here."

Cole spun around with surprise on his face. "I see."

I frowned. "You see what?"

"My mother." He came near and touched my face. "She played matchmaker."

"It kinda worked."

He chuckled and placed his forehead against mine. "Yes, it did."

He kissed my nose. I wiggled my fingers between the opening of his robe and touched his pecs. He nudged me back to the table and scooped some fruit salad into a bowl. I took the offered bowl and spooned a bite into my mouth.

He settled onto the lounge once more with his own bowl. Cole's features turned introspective.

"My mother mentioned that someone named Vanessa Warsaw booked an extended stay. She gave me the dates and told me I needed a vacation. When I asked her if she thought it was you, she told me probably not. So, here I am wondering if you're you. Then Mike shows up and wants to know why I've drank a whole six-pack. He took me out and bought me more." Cole chuckled and rubbed his scruff. "I suppose I was pretty verbal about what we had, and he dared me to go find out if it was you."

He raised his mug in salute. "The rest is history."

"Did you know it was me right away?" I asked. My heart pounded. He shifted again and the robe split, exposing his junk.

His brows formed a V. "Not at first, I mean, you looked like you, but you didn't act like you. I didn't think it was Veronica. You were subdued, but Veronica would have pouted and bitched instead of sitting quietly and observing. You acted wounded. Hurt. Skittish."

Cole leaned forward, and his robe jerked open a little more. I could see his balls, and I wanted to touch them.

"I didn't want to scare you, so Mike and I watched you. Then he came up with that stupid bet."

"Why didn't you tell me who you were?" I asked, my heart fluttered.

"I can't believe it took you so long to figure it out."

"Well, from the start, you reminded me of Nick."

"I am Nick."

"No, you're Cole."

He crossed his arms with a laugh, not at all offended.

"Listen to me Nicholas Arlington Tanner. The boy I fell in love with doesn't exist anymore. He was cute, sweet, smart, and protective, but this Cole guy—he's a man, not a boy. You're inches taller than when we dated. You've got a ton of muscles and a beard he didn't have."

"I'm not cute, sweet, smart, and protective?"

"I'm not saying that Cole, you're sexy as sin and super protective. You outsmarted Mr. Gorgeous and Mike. You've been kind and sweet to me, but respectful and not condescending. What I'm trying to say is that you're not a boy anymore, you've matured."

I wanted to add that I loved him more now than I ever had, but the words stalled in my throat.

"Tragedy and hardship create maturity and make you retrospective."

"Tragedy?" I didn't know what he'd lost, but I understood. "I'm sorry."

Cole shook his head. "Nessa, don't be sorry. The

greatest tragedy in my life was when I let you go. You were the one sure thing in my future. The one who loved and accepted me, no matter what. You knew me better than my identical brother and could tell us apart. I shouldn't have believed the lie." His brow furrowed, and he made a fist.

"What lie?" I uttered, trying to tamp down suspicion regarding my sister.

"I received a letter from you." He glanced at his lap and straightened his robe. "You broke up with me. I mean, you said you wished me a good life. Long-distance relationships sucked and all that."

"What? I didn't. I would never… I'll kill her," I growled.

Heat radiated off my body; any second I'd explode. I lifted my hands, and they trembled with rage. I balled my fists, clenching them to my sides.

"I'm going to kill my sister." I squeezed my eyes shut and visualized choking the life out of my twin.

When I opened them again, the scenery was washed with unspent tears. "Just because her relationship with Scott didn't work out, didn't mean she had to ruin every relationship I've ever had. We had a right to be happy, dammit."

Cole scanned me, staring at my angry eyes. His inspection stalled about midway. I glanced down to where my robe split, offering a view.

"Where would we be if my crappy family hadn't ruined things?" I mumbled.

His gaze snapped to mine. Without any hesitation, he answered, "Married with kids."

I gasped. Another wave of emotion rolled over me.

You might need a shrink.

I couldn't breathe. All I could do was nod. That future, that blessed future, had been flushed down the crapper by my crazy, lonely sister.

"It hurt her to see us," I said, softly.

That slut doesn't deserve empathy. Again, you need a shrink.

"Seeing us together and happy was like looking at a mirror of a future she'd never have. She fell hard for Scott, but he didn't want to commit. She hated that I had the good twin." I couldn't help the snide smile.

"Scott loved her, though." Cole glanced up at the sky. "That's why he tried again five years later."

"He was a free spirit, and she was…" I paused and waved my hand. "She was Roni. You know what happened between them, right?" I asked.

"The pregnancy?" Cole asked.

"Yes." I'd been sworn to secrecy by my sister, and, even though she was a total bitch, I kept my promises. "Scott's reaction broke her. Roni holed up in her room for a long time afterward. I actually had to bring her food and make her eat. After she recovered, she'd changed. Her heart hardened even more, and she took her hurt out on me. More than before." I blinked away new tears. "You'd make a great uncle." I admitted.

"It's too bad Roni lost the baby. I like being an uncle. Doug has three kids. No twins, though." Cole smiled, and he zeroed in on my sweet spot.

I stretched my legs and spread them, offering the ultimate view. His Adam's apple bobbed as he swallowed. Drowning my family's twisted behavior with flirting definitely would improve the day.

"It's getting warmer," I said, fanning myself and putting my sister out of my mind.

Cole stood and opened the umbrella, angling it over me. When he sat back down, he straddled the lounger. His balls once again peeked out. I liked it.

Dang, the hints of his beautiful body turned me on. I gripped the lounger arms. After a minute, I met his gaze. He'd caught me drooling over his male parts. His knowing grin had me smiling like a vixen. He tugged the edge of his robe, and it opened farther, exposing his erection.

My blood boiled. I needed to take my robe off; it was stifling. I slowly pulled the tie. He zeroed in on the movement.

As the robe slipped off my shoulders, he became alert, rigid, and his cheeks flushed. His gaze raked my body, his erection bobbed. He desired me. I wouldn't have to wait long.

As I closed my eyes and rested my head back, I heard him move. I didn't open my eyes until a shadow passed over me. He grinned down at me, his robe untied and abdomen exposed.

He lowered my lounger fast. I squeaked. When I was laying flat, he covered me with his body. His lips showered my neck and chest with kisses.

I pushed the robe from his shoulders. He hastily pulled a condom from its pocket before he shucked it all the way off and rolled it up to put behind my head.

I explored his sinewy back, and I held him against me while he entered me. We made love—slow and meaningful.

Suddenly, his hips moved faster as he neared the breaking point. "Nessa," he moaned against my ear as he orgasmed. His pleasure tremors set me on fire, and I climaxed with him.

We laid there while we caught our breath, and I stroked his head. I could fall asleep holding Cole like this. When he started to pull out, I held on, hugging him everywhere.

He winced at the sensitive clinch I'd given him. "Nessa, I need to throw the condom away. Warsaw women are fertile. We could get you pregnant."

I met Cole's serious blue gaze and my heart spoke. "So?"

His brow dipped as he studied my expression. "That's…" His eyes glanced around, "That's," then his softened penis slipped out, making a stronger statement than any words could.

My heart lurched with stabbing pain. Cole didn't want children with me. I kept my lip from quivering until he jumped off to go to the restroom.

I sat up and took a shuddering breath. What the hell was I thinking, spouting something like that? I pulled my robe around me, knotting the tie. I moved to a chair that didn't recline. I withdrew into my thoughts and stared at the drain on the floor.

Drowning in my silent misery, I retreated deep inside, trying to close the gate I'd opened to my heart.

Cole kneeled before me. He gently shook my knee. He shifted, so he was in my line of sight and his lips moved, but I heard no sound. I clenched my eyes shut.

I couldn't breathe, my heart was lead and weighed me down. My mouth had gone dry.

He shook my leg again. I rubbed my knees together and hoarsely barked, "No."

The feeling in my gut was worse than when I'd caught Veronica screwing Roger. This time my heart was shattered into a million facets as my dream vaporized around me.

Warmth touched my cheeks, and my lids fluttered open. Cole's cerulean blue eyes captured my gaze. His face was a mask of sorrow.

His hands cupped my face firmly, his thumbs skimming my cheeks and wiping the moisture. I hadn't realized I was crying.

Cole's lips had moved, but I hadn't listened.

"What?" I mumbled hoarsely.

He inhaled. "If you want to have a baby, I'm right there with you. Before we start working on it, I'd like to get married, but before we do that, I want to propose. And before I do that, I need to apologize."

My heart pounded, and my breathing stalled. I didn't know if I should dance, laugh, or cry.

All three!

Mimicking him, I placed my hands on his face. "You want to have a baby?"

"With you, yes." He smiled and continued, "But first—"

"Apologize." It sounded like an order, and he chuckled.

"I'm sorry, Nessa." His gaze dropped to my lips. "You surprised me. My heart, it did this thing."

I glanced away, anticipating another rejection.

"No, not in a bad way." He shook his head. "It leaped. Whenever I dreamed of having children, I envisioned you as their mother."

Words failed me.

CHAPTER NINETEEN

A STIFF BREEZE FLUTTERED THE umbrella. "Looks like it's going to rain," Cole announced.

A rumble rolled. It sounded like a car in need of a muffler but far away. I glanced toward the sky and a dark cloud glided overhead. Even the frothing waves sounded angry.

Cole helped me to my feet. I picked up a few dishes, then he shooed me into the bedroom as the first bolt of lightning cracked the sky. He lowered the umbrella, then brought the dishes inside as the first sprinkles of rain began.

He walked to the side of the bed where I was propped up on the pillows. Cole lowered himself to the bed, and I leaned against him. I could feel his heart beating, strong and steady.

Dark thunderheads rolled in. Walls of rain swept over the rough waves.

Soon the rain pelted the glass, distorting our view.

I sighed, content to live in the moment. I pushed out thoughts of tomorrow, next week, or next month.

Cole and I turned on a movie, then watched a few

home improvement shows. I enjoyed our time together and couldn't help touching his arm or taking his hand every so often.

The day continued to darken as the storm raged. The wind howled over the cliff and the brooding ocean churned and foamed.

We ate dinner in bed. Cole uncorked a bottle of wine. We clinked our glasses before digging into our steaks.

"Mmm," I moaned. "This steak is divine."

"I like that noise you make." He laughed when I gave him an evil smirk. "Maybe I should make you moan like that."

"I don't know if you're up for it," I teased, trying to sound bored. My heart raced at the thought of his hands all over me and his mouth tasting me again. I swallowed.

"Uh, huh." His eyes narrowed slightly. "I'll have to prove it to you."

"Well, if you prove it to me, then I can't deny it, now can I?"

"Challenge accepted." He laughed.

He took my fork and proceeded to feed me. I gazed into his mesmerizing eyes as he leaned closer with every bite.

"This is the kind of attitude that makes you take stupid bets," I pointed out with a wink.

He spooned a bit of mashed potatoes into my mouth, pulling out the spoon slowly.

How could he make eating so sexy?

"Mike's bet wasn't so stupid. It brought us together." He flashed a smile, touching my cheek.

I sipped my wine, then commented, "That's true. But what about your hair?"

"Yeah, about that…" Cole turned away, scratching the back of his head. I smiled as he fidgeted with a napkin.

He glanced at me with a sheepish smile. "The details are a little hazy, but I mentioned you to Mike. He flippantly announced he and Amoya would book a reservation to meet my Vanessa. Of course, I doubted he'd drop everything and dared him. We bickered like we do, and finally, I swore I'd dye my hair to a color of his choosing if he followed through with the booking. I didn't think he'd do it, but Amoya agreed.

"Lo and behold, Mike was a man of his word when it came down to wanting to meet you. It could have been worse. He could've picked fuchsia or green." He chuckled, pulling a clump of hair straight. "The stylist did a great job. It looks natural."

"Your roots are showing. You need a touch up." I teased, picking up the wineglass and swirling the red liquid. I finished the last sip and placed my glass on the tray table.

"Since I knew which ship would deliver you to the resort, I booked the same cruise line and embarked, hoping to find you earlier than later. Luckily, I saw you board the ship." He picked up his wine and emptied the glass.

"Creepy stalker," I laughed, then turned introspective. "I would have flipped if you approached me that first day."

"I did, but you wouldn't even look at me." He frowned and pulled at some fuzz on his robe. "You had earbuds in and wouldn't look anyone in the eye."

"Avoidance techniques," I offered with a shrug, remembering exactly when he'd tried to make contact the first time. In spy mode with a romance book open, earbuds in but not on, and mirrored sunglasses, I had observed the others around me.

Mike had elbowed Cole and pointed in my direction. Eventually, he approached my lounger, but I ignored him as he stood near me until he gave up.

My sunglasses had slipped down, and I enjoyed the fit of his khakis as he'd walked away. Mike had caught me inspecting Cole's ass as he greeted his friend at the bar. When he spoke, Cole's face had blazed red. I'd hastily righted my glasses and flipped the page.

After a moment, Cole had glanced at me, but my mirrored sunglasses gave nothing away. I turned another page of the book I had yet to read. He'd sighed and faced his friend once more.

By then, my hands shook too much to actually read. Cole's resemblance to Nick had shaken me.

"At least you were smooth about it, not like Mr. Gorgeous. He didn't like the word *no,* and I had to look for the nearest exit." I sipped my wine, trying to get the image of the beautifully insistent man out of my mind.

"He is a persistent fellow." Cole scowled.

"I suspected something when he pursued me and ignored the others. He flat out refused a busty blonde who handed him her room key." I shook my head. "I hope he gets paid well."

One side of his mouth lifted into a lopsided grin. "You gave him a run for his money."

I poked him in the chest. "No, you did."

A full-blown smile erupted on his lips, and he nodded. "Yes, I did."

Cole offered me another bite of steak. I moaned while

I chewed, then swallowed and licked my lips. His eyes widened slightly before narrowing.

He shifted, causing his robe to split open once again, exposing his package. I couldn't help the sly smile that rested on my lips. Two could play this game. The next bite he offered, I leaned forward, giving him a view of my cleavage.

Cole flashed a wicked grin, dropping a dab of gravy onto my breast. Of course, he licked it off, then kissed his way up my neck to my chin. He hovered in front of my lips with a wry smirk.

Dammit, that stinker isn't going to kiss you.

I shot my hand out, avoiding his thigh and going straight for his groin. My fingers clutched his shaft, and he shut his eyes, biting back a moan. I kissed his lips, then worked my way along his jawline.

Dinner forgotten, his hands slid up my thighs.

A knock sounded at the door. With a furrowed brow, Cole quit fumbling with my robe's tie. "Dessert," he mumbled.

"No, we were just getting to the dessert. That's an annoying interruption." I might have huffed as I crossed my arms.

Cole laughed, touching my nose with his finger. "You'll like dessert."

He opened the door wide enough to accommodate the dessert container, keeping the delivery person from entering our sanctuary. I appreciated the gesture.

He mumbled something to the person, then took the food, shutting the door with his foot. The lid was spotted with water droplets.

With a twinkle in his eye, Cole stretched out his arm and presented me with the dish. He lifted the lid. "Voilà!"

I inhaled the creamy-sweet scent of cheesecake. There were two large pieces, almost a quarter of a pie in all, with red raspberries and red drizzle swirling the plate. If Cole hadn't already had me swooning with desire, I definitely was now.

"They didn't have cherry topping," he said, inspecting me.

My heart warmed at his remembrance of how I liked cheesecake. "That's okay. The raspberries are red, too, and fresh is healthier." I sucked in my lip, trying to hold back until he set the plates down.

Cole snatched the forks before I could and scooped a small portion onto one. He intended on feeding me again.

Placing a hand on my hip, I announced, "A girl could get used to this." The tasty chunk slid off the fork onto my tongue. I closed my eyes, savoring the heavenly flavor as thousands of taste buds sang the hallelujah chorus.

I realized a truth. Being with Cole—I wanted that. I could envision us growing old together,

Falling madly in love with him, again, was an inevitability. In fact, I don't think I'd ever stopped.

CHAPTER TWENTY

I STEPPED OUT OF THE surf, plucked a towel from an Adirondack chair and tossed it at Cole. He wiggled his toes in the sand.

Grinning, I basked in the memories of the last few days. We'd woken up together and then spent the days talking, swimming in the ocean, or making love, with the occasional tickle fight and laughing until tears streamed down our faces.

The tropical getaway was paradise.

But paradise can't last forever.

Reality, in the form of your devious sister, will creep in and sabotage you.

I pushed away thoughts of my family and old life. Neither Cole nor I brought up the future unless it was something fantastical, like what we'd name our kids.

Cole toweled off, then glanced at the cliff-side cottage and squinted. He wiped the dampness from his face and studied the building again. "Is the light on?"

I craned my neck. "Yeah, the outside light is on."

"Looks like housekeeping isn't finished yet." Cole sat

and stretched his long legs. He reached and pulled me onto his lap. "We'll have to think of something to pass the time."

I slid my arms around his neck and pressed my lips against his jaw. I worked my way down to his chin. My body thrummed with want. "I can think of something."

He chuckled and pinched my bottom.

"Ow." I jumped. "The light is out."

"Time to get ready." Cole gave me a cryptic grin as he scooted me until my feet touched the dry sand.

"Ready for what?" I narrowed my eyes and poked him in the chest.

"Dinner and a show." He picked up our beach bag, then took my hand.

I warmed, reimagining his original show. My heart fluttered in expectation as we climbed the stairs.

On the patio, we stomped off the sand and stripped off our swimsuits, hanging them over the back of the chairs to dry.

I'd wondered why Cole had insisted on wearing bathing suits, but now it made sense. Housekeeping. Even if we were dots, it wouldn't do to have employees seeing their boss naked.

Cole glanced at the time. "Can you be ready in an hour?"

"Ready for what?" I asked again.

"Going to the resort for dinner and a show." Cole opened the sliding glass door.

I shadowed him into the bathroom, watching his buttocks firm and relax. "Not a personal show?" I stuck out my lower lip.

He reached for the shower tap and twisted it. "That

comes later." He stepped backward into the spray.

"I don't know if I want to put clothes back on." I'd grown accustomed to only occasionally donning the resort robe.

His hooded gaze caressed my nude body. I swallowed and shifted my feet.

"I prefer you that way, too, but I don't want to share you with anyone. The clothes will only be temporary, I promise you." He crooked his finger, beckoning me to him. I couldn't refuse. Our bodies pressed together, and our lips touched. His hands went straight to my hair. I sighed.

Wrapped in a towel, I stood in the closet trying to decide on a dress. The sleeveless red sundress with a low V neck was perfect with my demi-bra, but the navy knee-length dress with an empire waist had been my favorite on the cruise. Elegant and simple, refined yet comfortable. My platinum gray heels would work and be super sexy.

I smiled as I pulled open my underwear drawer. I picked up a thong as Cole entered.

His mouth flopped open, but nothing came out. A devilish grin found its home on his lips. He took a shirt off the hanger, then exited.

To hell with that. I dropped the thong back into the drawer. The element of surprise would be fun. I grinned as I slid the dress over my head.

Cole popped his head into the bathroom as I applied the finishing touches on my makeup. "The car is here."

He escorted me to the vehicle and helped me inside, then climbed in beside me. The smell of leather upholstery assaulted me.

Cole's knee touched mine, making the butterflies in my stomach take flight. I gripped my hands together and glanced out the window. I was going on a date with Nick Tanner, my first love. Nervous energy made me giddy and anxious at the same time.

The sun dipped low on the horizon, casting Dancing Winds in an orange glow. Associates and guests scurried to and fro. Many headed to the restaurant.

Cole offered me his elbow, and I linked my arm with his. Even in the four-inch heels, I was still shorter than Cole. We entered the dining room and the maître d's eyes widened with recognition.

"Right this way, Mr. Tanner." He smiled as he led us through the dimly lit room. I scanned the diners for Mike and Amoya and found them next to Cole's brothers, Scott and Doug. The men all rose.

I'd been in shock the night I'd met Grace and seen Doug again. His hair had receded and was starting to gray, but he was fit. Chasing little boys around must be good exercise. He extended a hand, which I took.

"Vanessa, it's so wonderful to see you again. Even if you still have bad taste in men."

Scott bumped his brother, breaking our hands apart. He wore artsy glasses, but they didn't obscure the mirth that twinkled in his blue eyes. Scott grasped my hand with both of his. "Shut up, Doug. Vanessa has always had impeccable taste in men."

"Says the man with my face." Cole laughed and placed a hand on my back. Warmth filled me at the possessive gesture.

I hadn't seen Scott since Roni's and his second

breakup. Five or so years. He appeared healthy and his hair was brown, as Cole's should have been.

Scott pulled me into a hug and whispered. "How's Roni?" He released me.

I shrugged. "Same old bitch."

Scott chuckled softly, but the merriment had left his eyes. Actually, he looked as if I'd slapped him. Maybe he still harbored feelings for Roni.

Hell, it seemed as if Tanners and Warsaws were cursed when it came to loving each other.

"About time you got here," Doug said to his wife as she approached from another direction. I caught him kissing Grace's cheek. She blushed, reached around, and pinched his bottom.

"Look who the cat dragged in?" A male voice offered, earning laughter.

I gasped. It was the bartender from the poolside area. Now I knew why he'd looked familiar. He was Mitchell Tanner, Cole's father. He gave me a peck on the cheek. My face was on fire. I wasn't accustomed to all the fuss.

"There's my girl," a woman's soft voice floated from behind Mr. Tanner.

My mother used to greet me in the same manner. Tears pricked my eyes and my breath hitched as a wave of grief threatened to consume me. I glanced down at the floor, trying to hold back the floodgates, when I was pulled into a mother's warm embrace.

Isabella Tanner smelled like lilies. I buried my face in her shoulder. "I'm glad you decided to visit the island."

I couldn't help but chuckle. She'd been the one who suggested I come rest at the resort. "I haven't had a chance to be alone."

"You haven't minded," Cole teased.

Hell no!

We sat down to dinner and a band started to play. Our courses came, and the band continued to entertain. As I panned the room, I noticed Mr. Gorgeous in a booth, glaring at my tablemates. I touched Cole's knee with mine, catching his attention. Without looking and keeping my hand low, I pointed to the fully clothed, frowning Mr. Gorgeous.

Cole gave a devilish grin and tipped my chin up. He placed his lips on mine. A sweet gentle kiss, making me shiver. Pulling back, he stopped a breath away. Scanning my face, his tender gaze ensnared my heart, capturing me completely. I was blind to all else.

I reminded myself to breathe.

His gaze dropped to my lips. In a flash, his next kiss consumed me, hard and needy. My hand clutched his dress shirt, tugging him closer. The heat of our bodies threatened to meld us into one. He gripped the back of my neck, holding me.

Someone cleared their throat.

"How are her tonsils?" Scott asked.

Cole abruptly ended the kiss but rested his forehead against mine. My face had to match his red one.

I closed my eyes and inhaled. My eyes snapped open as I realized I grasped his thigh precariously close to his groin.

He kissed my nose. "This isn't over," he whispered in my ear.

"I hope not," I uttered, before glancing around the

table at Cole's family and friends.

All eyes were on us. My mouth went dry, and I reached for my water. Mrs. Tanner winked at me, and I almost choked.

The wait staff cleared the table and started to bring out desserts. I'd ordered a cheesecake with a chocolate crust and caramel drizzle. Spying Amoya's creme brûlée had me reconsidering my order. Especially after the moan she made when taking a bite. Doug and Grace shared a dessert. Except for Cole and me, everyone had been served.

Watching how fast the delectables were being devoured, I anxiously awaited mine.

Cole leaned over. "Guess they forgot about ours," he said softly. "I'll go check."

"It's not a big deal." I put a hand on his leg. No need for him to check. They probably had to cut more. The kitchen staff wouldn't make such a rookie mistake as forgetting something on the owner's order.

"I want to hear you moan," he whispered in my ear, then he was gone.

Cole's lean form headed straight for the kitchen. I wanted to follow and steal him away to show him my secret—no panties. I smirked, imagining his face.

"Sometime Vanessa, you'll have to go shopping with me," Grace said, setting her fork on the plate.

I jerked my head around and smiled at the kind offer. I nodded, but I really didn't want to visit anywhere without Cole.

"Doug is going to take the kids over to Las Palmas to swim. They have a couple of pool slides." Grace leaned toward her husband.

"Sounds like somebody wants a little time away from the kids," Scott teased.

"Maybe the boys need some male bonding with their uncle," Doug replied.

"Maybe Mom and Dad need some alone time," Mrs. Tanner said, making Doug and Grace steal a glance at each other and blush.

"When you do go to Las Palmas, let me know. I'll go with you," Mike said.

"He has many fond childhood memories of that place." Amoya rolled her eyes. "I hear all about them every time his father visits."

"Yes, that's true. You're a saint." Mike picked up his glass and swirled the merlot. "I'd like to see it again before they close it down."

Everyone broke forth with an exclamation. Some shocked, others sad. I listened and waited for a lull, then said to Mr. Tanner. "You should buy it and make it a family destination. Keep the memories alive."

Mr. Tanner stroked his chin as a new exchange started. The Las Palmas owners were older than Cole's parents and wanted to retire but didn't have any family.

Scott suggested ways he'd improve the accommodations while Doug brainstormed how to streamline the property for families.

Amoya sat across from me. Her eyes lit up, and she elbowed Mike. His lips formed an O and his brows rose. They watched something behind me.

I didn't have to contain my curiosity more than a moment because Cole set a domed silver serving tray in front of me. My dessert at last. His hand paused on the handle.

I glanced at Cole. His tender expression coupled with a blush had me remembering our naked mealtimes. It seemed I was now destined to think of Cole feeding me whenever I saw a domed tray. My mouth dried and words clogged in my throat. The table hushed as if they knew my thoughts.

Cole lifted the lid, and I stared not at cheesecake but a blue velvet box. I gasped.

"A jewelry box," Mike the genius pointed out.

"Not any jewelry box," Amoya said in a soft voice. "A ring box."

My heart thundered in my ears and a lump formed in my throat. I glanced again at Cole.

With a smartass smirk, he said, "Open it."

I reached for the box with trembling hands. Pulling it close, I flipped the lid up. Empty.

What the hell?

I exhaled the breath I'd been holding and turned to question Cole. He no longer stood but kneeled on one knee, offering me the diamond ring from our shopping trip to Oliver's store.

"Oh my God!" I gasped again as my hands flew to my face. I leapt to my feet, sending the chair to the floor with a thunderous crash.

For a microsecond, I glanced at the astonished diners. All eyes had focused on Cole and I.

Cole raised the ring. The princess-cut facets caught the light and dazzled me. My hands covered my mouth, keeping my heart from joyfully leaping out of my body. My face hurt from the grin that I hoped would become permanent. I blinked away tears, refusing to lose sight of my first and only love.

"Vanessa Rose Warsaw." Cole's eyes glistened, and he cleared his throat.

The room silenced.

"Yes!" I screamed as I threw my arms around his neck.

Half the room collectively "ah"ed and the other laughed. I didn't give a rat's ass.

Cole's arms tightened around me. I was home. He nosed my hair, breathed deeply, and sighed. I melted against his chest.

"I'm so glad you said *yes*," he whispered, his breath against my ear, sending a shiver down my spine.

I leaned away and gazed into his shining eyes. "There was never another answer."

His breath hitched. He closed his eyes and nodded. Taking my left hand, he stood poised to place the ring on my finger.

"I love you, Nessa. Thank you for agreeing to be my wife."

Cole guided the ring onto my finger. The sensation traveled up my arm to my heart.

My throat clogged with emotion. Tears slipped out, and I nodded. He tipped my chin, claiming my lips in a hard, possessive kiss. The audience roared, but all faded as the fire of love consumed me.

CHAPTER TWENTY-ONE

I COULDN'T BELIEVE I'D BE Mrs. Nicholas Arlington Tanner. I flitted about, practically floating, my face sore from smiling. We didn't leave our villa the following day, but the day after, Grace and Mrs. Tanner pulled me away from Cole for shopping.

I cried when I said goodbye to Cole. There was an emptiness I likened to my soul being left behind.

I purchased a few things, including a negligee I intended to save for our wedding night. But I'd given in to temptation and showed him.

Soon I was modeling it. Then it ended up on the floor.

"I wish it was Thursday," I said, glancing at him. He patted the bed, and I sat on the edge.

"I know." Cole laughed. "Thursday will be here soon enough. Let's enjoy Monday." He pushed the robe from my shoulder and placed a trail of kisses along my collarbone.

"Are you sure eight o'clock will be a good time for the wedding?" My voice warbled as his hand found my breast.

Refusing to lift his lips from my neck, he hummed an affirmative.

"What if..." My voice stalled. I couldn't fathom my sister ruining the wedding, but it was my darkest fear. I swallowed the lump in my throat and clutched Cole to me, reveling in his nearness.

"Don't worry," he said, working his way down my cleavage. "I'll protect you."

I couldn't help my fears. Roni had sabotaged every romantic relationship in my life.

It was different with Cole. *He* was different. In the past, he could tell my sister and me apart. I hoped he still owned that skill.

Cole's talented tongue and fingers took me to places where my family couldn't reach me. All my anxiety faded away. Cole left me on the bed and went to get cleaned up. I shifted to my side and felt as if I'd melted into the mattress.

Cole re-entered the room, and a playful slap to my rump got my attention. I rolled over with a sanguine stretch. My eyes combed my fiancé's body.

"You clean up well," I said, reaching for the zipper of his khaki pants.

He took a step back. "Ah, ah." He wagged a finger at me, and I stuck out my lower lip. "You need to get dressed. We have plans."

I growled as I flipped to my stomach. "Not with each other."

He huffed out a breath and rolled his eyes. "Come on. It's your bachelorette party."

"I know. It's your bachelor party." I turned my face away and bit my lip.

"You'll have fun with the girls. You can gossip." He jostled the bed as he sat, then rubbed my calf.

"About what? The length of your schlong or how you make me squirm with your tongue? I'm sure your mother or sister-in-law would love to know the nitty-gritty details."

"Don't give away any of my secrets," Cole laughed. He stood, walked over to the mirror, and smoothed down his hair.

I slipped out of the room, going to dress. I didn't want to air my concerns, and I had a few. The red sundress was an easy choice. As I zipped it, I tried to think about my makeup.

I exited the closet, heading straight for my makeup bag.

"What's going on, Nessa?" Cole asked. I hadn't seen him leaning against the wall with his arms crossed.

I gave him a fleeting glance before searching in my bag for eyeliner. "Nothing." I tried to sound upbeat. Normal.

"Don't give me that." Cole pushed off the wall and stood behind me so I could see him in the mirror over my shoulder. "You're worried about something. And before you protest, let me inform you that the crinkle on your forehead tells me you are."

He kneaded my shoulders, and I sighed. "Out with it, Nessa."

I crossed my arms and narrowed my eyes. "I won't be able to get away with anything."

Cole shook his head and an impish grin broke out.

"Fine." I shifted my gaze to the ground. "I don't want to go to any place racy, you know…"

"Racy? As in strip joints?" Cole started to chuckle. "I don't think my mom would plan that."

"But Amoya?" I bit my lip again.

"No, honey, you'll be fine. As far as I know, you're staying at the resort. There's a great band lined up for tonight."

"What about Mr. Gorgeous?" I glanced at him. In the mirror, I looked like a frightened child. "You won't be there, will you?"

The tease left Cole's face. He slid his arms around my waist. "Mom will inform the staff. You'll be safe. The guys and I are going to Las Palmas for dinner. Mike, Scott, Doug, and Dad get to buy me drinks while the boys swim."

I turned in his arms, and we held each other. He lowered his lips to mine.

A low rhythmic drumming grew louder, and the building started vibrating.

Cole and I broke apart. Out the window, the palm branches all waved in the same direction.

My gut twisted around a boulder in my stomach. I swallowed bile and pulled Cole closer.

They found you. Run!

"Is that a helicopter?" Cole asked, the thump-thump-thump of the blades becoming apparent as the machine grew closer.

We walked out onto the patio and glanced out as the black mass approached. I cupped my hand over my eyes, shielding them from the sun.

"Oh no," I groaned as I pushed away from Cole and fled the helicopter's line of sight.

"Vanessa?" Cole called.

"It's my father." I covered my ears and squeezed my eyes shut. I didn't want to deal with him now.

Cole stood at the glass entry, inspecting the now hovering chopper. "It could be from one of the resorts. Some do offer island tours." He squinted and frowned. "Oh shit. You're right. It's your dad. He has binoculars."

The helicopter flew over our villa, then banked out of sight. It hadn't gone far. The sound of the air-chopping blades invaded our solitude.

I opened the front door, but it hadn't landed on the drive. I blew out a relieved sigh. "Maybe he's leaving."

Delusional hope.

"I don't think so." Cole pointed to the shoreline.

My heart sank. The helicopter had landed. The blades' rotation slowed. A man exited, then extended a hand to help someone.

My blood ran cold. "No. No. No! Not now. Not here."

That skank-ho is here!

"Roni," I growled. The evil twin. Tears stung my eyes. I spun into Cole's arms as a sob hit. He rubbed my back. The rock in my gut broke, revealing a crystalline middle that began shredding my innards.

"Vanessa, it will be all right." Cole tipped my chin.

I shook my head, refusing to meet his eyes.

He gripped my arms and squeezed enough to get my attention. "Listen to me. You are an adult. These people can't take you away or make you do anything you don't want to do. In three days, we are getting married, and no one will stop us. No one can change my mind. I hope they can't change yours."

I frowned and crossed my arms. "Of course, they won't. You're not getting away from me again," I declared.

Then I sighed. It was only a matter of time before my sister would attempt to steal Cole. "It's just… Roni."

Cole kissed my nose. The smartass smirk was back. "She sucks balls."

"Among other things." I giggled, then blew out a long breath and leaned against him. My heart rate steadied as I closed my eyes and hugged him. "You are good for me."

"I know." Cole laughed as his hands dropped to my butt. "We're good for each other. I've got your back here. You know that, right?"

I nodded and glanced out the window again. My father and sister followed another man, who had a suspicious resemblance to Mr. Gorgeous, toward the bottom of the stairs. They'd be on the patio in a matter of moments.

"Didn't you run a company or something back home?" Cole prompted, easing me away from the window. "This should be a snap compared to some business negotiations you've encountered. What did you do to prepare before sitting down with those business men and women?"

I gazed at my reflection in the mirror. A sad, frightened woman with balled fists, tight shoulders, and an absence of confidence returned my stare. Her gaze pleaded with me to help.

I closed my eyes, rolled my shoulders, and stretched my arms. These people are my family. They're dysfunctional, but they're mine. Mom would not approve of the way Roni screwed me over, but she wouldn't like the way I ditched Dad and the company, either. I inhaled deeply and opened my eyes.

I pointed to the reflection of a woman who now wore a smirk. "You've brought record sales to Warsaw Industries for the last two years. You've allocated and brokered too many deals to count, then hired appropriate staff to take over for you. You've created stable jobs across the Midwest and around the world. And you haven't killed your sister."

Yet.

"You are loved," Cole said from behind me. He shifted my hair to kiss my neck. "You are smart, kind, sweet, and sexy. I love you, Nessa."

"I am loved." I leaned back against his hard frame and hummed.

"There's that Mrs. Tanner smile."

Twisting in his arms, I cupped his face. "I'm glad I've got you with me."

I took a few deep breaths, then I turned to the sliding glass door. As I tugged it open, my father crested the stairs. He pivoted and his gaze swept the patio. When he saw me, his hard features softened until he noticed Cole behind me.

Even in the tropics, my father wore a white dress shirt and tie with black suit pants. At least the yellow tie had pink hibiscus flowers. At home, it would have made me smile.

"Hello, Daddy."

The corners of his eyes crinkled, and his thick arms encircled me, pulling me against him in a crushing hug. "Vanessa, I've been worried sick. You won't answer your phone. You didn't leave word where to find you. Your location is turned off."

I patted his back, feeling like a parent. "That was the point. I didn't want to be found."

And look, oh joy, they found you.

I let my father hold on until he was ready to release me. It had been a long time since he'd held me, maybe as far back as my mother's death. It was good to know he cared. I tilted my head onto his shoulder just in time to see Roni top the stairs.

Her eyes widened when she caught sight of Cole. Luckily, she was out of breath from the climb. She swung her gaze to me, and her eyes narrowed. I couldn't help but mimic her.

"Why are *you* here?" I practically growled.

Roni smoothed her skimpy white dress then tossed her shoulder length hair. Inwardly I smiled, she'd cut her hair. Mine was longer, and I planned to keep it that way. The spaghetti strap dress clung to her curves like cling wrap. She was the sexier version of me.

I couldn't tell if either family member recognized Cole as the young Nick Tanner I'd dated. I hadn't because he'd grown, dyed his hair, and didn't wear glasses any longer. But, according to Cole, both my father and sister had seen him about a year ago when he'd visited.

I pulled away from my father as Mr. Gorgeous arrived on the patio. Turning to Cole, I said, "See. I told you he'd been hired."

Cole gave a stiff nod, his once relaxed posture now on guard. With a furrowed brow, he scrutinized the other man, but he didn't have a thing to worry about. I loved Cole.

On the other hand, I worried my sister's advances toward Cole would fool him. And he'd fall into the same trap as the other men had.

"Okay, you found me. Look, I'm safe and healthy." I twirled, making my dress skirt flare. "Now you can go."

My father put his hands on his hips. I swear I saw a pout morph into a frown. Dad doesn't pout.

"That's a fine welcome, Prissy," Roni said, using her annoying nickname for me. Her rosebud lips formed a taunting smile.

Welcome? Smack her now.

Roni's gaze shifted to Cole. Her eyes lit up as if she was hungry and only sexy man meat could sate her hunger. I swallowed the ball of lead back to my stomach.

Why did Roni have to always want my man meat?

Anger, white hot and violent, bubbled inside. I gripped the back of the patio chair, trying to calm down so I didn't erupt like Old Faithful, spewing scalding venom.

If only.

Cole placed his palm on my lower back. The warmth of the gentle touch grounded me. I inhaled deeply. "What do you want?" I'd aimed this at my sister.

Roni smirked, noticing Cole's arm. "I see why you ran away."

Hot all over, I had to be bright red. My eyes narrowed. "I wanted to have you the hell out of my life. He was just an awesome bonus."

"Yes, who is your young man?" Father scrutinized Cole. No doubt taking in his nice clothes and confident posture. My father hadn't recognized Cole; a wave of relief washed over me.

"Don't you recognize him, Daddy?" Roni said, roaming closer, her gaze never straying from Cole.

Cole tapped me, and I had to intervene before Roni tainted the meeting. I moved, so the men faced each other, putting Roni behind me. "Cole, this is my father, Victor Warsaw."

"It's a pleasure, sir." Cole took my father's extended hand. Something must have passed between them because Father's features relaxed.

"I'll bet he's a pleasure," Roni said quietly into my ear.

With my hands fisted at my side, I spun around. I'd had enough of her running me over. Nose to nose, I staked my claim. "You will not go anywhere near Cole. You better not even look at him. I swear on Mom's grave, if you try to seduce Cole, I'll kill you."

"Vanessa!" Father hissed as if he'd been slapped.

"Nessa," Cole chided softly. He might be the only thing saving my sister from getting acquainted with my fists.

Roni stepped back, her eyes wide. She smoothed down her dress, trying to recover.

I don't remember the last time I stood up to my twin

sister. But I knew Roni, and unfortunately, she'd take it as a challenge.

"Vanessa, I don't understand this hatred you have for Veronica." My father placed his hand on my shoulder.

"Why not?" I said, twisting to confront him with the truth. "I've explained it to you."

Father slowly blinked, his version of the eye roll. He gestured in a dismissing manner. "Ah yes, the boys." He sighed. "So, your sister fancied a few of your beaus. It happens."

I'm not sure how long my jaw remained open. "Cole, do you see why I had to escape?"

He nodded and touched my face. If I stared into his tender gaze, I'd break down, but I couldn't do that. I had to get rid of my family first.

"Can you please get my laptop? I have something to show my father."

Cole left me. With a hurried stride, he disappeared into the bathroom, where he fetched my laptop from the closet.

"Veronica hasn't *fancied* the men in my life. She's slept with them. All of them except one, and she ruined that relationship, too."

I took a quick breath and continued, "I don't know how this slut has become your favorite. All she does is pretend to be me and seduce men."

"Hey," Roni whined.

"Shut up, whore." I poked her in the chest. "If you hadn't wanted to be confronted with the truth, you should have stayed in bed with Roger. You liked his puny dick."

"Vanessa." My father's face had turned red and his hands visited his hips again.

"Same for you, Daddy. I didn't invite you here, so if you can't stomach what I have to say, then you can leave. I know Roni's your precious *baby,* but she's a diabolical liar."

Cole returned to my side and opened the laptop. It made a soft whirring as it booted.

"I don't know what Roni said to you about Nick Tanner. You know, the night Roni lied while pretending to be me. Nick wanted to see me, not her. I'd been upset about Mom and asked him to come over. I needed a shoulder to cry on. Nick wanted to hold me. I can only speculate what she said happened, but given her track record, I'd say she tried to seduce him and failed. He could tell us apart."

My father's gaze darted between my sister and me. I swallowed.

"She's pursued all the other men I've dated. I've caught her in bed with Colin and Roger. Alex sent me a dozen roses after the *best sex* he didn't know I was capable of. But I hadn't slept with him." I ticked more men off my fingers, giving varying ways I'd found out they'd crawled into bed with my brazen sister.

I tapped the keyboard, opening a surveillance video from my office. Handing the laptop to my father, I said, "Watch this and decide for yourself."

My father glanced down at the picture on the video. A woman straddled a man on a desk. I hadn't wanted to relive the horror, but something had kept me from deleting it. Dad walked into the bedroom, sat on the bed, and pushed play.

I blocked Roni from entering the room. I didn't want her skank-ho ass to sully Cole's and my personal passion pit.

My father's face remained emotionless, however, it turned bright red. One hand gripped and twisted the white bedspread. He hastily set the laptop aside and rubbed his chin.

"No, you don't. You need to finish it," I ordered, pointing to the discarded laptop.

"Vanessa, I can't," my father croaked. His gaze darted from me to Roni. Disappointment flashed.

I couldn't enjoy the subtle reaction. "If you can't stomach what she's done to me over and over, then at least forward to the end."

My father nodded and retrieved the laptop. He continued to watch the clip. Red-faced shock, anger, and sorrow scrolled across his features.

After kicking them out of my office, I'd thrown a fit, destroying everything on my desk, then I'd crumbled to the floor. When I had dried my eyes, I had clarity. I'd set my plan to escape in motion.

My father closed the laptop and left it on the bed. He took my hands in his. "There are no words."

Damn straight.

"I'm tired of living under Grandma's curse. I didn't want the men you paraded in front of me. They wanted the business. Or they wanted between Roni's legs." I shrugged. "The only man I loved, the only man who loved me for me and could stop Roni in her tracks, you banned from my life. Why is that, Daddy? What did she tell you to make you hate Nick?"

"Nicky," Roni sighed. We glanced at her. Her finger

rested on her lip and her eyes had closed, as if savoring something sweet.

"Roni said he tried to rape her," my father replied in a gruff voice.

I gasped and leaned against Cole. After the shock wore off, I laughed. "Like he'd want her skanky ass."

Roni's eyes snapped open, and she glared at me. "Nice dress."

I glanced down at the red sundress. It was Roni's. Well, technically, it was mine. She'd taken it from my closet first. Stealing it back was inadequate restitution.

"Nick came to our house to comfort me. He found you first. You pretended to be me, didn't you? Scott had been smart enough to see through your shit, Roni. What made you think Nick wouldn't? Why did you ruin our relationship? Didn't you know we were in love?"

I glanced at my father. "He was the one, Daddy. Mom knew it. She helped me pick out a wedding dress."

"She did?" My father took a step back, as if talking about my mother frightened him.

"Liar!" Roni shrieked, balling her fists at her side.

"Look who's talking," I spat.

"Vanessa isn't lying, sir," Cole said.

My father's brow furrowed. "How would you know?"

"I know because I'm Nicholas Tanner." Cole's hand moved slightly on my back. The sensation caused a shiver to run down my spine.

My father's eyes widened.

Cole shifted to meet my gaze. "That night, I snuck in your bedroom window like we planned. Roni heard me. She sat on the bed with her hands in her lap, pretending to be you. I guess she didn't know that you'd jump and wrap me in a giant hug, not sit like a mouse." He chuckled and rubbed my arm. "She tried to convince me she was you. I didn't buy the act for a second. Nobody is like my Nessa."

He caressed my cheek, and I sighed. Those big blue eyes focused on my lips. My heart raced.

"Eventually, Roni angrily stomped out of the room. I waited for you to come for nearly an hour. When your dad finally burst in screaming, I was confused as hell." He scratched the back of his head. "I'd fallen asleep on your bed."

"Why did you do it, Roni?" I asked.

Roni shrugged, while taking great interest in a fingernail.

"What's done is done," my father said. "For my part, I'm sorry."

What's done is done?

I huffed. "You should be. Cole and I would be married. You'd be a grandpa and the business wouldn't be in jeopardy."

"Nessa," Cole said.

"But we've wasted so much time." I hugged him. "We'll never get that back."

"All the heartache we've suffered will help us appreciate each other all the more." Cole's embrace tightened.

I rested my head against Cole's chest, glancing around the patio. Mr. Gorgeous leaned against the half wall, staring down at the sea. He must have informed my father about my whereabouts. Dad lowered himself to a chair and seemed lost in thought. Roni faced the wind, so her hair trailed behind her. She stole covert glances at Mr. Gorgeous.

That's good. Roni likes penises. And he definitely has one.

I turned in Cole's arms again and he placed his chin on my head. His arms encircled my waist, and I settled my hands on his. I closed my eyes and breathed in the warm, salty air. As the breeze caressed me, I calmed and relaxed.

The cries of seagulls and the distant sound of the surf added lines to the melody my heart sung. I squeezed Cole's hands.

"Holy shit!" Roni yelled.

My eyes popped open, and I swallowed my heart in my throat. Cole had stiffened and pulled me tight against him protectively.

Roni pointed to my hand. The engagement ring gleamed in the sunlight.

"Look, Daddy, Vanessa is engaged." Roni stepped forward and jerked my finger to her face.

"Congratulations." Smiling, my father jumped to his feet and shook Cole's hand again, then enveloped me into a bear hug. "When's the big day?"

Cole and I shared a glance, then I sighed. "Thursday."

I stifled a giggle at the look of shock on my father's face. "*This* Thursday."

My father rubbed his forehead. I could tell he was calculating the days until my thirtieth birthday.

As far as Warsaw Industries was concerned, I was

cutting it close. I'd given it up, and that much was certain. Father could give it to Roni. I was done.

"Yes," I whispered. "We didn't want to wait."

CHAPTER TWENTY-TWO

I SAT SURROUNDED BY WONDERFUL women and also, unfortunately, my sister. Amoya, Grace, and Mrs. Tanner all acted like giggly schoolgirls while Roni sat quietly. Her reserved behavior was probably an act.

Although, when we had arrived at the resort, Roni had caught a glimpse of Scott Tanner and her face blanched. She'd quickly hid behind a potted palm, biting her lip. Scott hadn't noticed her, or, if he had, he'd ignored her presence.

I tapped my foot in time to the music, sipping a fruity alcoholic concoction. As planned, Amoya, Grace, and I discussed bridesmaids' dresses and shoes—colors and styles.

"Wait until you see my shoes," I giggled, partly because of the alcohol and partly because of the ruse we'd devised for Roni.

With a gleeful expression, Amoya rubbed her hands together. "They have to be better than Grace's wedding shoes."

Grace gasped in mock horror, a hand clutching her chest.

"It's true," Mrs. Tanner admitted, nodding. "Vanessa

has better shoes."

"Why?" Roni asked, one brow raised in question.

"Because I didn't wear any," Grace smiled. "We got married on the beach. What's the point of heels if you're going to sink in the sand?"

I snort laughed. "Bare feet. I like my shoes."

The band invited us up to sing background vocals. My posse could have rivaled Karen's for alcohol consumption and laughter.

The only reason I even took the steps to the stage, though, was because Amoya was pulling me while Grace pushed. Once there, sandwiched between extroverted personalities and bolstered by liquid courage, I belted out the songs, one after another.

Throughout the evening Mrs. Tanner snapped photos and I started posing. I even grabbed my sister for one.

Damn. You must be drunk, girl.

At the end of the night, Cole joined me for the drive back to our private villa. I kicked off my shoes and propped my head on his shoulder.

"Looks like you had fun," Cole said, patting my thigh.

"Mmhmm." I hummed, then yawned. I must have fallen asleep because soon he was shaking me gently. He held my hand, helping me out of the car. He carried my shoes by the strap. When the door opened, I flopped on the bed.

The scent of Cole's cologne lingered on the pillow, and I sighed and closed my eyes.

Morning light bombarded me. I opened my eyes,

yawned and blinked. I stretched my arm and found cool sheets. Emptiness washed over me, then dread.

I sprang upright.

Cole leaned against the half wall, holding a steaming white cup, and stared at the teal sea. The steam fluttered in the breeze as he brought the cup to his lips and sipped.

My dread melted away as warmth filled me. Cancelling the day's plans seemed a great idea. Maybe I could coax Cole into a day in bed.

Sliding out of bed, I realized I was nude. Somehow, I'd removed my dress—well, all my clothes. I slipped into the bathroom. After brushing my teeth, I tried to smooth my bed head.

Threading my arms through a clean white robe, I headed toward the patio. Stepping into the sunshine, I met Cole's gaze as he lifted a fresh cup for me.

I took the offered java. "What happened to my clothes?"

Clothes gremlin!

An impish grin found purchase on Cole's lips. "I can't tell you my secrets, but I can tell you I thoroughly enjoyed it."

How the hell did he strip me? My whole body heated at the thought. I pressed my lids closed and swallowed. I needed coffee pronto.

The dark brew steamed as I inhaled the rich aroma. "Mm," I hummed as I sipped.

Cole started, "So today—" I groaned. He knit his brows and threw a cloth napkin at me. "Don't start, young lady."

I giggled and waved my hand. "Please continue, Sir."

"Today." He nodded and pulled his phone out of his pocket. He tapped the screen. "You are to visit my mother and father's suite for a dress fitting. I'll be there but, in another room, getting measured as well. Then we have an appointment at Las Palmas. The owner, Mr. Sultana, wants to meet you."

"Me?" I squeaked. "Why?"

Cole kept his eyes glued to the screen and continued to scroll. "That's the requirement for the meeting."

"Oh, okay." I didn't understand, but whatever. I'd go with Cole to meet what's-his-name just to keep from giving Roni the opportunity to find Cole alone.

The less she knew about our nuptials, the less likely she'd sabotage my wedding. I hoped she wouldn't show her face around the Tanner's villa again.

Cole cleared his throat and caught my attention. "You don't have to worry about the Las Palmas meeting. I'd prefer to bring you with me." He offered me a sappy grin.

I narrowed my eyes. "This isn't some scheme of my father's, is it?"

"No," he said with a frown. He glanced back at his phone before putting it in his pocket. "The last thing will be dinner with our families."

I groaned again. "Will *she* be there?"

He faced the ocean. "Unfortunately." He tilted his head, his profile exposed the wry grin tugging on his lips. "But Scott will be there too. That should make her behave."

I rubbed my face, then shrugged. At this point, I didn't know what would or wouldn't keep Roni in check.

After breakfast and a shower, we climbed in a car and

headed to the resort. When I stepped out of the car, Grace greeted me with a hug.

"I'm so glad you're here." Grace glanced around, then lowered her voice. "Your sister is driving me mad, asking questions about you and the wedding."

Cole and I shared a troubled glance. "That sucks balls," I said, balling my fists onto my hips.

"Among other things," Cole quipped.

We exchanged another look and started laughing. Our inside joke relaxed me, and I happily followed Grace. Cole veered off when his father called to him from across the lobby. He waved, then winked.

The Tanner's free-standing villa was a hike from the lobby. The oceanside dwelling had many glass doors, and they'd all been opened to allow the gentle breeze to cool the rooms.

It felt as if I'd entered a wind tunnel as Grace led the way through a large, decadently furnished living space. I glanced around quickly as she beckoned me into a hall.

The brisk walk through afforded me little opportunity to visually explore the villa. I focused ahead of Grace, to where women's laughter spilled out of a room. Friendly faces greeted us when we entered.

"Ah, the bride is here," Mrs. Tanner said, clapping her hands together.

"About time," Amoya teased with a devilish smile, before she hugged me.

Behind Mrs. Tanner, a woman stood with her hands clasped and head tilted as if she could see through me. She was dressed as a native islander in a bright orange and yellow dress. Her hair was cut short and starting to gray.

"Vanessa, this is Tabby Mack." Mrs. Tanner gestured to the woman. "She's the best seamstress around. She works miracles with a needle and thread."

I nodded. "Thank you for agreeing to help me on such short notice."

"It's a pleasure, Ms. Warsaw. What a blessing to play a part in such a happy time." A bright smile broke out on her face. "Shall we begin?"

Her fingers tugged on a soft measuring tape draped around her neck. It had blended into the pattern of her dress.

"Right." Grace approached a round rack with a variety of dresses. The metal holder had wheels. It appeared a designer had dumped an entire store of dresses onto the giant fixture.

With wide eyes, she picked out a coral-colored strapless. "What color do you want for the bridesmaids' dresses?"

I shrugged. "I don't care. Just pick something you like."

Amoya joined Grace, and they pulled out different dresses. Their banter sounded as if they were researching and making a spreadsheet with the pros and cons of the varying lengths and colors. I sighed and turned to Mrs. Tanner.

She reached for my hand. Her warm fingers squeezed, and I sucked in a deep breath. "Are you ready for this, dear?"

I bit my lip. My wedding dress had been hidden in Mrs. Tanner's closet for a decade.

"Your mother would be happy you are wearing the dress she'd planned for you to wear."

Tears filled my eyes, and an ache settled in my chest.

I expected nostalgia at seeing the dress again but not the emptiness that engulfed me. My breath hitched as Tabby unzipped the dress bag.

White lace and beadwork were exposed bit by bit. Suddenly, tears blinded me, and Mrs. Tanner's arms encircled me.

"This is lovely work," Tabby whispered in awe, examining the stitching. "It's delicate."

The empire waist gown was a halter style with a plunging neckline. Back then I wouldn't have been able to fill the cup, but now I was a little more endowed.

"I always thought I'd look like a princess." Taking both of Mrs. Tanner's hands in mine, I faced her. "Thank you for keeping it safe. I…" My voice faltered.

"Your mother would be proud of you, Vanessa." She hugged me. "Now, try it on so we can see if it needs to be altered."

Both women helped me slither into the dress. Tabby fastened the back and Mrs. Tanner unboxed a few new shoes for me to try. I didn't want a stiletto, I'd sink into the sand, anyway. Truthfully, I'd be happy mimicking Grace and going barefoot.

I stepped into a pair and promenaded to a full-length, three-paneled mirror. The few weeks I'd spent on the cruise and with Cole had turned my skin a healthy, sun-kissed tan. The white of the dress complemented my new skin tone. I grinned, wiping tears from my face.

Tabby measured and pinned. I did as she instructed.

I turned and gasped. "What is that you're holding, Amoya?"

"Do you like it?" Amoya spun with a pale blue dress

in her arms. It had a halter style neckline like mine. The hemline seemed flowing and longer in the back. But that's not why I liked it.

"It's the color of Cole's eyes," I said quietly.

Amoya and Grace shared a look, then smiled.

"There's only one more this color. It's a short spaghetti strap dress." Amoya lifted it.

"Oh my. I love it." Beaming, Grace took it and held it against her body. She spun, giggling.

I grinned, but my spirits remained tempered by thoughts of my evil twin. I raised my skirt and made my way to the window. Peering out, I searched for Roni. Nothing but flowers and groves of palms. Relief washed over me.

"Try that on," Grace told Amoya. "I'm going to run to my room and get something. I'll be right back."

Grace disappeared out the door, turning down the hall.

Tabby examined my dress a few more minutes then helped me remove it.

I zipped Amoya's turquoise dress. She slipped a pair of sandals on, then stepped before the mirror. She moved a few steps of a formal dance, watching the skirt flow.

"It's beautiful," I said, and Mrs. Tanner nodded.

"The short front makes your legs look a mile long," Grace stated from the doorway. She breezed into the room holding a gauzy scarf. "Now it's my turn." Grace stepped into the spaghetti strap dress. After closing the fasteners, she added the scarf around her neck. "What do you think?" she asked us.

With yellow hibiscus-like flowers set on a pale turquoise background, the scarf was the perfect accessory for the tropical wedding. The material muted the colors and softened them. "I like it. The dress looks good on you, too."

It warmed my heart to see my bridesmaids strutting around in their dresses like little girls putting on a fashion show. "Thank you both for agreeing to be in the wedding."

Amoya and Grace bombarded me with a giant hug and squeezed tight. I laughed even as the tears came.

"You're welcome," Grace said. "I'm glad I'll finally get a sister-in-law."

It stung knowing Grace supported me more than my flesh and blood twin. After the girls changed back, and while Mrs. Tanner made arrangements, we sat on the terrace and sipped iced tea. I closed my eyes, basking in the sun while the breeze cooled me.

"It's going to be beautiful," Amoya sighed.

"What is?" asked a familiar voice.

My stomach roiled, and I tried to keep my face neutral. I popped one eye open. My sister, wearing an innocent expression, stirred a piña colada.

Innocent my ass. You know she has double the rum.

I closed my eye. "My wedding. That's what." I took a sip of tea.

"You're going to behave, aren't you?" Amoya's firm, schoolteacher voice amused me.

"Moi? Of course," Roni purred. "I wouldn't ruin my sister's happiness."

"Bullshit," I coughed, sitting straight.

Roni grinned impishly and shrugged. She stood for a few moments in the awkward silence before turning and leaving. My blood pressure would remain elevated until the wedding was over and my sister gone.

Amoya glanced at where Roni had been and pointed at the floor. Outside the edge of the doorway, a shadow hovered.

I winked at Grace. She smiled.

"What a bitch. I can't believe you share DNA with that slut." Grace fingered her drink, shifting in her seat, making it creak.

"Me neither. After what you told me, I'm glad you're being sneaky with your dress," Amoya said.

"Yes, I won't leave it here in the resort where she can charm the pants off an employee to gain entry." I leaned forward. The shadow moved, and I covered my mouth to stifle the giggle.

Amoya's voice rose. "What did you do with it? Is the seamstress keeping it for you?"

"No. It will be returned to our villa after it's altered. It won't take long. The dress is perfect for a beach wedding." I lied. "Mrs. Tanner is great at putting together the whole shebang on such short notice."

"This is a destination wedding resort. It's one of the main money makers on the island," Grace added. "She's had lots of practice. It doesn't hurt that she has a team of assistants at her beck and call."

"Love those pumps, by the way," Amoya winked.

"Yes, it's weird they fit a size smaller," I lied again. "I already sent them. They'll be in my closet when we return this afternoon. The good thing is they aren't Roni's taste."

"Too classy?" Grace said, trying not to laugh.

"Let me guess. Veronica would prefer stilettos."

Amoya crossed her arms and relaxed against the back of her chair.

"You got it," I nodded. Our ruse completed, I closed my eyes again. "Grace, tell me about the boys. When are their birthdays?"

Grace's expression softened as she dove into a lively discussion about her children. After a few minutes, Roni's shadow disappeared.

Amoya checked the hallway. "All clear."

"Since we weren't giving her any more information about the wedding, she slunk off," Grace groused.

"That's Roni," I offered, shaking my head.

The scent of Cole's cologne tingled my nose, and I turned in time to see him standing in the doorway. He pulled me to my feet and into his arms, then placed a kiss on my forehead.

"Hello, future Mrs. Tanner," he greeted me, sending a shiver through my body.

"Mrs. Nicholas Tanner," I corrected, "you've got to distinguish."

"Yes, our numbers are growing," Grace stated.

Cole pointed to a waiting yacht. "Are you ready for our next adventure?"

CHAPTER TWENTY-THREE

AFTER CLAMBERING ABOARD THE GIGANTIC yacht, I settled into a deck chair. As we cut through the waves, I was reminded of the bumpy catamaran trip that had delivered me to the Dancing Winds and the twenty-four hour bet that reunited me with my first love.

Cole's phone rang, and he paced the deck most of the journey. He mentioned Las Palmas a few times, then shot a glance at me, offering an apologetic smile. A seed of worry planted in my gut, and the longer he paced, the more the worry grew.

"We've already discussed what to ask. I'll see you shortly, Doug." Cole stowed his phone in his pocket.

Approaching the dock at the Las Palmas resort, I saw Doug and his three boys. The children waved.

Cole took my arm and helped me off the boat. "We have a welcome party."

"I see that," I said. "Are they a part of the meeting, too?"

The two younger brothers ran to me, each hugging a leg. Tommy, the oldest boy, stayed back but grinned. "Aunt Vanessa," he said, "are you going to buy Las Palmas?" He tilted his head like a puppy.

"I—uh—"

"Tommy, we don't know for sure what Mr. Sultana wants," Cole replied, saving me.

"It's a miss-tree," said the youngest boy, Clint. He hugged my right leg and smiled, exposing two missing teeth. I tousled his hair. He had the piercing Tanner blue eyes.

"Yes," I agreed. "This whole visit is a mystery."

Cole and Doug talked as we hiked toward the main lobby.

Doug held Clint's hand. Tommy and Joshua peppered me with questions about the wedding. All three were participating as flower boys and ring bearers. They pointed out the swimming pool and the big red tube slide.

Cole held the door for us, and the Tanner entourage entered.

At first glance, the room was smaller than the Tanner's resort. It showed its age with low ceilings, brass accents, and dated artwork, but the furniture placement was inviting and cozy. Large windows let in light and gave the guests a panoramic view. The terracotta tile floor wasn't as posh as marble, but it fit the island decor.

Cole strode straight to the front desk and spoke with the clerk. She beamed a smile at him while listening, then picked up a phone.

"Auntie Van," Joshua said, tugging on my hand. "Lookee. See the slide in the pool? Tommy and I have gone down it, but Clint was too afraid."

"Nah, uh," Clint said, staring at his shoes. "I had sunburn and didn't want it to hurt."

"Baby," Joshua teased.

Clint's eyes welled with tears. "Am not."

"Yes, you are," Tommy agreed.

"Okay, knock it off." Doug frowned and kneeled next to Clint. "Why don't we go get some ice cream?"

Doug glanced at me. "We'll be back in a few."

A gleeful chorus of happy boys followed him out of the lobby. They disappeared out the back. I moved to the window, watching them walk on a palm tree-lined path.

Families gathered around the pool. Mothers slathered sunscreen over giggling kids. Fathers threw balls or helped kids swim.

Someone opened a door and the effervescent laughter of children tickled my ears. I smiled as the sound warmed my soul. No wonder Mike Higgins has fond memories of this place. It was full of life and love.

I jumped when Cole touched my shoulder.

"Sorry about that. Vanessa, I'd like you to meet the owner of Las Palmas." Next to Cole was an elderly gentleman with a kind face. His tanned skin held a roadmap of wrinkles.

I extended my hand. "It's nice to meet you." Again, children's laughter rang like church bells. "Thank you, sir, for supplying happy memories."

His smile broadened as both hands clasped mine. "You've hit the hotel's goal. This has been my passion for many years. Now it is time to pass the torch."

Cole smiled and blushed. Something was going down. Perhaps the Tanner family intended to buy Mr. Sultana out. I linked arms with Cole, and we followed the older gentleman to his office.

"Please have a seat." Mr. Sultana motioned to a couple of worn leather chairs.

We sat, then I watched Cole work. He explained what

the Tanner Hospitality Group could do to ensure the longevity of Las Palmas. He was confident and sure, yet honest, but not boastful.

Mr. Sultana pressed his fingertips together and frowned. "It's like selling my child," he said. My heart hitched. He loved the property.

I had remained quiet, but now I leaned forward and caught his eyes. "You're not selling your child, we're adopting it. And we will love it as our own."

I swear the old man teared up, and he nodded. He turned his attention to the stack of papers. Shortly, he pulled a hanky out of a drawer and dabbed one eye.

On the corner of his desk, a small drooping plant in a blue pot stood sentinel. It looked sad, like Mr. Sultana.

I cleared my throat. "I'd like to say something if I may."

Mr. Sultana pushed up his glasses, and Cole grinned.

"I may not be knowledgeable about the hospitality business or my fiancé's involvement in that business, but what I do know is his passion. When he cares for something, he's passionate about it."

I scooted to the edge of my seat and smiled at Cole. He took my hand, caressing my fingers.

"His family and another reminisced about your hotel, Mr. Sultana, and they cherish their memories made here. I know they'd much rather you sell it to someone with passion than let it go to someone who just wants another hotel. If someone else is more in tune with your ideals, then the Tanners would be happy with your choice."

"Thank you, Ms. Warsaw." Mr. Sultana stood. Cole and I mimicked him. "Would you excuse Mr. Tanner and me for a moment? I promise I won't keep him long."

Keeping a watchful eye on the office door, I milled about the lobby. I waited no more than five minutes before Cole strode up to me wearing a sexy smile. Maybe I could take him home.

"Nessa, Mr. Sultana has accepted our offer."

"That's wonderful news." I took his hands, ready to shout with joy.

"But…" He glanced around, then led me to a quiet corner.

"But what?" I bit my lip.

"Mr. Sultana wants you to be the general manager." He rubbed his hands on my arms. I didn't think his smile could brighten any more. "You do need a job."

My mouth opened, but I couldn't speak. I'd never worked in the hospitality business. Finally, my rusty jaw started working. "I am currently unemployed, but my father will want me to help transition Warsaw Industries."

I gazed out the window. This beautiful paradise could be my home. Accepting the job would help my new family acquire Las Palmas.

"Don't worry. I told him we were taking a long honeymoon." Cole scratched the back of his head. "We really haven't talked about where we are going to live. I guess we should do that." He laughed.

I hugged him tight. "I just want to be with you."

"That's the plan," Cole said. He kissed me on the top of my head. "If you decide to try it, we can build a house."

I tipped my head up. "You mean you don't want to live at the villa?"

"It's a little small for all the kids we're going to have." He grinned.

"Oh." Yes, it was. I nodded, overwhelmed with

thoughts of a new job, home, and kids.

"Can we walk the property?" I needed to process and I could do that while taking the path around the buildings.

As we strolled, Doug and the boys found us. He planned to take the kids swimming. We ventured to the front, then the beach area.

"You know what this place needs?" I studied the green space.

"Tell me." Cole threaded his fingers with mine.

"A playground." It was a simple fix.

Cole's gaze circled the property, arriving at the same conclusion. "Never noticed there wasn't one."

We boarded the yacht for the return trip to the Dancing Winds resort. I eyed the sandbar, tempting me, once again, to seek solitude from my thoughts.

Cole tugged my hand, pulling me from my zone. Hand in hand, we strolled toward the family villa, eager to share our news.

CHAPTER TWENTY-FOUR

After alerting my future in-laws to the successful meeting at Las Palmas and then cocktails with the Higginses, Cole and I strolled the sandbar where I'd sacrificed my solitude.

I lifted my left hand. The diamonds glinted in the sunlight. The tropical setting, the man, my new life—it all felt surreal.

"Let's walk to the villa," Cole suggested. "Maybe we could stop at the tree again." He wiggled his eyebrows.

His gaze locked with mine and heat shot through me. I tried to swallow.

"I wouldn't mind a repeat."

He took my hand, and we started toward the path.

"What would you do if I became the general manager of Las Palmas?" I asked.

Cole glanced at the palm branches overhead. "There's always Dancing Winds to run. Plus, I could teleconference and work from anywhere. Computers are a wonder."

I chuckled, giving him a sidelong glance. "Could this really work?" I whispered.

"Only if you want it to." He swung my arm as we

continued to stroll.

By the time we'd reached our beach, I'd decided to take the job. No more living near Roni.

I flopped down into an Adirondack chair and closed my eyes. The sun's rays caressed me.

"You are so beautiful," Cole stated from the chair next to me.

A smiled tugged on my lips, but I tried to hide it. "That's a nice thing to say to your fiancée. You must want something."

A finger skimmed my cheek, tingling my skin. "Would you like to go upstairs and find out?"

"Oh, a mystery. I love mysteries." I jumped to my feet and pulled him to his.

"This one won't be hard to solve." He placed my hand on his crotch.

"It's hard, all right." I fingered his zipper. I wished there was an elevator, but, alas, we had to climb the stairs.

I'd been so focused on Cole's hands all over my body when we reached the top, I hadn't noticed he'd frozen.

"Shh. Somebody's here," he whispered. He stepped in front of me protectively.

I heard rustling and a door close. My heart leapt to my throat, and I clung to his waistband as he took a step closer. A shadow passed by the bathroom door and reflected on the window.

"Son of a bitch," I mumbled, dropping my arms. "It's my sister. Looks like she's taken the bait."

Cole nodded and flashed a wicked smile. Treading stealthily, we stepped into the bedroom. With a nod, I took the left door while he entered from the right. I held my breath and peered into the bathroom. I saw no one.

However, all the drawers had been pulled open. Several items hung over the edges.

Standing by the toilet, Cole pointed to me, then to the closet. Stealing a breath, I peeked inside.

Roni had her back to me. She kneeled on the ground before a shoebox and lifted the lid. She tsked.

I'd caught her in the act. My blood pressure skyrocketed. I trembled, outraged at her presence. I retreated from the closet and inhaled.

Cole touched my shoulder. Tears of betrayal formed in my eyes, but I refused to give in to them. With another breath, I stepped into the closet again.

"Figures I'd find you trying to sabotage my wedding," I said through clenched teeth. The icy nature of my voice shocked me.

Roni jumped, her eyes wide and chest heaving. She dropped the shoe she held.

"I knew it. You always try to ruin my life."

Her eyes narrowed. "You've ruined my life, too."

I crossed my arms and rolled my eyes. "I've never slept with Scott or any of your other boyfriends."

"You'll never understand," she uttered. Her gaze dropped to her feet, and she rubbed her arm.

I blinked. Roni reminded me of an anxious little girl, but it could be an act. I couldn't afford to let my guard down. "And I'll never understand why you hate me. What have I ever done to you?"

Her gaze snapped to mine, and she pursed her lips. "Besides being born first?" she snapped.

I gasped as if slapped. "Like I could help that." I shook my head. Why would coming into the world three minutes before her matter?

"You've always been the favorite. The chosen one," she said in a mocking tone. "Do you know how hard it is to follow in my perfect sister's footsteps?" She huffed, placing her fists on her hips.

I leaned toward her. "Here's an idea: instead of walking in my footsteps, why don't you create your own?" I yelled.

Her face turned magenta, and her lips pressed into a thin line. I didn't give her the opportunity to answer. "Get out, or I'll tell Scott the truth."

For a fleeting second, Roni's eyes widened, and she panicked. A hand flew to her throat. With a hop in her step, she briskly walked to the front door. "You wouldn't dare," she hissed. She pulled it open.

"Wouldn't I?" I crossed my arms. "You haven't earned my loyalty."

"But you promised." Roni pouted.

Yes, I'd promised, but I should never have promised my sister anything. I shrugged, offering her a wicked smile.

She folded her arms and huffed, "How am I supposed to get back?"

"Cole, can you please call a car for Veronica? Too bad there aren't any predatory animals on the island big enough to eat a human."

I left the door ajar so I could keep an eye on her. I knew she'd try to eavesdrop.

Cole nodded and called for a vehicle. "Where should we send her?" he asked.

"Off a cliff?" I laughed. "How about to town?"

"But not close to Lou's tattoo parlor. You don't want her to get the same one. I'd never be able to tell you two apart then." He winked.

My jaw dropped. I glanced through the door crack, and Roni inspected my ankles. I turned away but scratched my chest above the left breast.

"Shh," I hushed him. "I don't want her to find out what it is." I covered my mouth to stymie a giggle.

"She couldn't unless she talked to the guy who did yours."

I shushed him again. "It has too much sentimental meaning. If she finds out, she'll ruin it."

Within moments, the car picked up Roni.

The previous day, I'd accompanied Grace to get a tattoo. She added her boys' names to an existing tattoo. I'd flipped through books and liked a small single rose bud and had mentioned if I ever got inked it would be a single yellow rose.

It had been the first flower Nick had given me. Scott had given Roni one as well, but it wasn't yellow.

Cole phoned the tattoo studio. He proceeded to give them the quick version of our story.
Luckily, I'd had a nice conversation with one of the artists. She remembered me and agreed to help.

The driver called to let us know he'd delivered her to Lou's instead of Las Palmas, and he stayed long enough to see her enter. Cole and I laughed.

When we sobered, Cole reached out and touched my arm. "What truth should you tell my brother?"

"I promised," I sighed.

He frowned, sticking his hands in his pockets.

"I can't tell you." Shaking my head, I bit my lip. Withholding the information from him hurt, but it wasn't my secret to tell. No matter how much Roni had been a bitch to me, I wouldn't break my word.

I retreated back to the bathroom and cleaned up Roni's mess.

Nothing new there.

As I worked, a horrible idea formed. But the more I thought about it, the lighter I felt. Next thing I knew, I had changed into the shortest dress I owned and coupled it with the highest heels. I applied makeup similar to a movie star.

Or a porn star.

I hastily wove a braid to replicate Roni's, and then, one foot in front of the other, I strode like a model toward Cole. Roni had made it look easy, but I wobbled like I used stilts.

With hooded eyes and what I hoped was a seductive smile, I touched the top button on his polo shirt, then traced a line down to his zipper. He caught my fingers mid caress as his eyebrows shot up. I batted my eyelashes while I pouted.

"Okay. Why are you trying to play Roni? What's going on Nessa?" he asked.

I blew out a sigh. Pretending to be my sister sucked. How did Roni do it? I studied the quilted threads on the comforter.

Cole stepped out onto the patio and stared at the waves crashing onto the shore. His brow pinched with worry and his lips hinted at a frown.

Touching his elbow, I met his gaze. "I can't tell you

her secret," I said, then swallowed, "but I can show you."

CHAPTER TWENTY-FIVE

THE CAR STOPPED UNDER LAS Palmas' portico, and Cole helped me out. With the confidence of my faux persona, I strolled to the main desk.

The clerk behind the counter stuttered in his phone conversation when I smiled beguilingly. The other man at the desk eagerly greeted me. "How can I help you today, Miss?"

Hoping to appear bashful, I adverted my gaze but made eye contact with Cole. He waited on the other side of the lobby with an amused expression.

"I seem to have misplaced my room key," I said, meeting the man's gaze. "Can you help me?"

"Why certainly. What's your name?"

"Warsaw, V—Veronica." Heat rolled off me, and I glanced at the mirrored wall behind the reception desk. I'd turned crimson at the lie.

The clerk tapped on the keyboard and pulled up Veronica's information. A moment later, he handed me a plastic keycard. "Here you are, Ms. Warsaw. If you need anything else, please ask."

"Thank you." I flashed a smile, then sauntered out of the lobby, meeting Cole by the door. We followed the trail on the outside of the building, rounding a corner. The sounds of families at the pool diminished the farther we explored.

"Here we are," I said, waving the white card.

I swiped the keycard, pushed open the door, and peered into the room. A woman lowered her book and glanced at me with a grimace. Her dark hair was pulled into a severe knot.

"Mommy," a high-pitched voice shrieked. My nephew attached himself to my leg. I met Cole's shocked gaze, before glancing at my nephew.

"Preston," I said softly, "It's Aunt Vanessa."

Preston tipped his head back, then tilted it, examining me. "Sorry, Aunt Van." At four, almost five, he was the spitting image of his father, Scott Tanner.

The living area was scattered with toys, Legos, and books. Goldfish cracker crumbs and an empty wrapper, remnants of a recent snack, littered the table.

"Good afternoon, Mrs. Rodriguez." I waved at the woman, who nodded, then went back to the book.

"Preston," I sat on the sofa and tapped it. Cole settled next to me. "I want you to meet Cole. We're getting married tomorrow. He's going to be your uncle."

Cole stuck out his hand, and Preston shook it. "Hello, Preston."

"Hiya, Uncle Cole." Preston's big blue eyes blinked. He pulled Cole over to inspect his toys. "Do you like my cars?"

Cole's face lit up as he pushed a Hot Wheels truck down a ramp. Preston and Cole's laughter melded together as they made car noises. My heart sped up at the sight of my man eye-level with my nephew.

I wiped a renegade tear and stood up, hugging myself. I could imagine a little boy with Cole's blue eyes and a petite girl with long wavy Cole-colored hair. This was my future. I caught Cole grinning at me.

"Mrs. Rodriguez, could I speak with you for a minute?" I asked. She set her book aside, and we stepped out into the late afternoon sun. "My wedding is tomorrow evening. Has Veronica mentioned it to you?"

"No, Ms. Warsaw." Mrs. Rodriguez's brows knit together in confusion.

I swallowed my unease and donned a smile. "Well, I'm sure it was an oversight in all the haste." I took her hand. "I would love for you to attend. It's at the Dancing Winds resort. Would you mind bringing Preston? I'm sure my sister will be near me." Not a lie, per se, but I hoped it wouldn't be true.

I explained the details and Mrs. Rodriguez seemed honored to be included.

"I know Preston will be cared for after the wedding, so if you'd like, you're welcome to take the evening off. But please, don't take this as a dismissal. I hope you'll stay and enjoy the festivities."

She nodded, unable to speak. We entered the suite again, and Cole put a finger to his lips.

"Ready or not, here I come. I'm going to find you, Preston," Cole pulled the drape out. Preston wasn't there.

Mrs. Rodriguez and I passed by, continuing to the bedroom. We inspected Preston's clothing, hanging in the closet. My father made sure his grandson always had a suit to match Papa's, and fortunately, it had been packed.

Mrs. Rodriguez and I firmed the details. I wore a satisfied smile when Cole and I left for our rehearsal dinner.

"Vanessa, thank you for sharing Preston, but…" Cole sighed.

"I know it's wrong to keep him from Scott, but I promised Roni I wouldn't tell." I faced Cole. My heart ached for my nephew.

"Showing, but not telling," he said, taking my hand.

I shrugged. "I've kept my word, but you didn't promise Roni squat. What you decide to tell Scott is up to you."

On the beach, we ran through our placements for the service while the resort staff worked on completing the final details for another sunset wedding. We had one chance before we needed to leave the premises to make way for the other wedding party.

My father covered my hand with his, and we took a step. I gazed, misty eyed, at my first love. The wedge heels made me wobble, but with my father's support, I didn't sink in the sand and managed to make it to Cole's side. My face became hot when my father passed my hand to him. The wedding planner told us where to stand. He positioned Amoya and Grace, then Cole's nephews.

With her arms pulled tight around herself, Veronica fumed from the back row. Her narrowed eyes skittered from Scott to the rest of the group. I hoped her fear of dealing with Scott would hold her deviousness at bay.

Within a few moments, we were escorted to a private dining room. Mrs. Tanner turned on a large screen TV. She watched as a man straightened a row of chairs.

As our meal was served and the conversations circled

around the room, I leaned over so Cole could hear me. "Are all the weddings filmed?" I asked, curious.

"All weddings are broadcast on the resort's channel unless the couple requests us not to. A copy is given to the newlyweds as a gift. It's part of the wedding package." Cole kissed my cheek. His face hovered near mine. "Are you worried about being on TV?"

"I don't know," I hesitated. "Should I be?"

"Don't worry." He tipped my chin. "No one watches the channel unless it's a rainy day. Even then, people probably wouldn't turn it on more than a minute or two to find out the day's activities."

Now his lips found mine, and I sighed. At this time tomorrow I'd be his wife. My heart took flight.

"Get a room," Scott teased.

"Sounds like a good idea," Cole replied.

Heat consumed me. I wasn't sure if it was the publicized innuendo or the thought of Cole naked and laying on the white bed.

Duh. Sexy as sin, naked man!

Mike's church bell laughter rang out from the end of the table. My father entertained him with a childhood anecdote. Daddy glanced at me and winked. I returned it.

"How was it raising girls?" Mike asked.

My father waved and rolled his eyes. "Who knew there were so many shades of pink and there was a difference between leggings and tights…"

The smile fell off my face. My mother should be here, teasing him about the time when I was three and Dad put both left shoes on my feet and both of the right on Roni's.

Our preschool teacher had been amused. It had been one of Mom's favorite stories. I turned away and closed my eyes.

"What's going on, Nessa?" Cole asked softly. He touched my shoulder.

"I'm missing my mom." My voice cracked, and he pulled me onto his lap and held me. One hand stroked my arm. Surrounded by Cole's embrace, my wounded heart found solace.

CHAPTER TWENTY-SIX

"GET UP," I SAID, SLAPPING the bottom of Cole's foot. I'd let him sleep while I bathed and gathered all the items I needed for the day, including my fake dress and decoy shoes.

He grunted and rolled over, pulling his feet under the bedding and out of my reach.

"We're getting married today," I sang.

Cole bolted upright, wearing a sappy grin. Hair flat on one side and sticking up in the front, I itched to run my fingers through it.

He scratched his tanned chest, and I longed to rub my hands over the contours of his warm skin. He stretched and yawned.

Damn. That's one fine man.

Someone knocked on the door. I skipped over and opened it.

"Good day, Ms. Warsaw," a dark-skinned man greeted, tipping his hat.

"It's my last day as a Warsaw," I crooned to Cole. He slipped his arms around my waist and kissed my cheek.

"This is going to be a long day," Cole said, sounding sad.

I frowned. "Having second thoughts?" I bit my lip.

"Never." He kissed my neck, sending a shiver vibrating through my body. "It will be long because you won't be with me." I spun into his embrace.

I stepped back, gazing into his eyes. "I'll see you later." I grabbed my tote and moved toward the car. He waved as the car sped away.

Once at the resort, I met Amoya and Grace at the spa.

"I can't wait to get a massage," Grace said, rubbing her hands together. "Hell, I'm just happy your me-day gets me away from the boys. I love them, but sometimes it's nice for Daddy to have quality time with them."

"Makes him appreciate you a little more, too," Amoya said with a sympathetic pat on Grace's arm.

"I wish." Grace rolled her eyes.

The time flew as we enjoyed massages, facials, pedicures, and manicures. I tried to relax and laugh with my new friends, but Roni was never far from my thoughts.

I had safety measures in place to ensure she didn't launch a coup. But would they be enough? All my previous precautions had been in vain; she'd always found a way to circumvent them.

We enjoyed a quick lunch on the patio overlooking the surf. I studied the long sandbar peninsula, remembering Cole and Mike's twenty-four hour bet. It might have been childish, but it worked to bring Cole and me together. I smiled and took another bite.

Grace linked arms with me as we entered the salon portion of the spa. We flipped through the brochures looking for an updo for me. With my bridesmaids' help, I selected one with a braid. The stylist worked magic on my hair while Amoya and Grace watched.

The braid started on the side of my head, then gathered at the back of my neck. It was soft and whimsical. I looked like a princess.

"Cole's going to love it," Amoya cooed.

Grace sat in the styling chair next. She'd chosen an intricately woven updo. It took some time. "I'm taking advantage of this," Grace said as she flashed a smile. "This is as girly as you can get. Braids, bun, and flowers."

"What about glitter?" I giggled.

The stylist placed tiny white flowers in her hair and then sprayed it. "Next."

Amoya relaxed into the chair. She opted for the classic French twist. A few spiral tendrils framed her face.

Grace glanced at her watch. "Oh, we need to hurry. The makeup people will be here soon."

On our way to the Tanner family villa, many resort guests stared as we passed by. I glanced around, on the lookout for my sister and hoping to spot Cole. I didn't spy either.

It was a whirlwind of activity in the house. A photographer snapped pictures. Mrs. Tanner barked orders and pointed. She popped in and out of the room, keeping everyone on schedule. Suddenly, she appeared in a beaded, deep aqua dress.

"I love your gown," I offered.

"I'm glad," she replied with a blush, glancing down at the shimmering garment. "I've been eyeing it for ages and your wedding gave me a reason to spend the money."

Amoya donned her dress and one of the event helpers zipped it. She twirled, swishing the material. Grace stepped into her gown next, then they helped me into mine. After everything was fastened and zipped, a soft knock sounded on the door.

Mrs. Tanner gasped when she saw me. Then she wiped an eye. When she found her voice, she grasped my hands and said, "Your father would like to see you a moment."

I nodded. My father froze in the entry and blinked. "So, beautiful," he finally whispered.

"Grace, let's get a family portrait with the boys before they get dirty." Mrs. Tanner motioned to the photographer to follow.

"Maybe we should get one of Mike before he gets dirty, too," Amoya tittered.

Both my bridesmaids retreated with a wave.

"Daddy," I said, twirling my diamond bracelet.

The room filled with a peaceful silence. Smiling, my father stepped forward and took my hands in his. "I remember when you hated boys, and now I'm losing you to one."

His eyes misted, and he squeezed my hands. "Your mother asked me to give you something on your wedding day." He released me and reached into a suit jacket pocket. "I had it overnighted for your wedding."

My breath hitched. "She liked to plan ahead."

A sad chuckle escaped his lips. He pulled out an envelope and handed it to me. A single word was handwritten in a style I hadn't seen in a decade—my mother's. *Vanessa.*

I glanced up at my father. "A letter?"

"Yes, and this." He opened his palm. A small angel pin sat in the hollow. "She wanted this pinned on your gown. "It's the something old. It was your grandmother's."

"Oh," I squeaked. Conflicting emotions rolled over me. Elation. Sorrow.

"I'll give you a few minutes." Dad hugged me. He paused at the door. "Take your time reading. Cole will wait for you. He'll understand."

Emotion clogged my throat, so I nodded. My father quietly left.

I traced the letters of my name in the elegant script. Cancer had stolen a classy lady. I flipped the envelope over and carefully pried the flap up. The yellowed paper inside had been tri-folded. I sat on the bed, inhaled a steadying breath, and started to read.

"My dearest Vanessa,

Congratulations on your upcoming life with Nicholas—a wonderful man who loves you. I'm sorry I won't be the one to fuss over you. Know that I'd give anything to be there. I love you…"

I pressed my eyes closed and took a stuttering breath. Tears escaped.

Jumping to my feet, I scanned for tissues. Hopefully, I'd find some in the bathroom.

In the large room, I plucked a tissue from the box. Glancing up, I dabbed my eyes, trying to save my makeup.

A wall mounted TV playing the resort's channel showcased the day's weather and the beach where I'd soon pledge my love to Cole.

I swallowed. My new life awaited, but first…

Closing the lid, I sat on the toilet and began reading again.

My mother offered me words of advice about marriage and tips about living with a man. "Your father and I were soulmates; just like you and Nicholas. Your father will be lost. Please be patient with him and encourage him. He's young, handsome, and a good man. He can find a new love."

I gasped. I hadn't expected Mom to want me to counsel Dad to find another woman.

She continued, "Somehow Veronica found out about the business going to you when you turn thirty. She feels hurt and excluded. Remember to share with her…"

My jaw locked as I clenched my teeth. I counted to ten, so I wouldn't crinkle the precious letter.

If she only knew what you'd shared with Roni. All the men in your life—except Nick Tanner.

"The sharing stops today," I growled.

The soft treading of someone in the bedroom caught my attention. I glanced up in time to see Roni grinning maliciously as she slammed the pocket door shut.

"Roni!" I vaulted up and tried to push the door. The latch wouldn't open. I pounded the wood. "Roni, let me out."

Her villainous laughter met my ears.

CHAPTER TWENTY-SEVEN

After a few minutes of cursing and hammering the door with my fists, I stopped, chest heaving, and turned around.

I tried to take deep breaths while staring at the waves on the TV. "Calm down and think."

My mother's letter lay on the floor. I stooped to pick it up.

The music on the TV changed, and the view panned to a group of people. Mr. and Mrs. Tanner walked arm in arm down the short aisle.

"Oh my God."

Shaking, I rose to my feet. I gripped the counter, closing my eyes.

"Oh my God," I repeated, then my eyes snapped open. A snort of hysterical laughter escaped. "Roni took the bait."

In the short glimpse I'd caught, Roni had completely fallen for the fake wedding dress and shoes, but her hair had been styled exactly like mine.

I pivoted, hiked my dress, and kicked the door. Trying again, I rattled the handle mechanism, but it remained locked.

In the crack between the door and frame, a single metal piece taunted me. I searched the bathroom for something thin and narrow. In the second drawer, I found a rattail comb with a long, pointed handle. Conscientious of my dress, I kneeled and tried to jimmy the lock. It popped, and I rolled the door open.

After several calming breaths, I picked up my mother's letter. "Sorry, Mom, I can't finish it now."

I laid the paper on the bed. In the three-way mirror, I spied my wild, red-rimmed eyes.

Stalking to the exit, I twisted the doorknob, but it didn't move. I pulled, then shoved the door.

"No!" I shrieked. "I'm going to kill you, Roni!" I clenched my teeth as I beat the door with renewed energy.

I shouted for Cole, my father, the staff—anyone within earshot.

Once more, the music on the TV changed; I abandoned the door and flew to the bathroom. Grace started down the aisle. I frantically searched for a phone. I clasped my hands together to keep from clawing at the walls.

The window? I opened the blinds. I let out a frustrated sigh. It was too far of a drop from the second story.

I started pacing from the bathroom, where I watched the wedding unfold without me, to the door, screaming in desperation the whole time.

I froze before the TV as Cole stood with Doug, Scott, and Mike. The breeze ruffled Cole's sexy-as-sin hair.

Grace and Amoya ogled their men, while Tommy, Joshua, and Clint walked in a row. Joshua carried the ring pillow.

Cole's face lit up with a tender expression meant for

me, but one eyebrow quirked upward. A hiccupped sob escaped as I sunk to the marble floor, unable to stand.

Grace and Amoya glanced at each other and frowned. Likewise, Mrs. Tanner sat up with a furrowed brow.

"Come on, come on, come on. That's not the dress." They had to speak up. "Please," I begged in a hoarse whisper.

Arm in arm, my father and that bitch of a sister marched closer to Cole. The weight of my future pressed heavy on my chest and I couldn't move. Why couldn't my father recognize Roni in another dress? He had just seen me.

Cole had never seen the dress. He wouldn't know. I bit my fist.

My father handed Veronica over to Cole and they grasped hands. A big grin made a home on Cole's lips.

My dry mouth wouldn't close. All was lost if Cole didn't recognize that the bride was Roni. His eyes narrowed briefly, but my hope was trampled as the couple faced the officiant.

Another sob croaked out. "No," I wheezed.

But then Grace tapped Roni on the shoulder and spoke to her. Roni shook her head and turned back to Cole with a slutty smile.

"What did you say, Grace?"

I gathered my courage and pulled myself to my feet.

Amoya, with one hand on her hip, pressed in, pointing at Roni. The couple faced her, breaking hand contact.

Cole fanned himself like he was overheating. He leaned over and whispered something in Roni's ear. She nodded, wearing a coy smile.

Cole fanned himself again, then stumbled. Luckily,

Scott caught him and then helped him to a chair in the front row. He said something to Scott, who jerked his gaze toward Roni. Balling his fists, Scott jogged out of view.

"Besides your eyes, what's wrong, Cole?" Hoodwinked and ill. Fear churned in my gut, and I stepped closer to the screen.

Someone handed Cole a cup of water.

Roni pouted but acted concerned. Grace and Amoya stood, their heads tipped.

Pounding on the door made me jump. "Vanessa?" a man's voice called.

I ran to the door. "Scott? In here. Help, I'm trapped."

"I'll get you out," he stated. The handle jiggled.

"What's wrong with Cole?" I asked.

"Nothing. Now stand back," Something crashed like glass breaking. "Son of a bitch, that's heavy," he grunted. There was a scraping, then the door swung open.

"Scott," I breathed when he pulled me into a hug. "Thank you."

"Come on Cinderella," he uttered, with a frown of determination. "Wedding time."

"Thank you," I repeated as he hurriedly escorted me out of the room and down the stairs. We took a myriad of paths I wasn't familiar with. The less traveled narrow trail led to the main lobby.

I imagined my sister's face as I appeared.

"Ms. Warsaw," someone called. Scott and I stopped and turned.

Mrs. Rodriguez let go of my nephew's hand and he ran toward me. "You look pretty, Aunt Vanessa." Preston glanced at me with wide eyes.

I swallowed and glanced at Scott. His mouth hung open. I really didn't need to deal with any more of Roni's shit, but there I was, knee deep in it.

"Ms. Warsaw, we've been waiting like you requested," Mrs. Rodriguez huffed. She clutched her large handbag closer.

"I'm sorry but—" I'd completely forgotten them but didn't have time to explain. "You're welcome to go to the wedding now. If you don't mind, I'll take my nephew."

She nodded and ordered, "Be a good boy."

Preston grinned up at me, then his bright eyes shifted to Scott. "Prescott, this is Preston, Roni's son. Preston, this is Cole's brother."

Scott obviously didn't know what to do, but Preston stuck out his hand in a very adult move. "Hiya, Prescott."

"Ok, boys. I'm late. We can talk later." I took Scott and Preston's hands as we headed in the direction of the beach. When we arrived, we paused behind a barrier used to keep the bride hidden until the right moment of the ceremony. I sucked in a deep breath.

"Wait here," Scott said. He disappeared from sight as he moved up the aisle. The group of people quieted, then all started talking at once.

"Aunt Vanessa, are you worried?" Preston asked. His brow crinkled as he scanned my face.

My heart warmed. I must remember not to kill my sister, if only for my nephew's sake. I kneeled and took both his hands. His little suit fit perfectly. He wore a yellow tie with blue diamonds. The wind ruffled his hair.

Scott reappeared behind Preston, and I blinked. They bore such a close resemblance.

"I think I'll be fine once I see Cole." I winked at

Preston.

"They're ready," Scott stated.

I nodded. "Preston, I need you to do me a favor. Your mom is going to be up front, too. Once we get down to the beach, I want you to go with Scott. You can sit with Papa Vic or stand with Scott. No matter what happens, I love you. Thank you for coming to my wedding." I pulled him into a hug. "Now I need to find a guy in a suit to walk me down the aisle."

"We both have suits on." Preston glanced up at Scott. "We can share. Right, Prescott?"

Scott's hardened features softened. "Right, buddy."

I stood. "Take my hand. Don't walk too fast because I have these fancy shoes." Preston placed his little hand in mine. "Now take Scott's hand."

"Scott?" I paused before taking the step into view.

"What?" His frown returned.

"Roni didn't lie," I admitted in a hoarse voice.

Scott's gaze shifted to Preston, then to me. He arched an eyebrow as if to say "bullshit."

"Twins," I whispered.

His face fell, a mixture of pain and anger flashed, then he nodded stiffly. "First things first."

"I get the right to mortally wound her first," I growled.

Scott's lips twisted into an evil smirk and a chuckle escaped. "Okay. I'll take second dibs."

"Cole is waiting," Preston reminded us.

"Oh."

Preston took a step and pulled us down the aisle. Scott and I grinned over his head, then I turned to face the crowd. Mostly Cole's family and a few of the Tanner's acquaintances. I didn't care a lick about the audience.

My gaze zeroed in on Cole. He'd made a marvelous recovery. He held his hands behind his back and stared at me with a tender expression.

Grace and Amoya started clapping and others joined in. My face heated. My eyes narrowed as my gaze swung to my paling sister. Her green eyes widened, and her mouth bowed open in fright as she scrutinized her son holding Scott's hand. The nearer we got, the more she seemed to shrink.

Suck it, biotch!

My focus returned to Cole, and he didn't wait for me to reach him before leaping to my side and embracing me. I sighed against him.

"Watch it, Uncle Cole." Preston's arm was stuck in between us.

"Sorry, squirt." Cole loosened his grip so Preston could escape. My nephew stayed with Scott instead of sitting with my dad.

Cole led me to the officiant. He leaned close to me. "You're late. What took you so long?"

I touched his face, for the first time noticing my ruined nails. Anger simmered under the surface. "The bathroom door was barricaded. Then the bedroom's. I watched on TV. Cole, I saw how you looked at her." I tried to swallow, fighting back the tears.

"I knew instantly when she smiled at me, it wasn't you. Besides, she kept glancing…" He shot a look at his twin. "Her eyes were sad and her smile fake. It wasn't your Mrs. Tanner smile." He tipped my chin up and kissed my nose.

"God, who wouldn't want you?" I smirked. "You're perfect."

Scott coughed, "Bullshit."

I chuckled as I glanced past Cole at Scott. His gaze was trained over my shoulder to where my sister still stood. I didn't want her breathing down my neck.

Cole grasped my hands. "I tried to give Roni a chance to admit she wasn't you, but when she called me Nicky and faced the minister, I feigned dizziness. I knew she had done something. I sent Scott to find you because I didn't want Roni to escape before we could confront her." His brows furrowed as he pierced Veronica with a stony gaze.

"There's something I need to do. I have a few things I need to get off my chest." I tilted my head, pleading for Cole to understand.

"Go for it. Just remember, there are little ears." His gaze shifted down onto the front row, where his nephews sat.

I hesitated. "Oh. Well—"

"That sucks balls," Cole interrupted.

"Among other things," I replied. I giggled, then squeezed his hands.

I pivoted to face my sister. Roni took a step back and bumped into Grace. Roni's eyes darted all over. I watched her gaze drop to Preston, then move up to Scott.

"Vanessa—" Roni started.

"Don't even," I said, my anger flaring anew. I leaned into her space and jabbed her with my finger. "You better be glad I don't own a gun," I growled through clenched teeth. "You are the worst sister. I can't believe you tried to hijack my wedding. What were you hoping to do? Live with him forever? Like he couldn't smell your stink a mile away." My chest heaved.

Cole put a hand on my shoulder. The gentle touch reminded me I wasn't alone.

"Vanessa, I—" Roni attempted again.

"Shut up. You don't get to talk." My gaze bored a hole in her head. "You've always been a taker. Money, time, men. You tried to live my life. You tried to steal my future. My husband." I shook my head. "I'm not a taker. I'm going to be generous. I have something to give you, Veronica." I couldn't help saying her name, as if it disgusted me.

Roni's lids fluttered. I hadn't realized how stiff she'd been until she relaxed. "Really?" she replied timidly.

I scanned her from head to toe. She wore the stolen dress and shoes. Her feet had to be throbbing in a size too small. I almost grinned. Her hair was up similar to mine. She must have bribed the stylist at the salon.

I straightened and rolled my shoulders. Fast as a snake strike, I reared back and launched my fist. Her eyes widened, and a hand flew to her face as she stumbled backward into Grace. She lost her balance and fell unceremoniously on her ass.

My knuckles ached, and I rubbed my hand but smiled. Mom might not have approved of punching my sister in the face, but then she might've if she'd known what Roni had done.

A weight had been taken off my shoulders, chest, or wherever it had settled. I felt light and free. My cheeks hurt from smiling.

As I said my vows, Cole lifted my bruised knuckles to his lips. My heart melted, and I inhaled the balmy air. The breeze swirled, caressing us, and rustling our hair.

The setting sun's rays kissed us with a rosy glow.

Gazing into those cerulean blue eyes made me yearn to be alone with Cole, the ultimate companion. I longed to share my mother's letter with him. Plan our future. List our hopes and dreams, then try to make a baby. Maybe two.

One twenty-four hour bet turned forty-eight hours turned more. Cole and I stood hand in hand, facing each other. I could hold his hand…

Or other body parts…

Any time I wanted. Forever.

The End.

EPILOGUE

Three months later…

I dropped the photo of Mr. Gorgeous wearing a speedo into the box, shaking the visual of him naked, laying on the bed, out of my head.

"Why do you need a picture of Mr. Suck-it?" Cole asked, staring over my shoulder into the box.

"It's for my friend Johny," I replied. I glanced at my frowning husband. "Hand me the packing tape, please."

I taped up the box and addressed it to Johny's realty office. My gay realtor had thwarted Roni's attempts to learn my escape plans.

A smile flitted across my lips, remembering Johny and his brother, Cal, and how they helped mislead Roni so I could escape.

"He was the one who helped me sell my house and my car, and store my items. His brother Cal owns a salon and he and his team worked on my nails and hair. One of the girls came up with a trick nail so my personal assistant could recognize me."

Cole shook his head. "I can't believe you had to go to such great lengths to throw Roni off your trail."

I sighed. "If she would have focused on her own life instead of mine, she might have been happier. I know I would have been."

"You don't have to worry about her now." Cole touched my arm.

I leaned against my man, wrapping him in a hug. The afternoon sun beamed in through the glass, warming me. I tipped my chin up and caught his cerulean gaze, trapping it. "Are you wanting a break from planning our next adventure?"

He smirked, leaning to kiss the tip of my nose. "I could use a massage here." He lowered my hand to his crotch, and I giggled. He hardened at my touch.

"How would you like your massage? With my 1. mouth, 2. hand, or 3?" I wiggled my brows, placing his hand over my sweet spot. "Although for a limited time, if you purchase the deluxe package, you'll receive all three treatments in one visit."

Cole's brows rose, then narrowed. "I think lifetime membership trumps limited time."

He lowered his lips to mine. I deepened the kiss and his phone buzzed.

"Shit." Cole stepped away, fishing the phone out of his pocket. He glanced at the screen, then hit accept. "Hey Scott." He tapped the speaker button. "You have the worst timing."

"Did I interrupt sexy time again?" Scott laughed.

"Hi Scott," I called.

"Um. Oh hi, Van. Glad you made it back to the States in one piece. Are you tired of traveling yet?" Scott asked.

"Sick of time zones. Yes. Traveling. No. Sexy times. Never." I winked at Cole.

Our whirlwind honeymoon had lasted two months. We traveled to points in Europe, the Mediterranean, and the Middle East. Each locale boasted a Tanner Hospitality Group property. While taking in the sights and culture, I had a crash course in the behind the scenes of every hotel we visited. I learned tips and tricks from each manager.

"How's New York? It's been years since I've been there," Scott mumbled.

I recollected he and Roni's clandestine getaway to see a Broadway show and play tourist. It was the trip that created Preston.

"Crowded," Cole replied.

"It smells funny," I added.

Both men laughed.

"What's next?" Scott asked.

"Well, we have a list, thanks to the board, to visit. Exotic Dayton, Ohio, is on top," Cole offered, scrubbing his face. "Eventually, we will swing by Houston, by way of Louisville and St. Louis."

"I've never been to Dayton before," I mused.

"Not missing much," Scott scoffed.

"I don't know," I said. "That's where the Wright brothers built the first airplane. The car starter, cash register, and barcodes were a few things invented in Dayton. I may have Googled some things about the place. I do it for each town we visit."

"That's smart," Scott said. "Oh, I've got another call coming in. I need to go, it's Preston."

"Tell him Uncle Cole says hello, and we bought him a present."

"Will do." Scott hung up without saying goodbye.

Cole and I glanced at each other and grinned. I bit my

knuckles to keep from laughing.

"He's in love with that kid," Cole stated. He plugged his phone in to charge, then relaxed on the sofa, glancing out at the panoramic skyline view. Leaning his head back on the pillow, he yawned.

"It might be time for a nap," I suggested, wiggling my brows.

"With the wall of windows, it's so light in here. I might be able to sleep after your *nap*. The jet lag is real today." He yawned again.

"Okay, I'll move the box and join you for a nap." I shifted the box from the sofa cushion to the kitchen counter. Whenever we stepped out next, I would mail it. I wish I could record Johny's reaction to Mr. Gorgeous' photo.

Inside the package were a bunch of gifts to distribute to Cal and his army of salon employees. They all helped me expedite my escape, and I wanted to give back. I'd picked up souvenirs—shells, jewelry, and other little knickknacks.

And while I still hid my location from my sister, I had returned to social media. I wanted to share my joy with the world.

My phone chimed, and I glanced at the screen. My father. Dad's attitude had changed since my grandmother's curse had been broken. He'd won at golf against his buddy Richard. I kept scrolling through his text, dumbfounded. Roni had taken a management position within Warsaw Industries, near where Scott lived in Atlanta. Holy shit.

Was she trying to be responsible so she wouldn't lose custody of Preston? Maybe she was bored now that she no longer had me to harass. I shrugged. Whatever the reason, as long as she stayed the hell away from me and my husband, I'd be good.

I lifted my phone. "Cole, Roni's taking over an upper management job in Atlanta."

"Hmm?"

"Let's bet on how long she'll last. Two weeks? A month?" I rubbed my chin, wondering if Mike and Amoya would like to wager. "Cole?"

When he didn't answer, I turned and glanced at the sofa. He'd slumped out of sight. The poor guy was truly tuckered out. Then I noticed an article of clothing draped over the sofa. His khaki pants.

The temptation to leave him nap was foiled by the greater temptation to ogle him in his boxer briefs. Tiptoeing to the front of the sofa, I found Cole utterly nude. His clothes were in a heap on the floor. He reclined with his eyes closed, a smirk owning his lips.

My gaze raked his body, starting at his short brown hair to his long, tanned legs. His Vanessa-sized dick jerked awake. My gaze snapped to his face.

He blinked, taking hold of his erection. "Vanessa, come play with my cock," Cole said, mimicking Mr. Gorgeous.

I raised my hand. "I suck balls."

"Among other things." Cole grinned and opened his arms for me. I fell into his embrace.

Savoring my first love's touch, I devoured his lips. As we made love, I couldn't help noticing the wonder in Cole's gaze. No matter where we were in the world, I'd found my home.

Love a book?

Please leave a review.

Reviews are virtual hugs for authors.

Destination Escape
Learning to Love Again
Book 1

Family—what a joke. First off, my conniving, slutty identical twin sister, Veronica, makes my life hell. She likes men but mostly the men I've dated. She's had them all but one—my first love, Nicolas Arlington Tanner. Then secondly, my match-making father wants me to marry to save the family business.

After years of my sister's treachery, and my oblivious father having his own schemes, I need to get away.

I will give up my career, my inheritance—everything, and run far from my family and the leash they're trying to loop around my neck.

So, I've made a secret, detailed plan to escape.

Destination Escape

Darlene hesitated, biting her lip. She tapped the stylus on the side of the tablet.

"Anything else?" I asked, hopeful she'd keep whatever was bothering her to herself.

"Well…"

I sighed, wiping my palms on my dress pants. "It's okay, Dar."

She met my gaze and nodded. "Roger is on line one."

My jaw clenched as a wave of nausea hit me. I balled my hands, fisting my pants and holding on until I could swallow the bile. My tongue stuck to the roof of my mouth. I stole a deep breath, then another. Finally, the rusty hinges of my jaw loosened enough for me to mutter, "What the hell does he want?"

"He's been holding since the last time I told you he called." She glanced at her watch. "That's three hours or so."

"Really?" I'd figured Roger was desperate, but I couldn't believe he'd waited, listening to our answering loop, for three hours.

"Fine." I waved her off. "I'll get rid of him." The door closed behind Darlene with a snick. I stared at the blinking light, debating whether to talk to him or pick up the receiver then immediately slam it back down.

Great idea, genius. He'd just call back and guilt you with his ruptured eardrum.

It would serve him right. But hurting him, while justifiable, wasn't what I intended to do. Now my twin, Roni…

You can drop kick that biotch off a cliff.

The corners of my mouth lifted in an evil smirk. I squared my shoulders. If I could broker multimillion dollar international trade agreements, surely I could talk to my ex-fiancé.

I lifted the handset to my ear and pushed the button.

"Hello." I breathed, using the tone that had gotten me the nickname Ice Queen at Warsaw Industries.

"Vanessa don't hang up, please," Roger begged.

"I have nothing to say to you." I swiveled in the chair, glancing out the window at the swelling rain clouds.

"I know. I understand. Please, all you need to do is listen." He paused.

"You've got one minute, Roger," I acquiesced.

Why give the louse a single second? It won't change your mind.

"I'm sorry. I don't know how many times I have to say it." He sucked in a breath. "I thought she was you."

Hit with an overwhelming sense of déjà vu, I wondered how many times had I had this conversation? Different men, same sister.

"I wouldn't have… if I would have known…" Roger stammered.

"I know," I fired back with venom.

"I'm sorry," he uttered again. "I didn't know it was

Veronica."

"You slept with her. Just because you believed it was me doesn't make you less guilty. You had sex with my sister. In my office. On my desk." Breathing became difficult, so I leaned back and focused on the overhead lights.

"But I thought I was making love to you," he said in a small voice.

I snapped forward, righteous indignation coursing through my veins. "It boils down to this: you didn't love me enough to be able to tell the difference between my twin and me."

ALSO BY
ROCHELLE BRADLEY
Romance with Sass & Shenanigans.

The Double D Ranch Book
Plumb Twisted
More Than a Fantasy
Municipal Liaisons
Here We Go Again
The Playboy's Pretend Fiancée
Cole's New Song
Brad
Canon
Destination Escape
The 24 Hour Bet
Love, Lattes, & Holiday Tales

Books by Rochelle Bradley & CJ Warrant
Boba Book Babe Mysteries

Pandemonium in Peoria
Silenced in San Antonio
Holiday Glamping

Magic. Mystique. Mischief.
books by
Rochelle K. Bradley

Dragonfly Wishes - Dragons of Ellehcor 1

Dragunzel - Dragons of Ellehcor 2
Descended - Secrets of the Fallen 1
Charmed by Murphy - The Murphy Brothers 1
Murphy's Paws - The Murphy Brothers 2
The Secret Shelf

ABOUT THE AUTHOR

Born and raised in Cincinnati Ohio, Rochelle developed a love of nature and art. She is a Bearcat, a Buckeye, an interior decorator, and fluent in sarcasm. She currently lives in southwest Ohio and shares her home with a black cat, a leash trained orange tabby, and her Prince.

Rochelle co-hosts (with author CJ Warrant) Wednesday Coffee & Books an Instagram Live show where they interview romance authors. Watch the show Wednesdays at 11 AM EST.

Rochelle is an award-winning author including three IHIBRP (Indie Helping Indies Book Review Project) 5-star awards. *Haunted Memories*, a contemporary romance, won a contest from Ellechor Publishing House. *Against the Laws*, finaled in the Chicago-North's Fire & Ice Contest.

She loves to connect with readers. Scan Rochelle's Linktree (https://linktr.ee/rochellebradley) where you can follow her on TikTok, Facebook, Instagram, and other social media. Visit Rochelle's website to sign up for her newsletter to keep up to date about future novels and book signings: RochelleBradley.com.

www.ingramcontent.com/pod-product-compliance
Lightning Source LLC
Chambersburg PA
CBHW061648190726
48289CB00006B/1791